THE PRADA PLAN

THE PRADA PLAN

ASHLEY ANTOINETTE

www.urbanbooks.net

Urban Books
1199 Straight Path
West Babylon, NY 11704

The Prada Plan copyright © 2009 Ashley Antoinette

ISBN- 13: 978-1-60162-157-3
ISBN- 10: 1-60162-157-4

First Printing April 2009
Printed in the United States of America

20 19 18 17 16 15 14 13 12 11

This is a work of fiction. Any references or similarities to actual events, real people, living, or dead, or to real locales are intended to give the novel a sense of reality. Any similarity in other names, characters, places, and incidents is entirely coincidental.

Distributed by Kensington Publishing Corp.
Submit Wholesale Orders to:
Kensington Publishing Corp.
C/O Penguin Group (USA) Inc.
Attention: Order Processing
405 Murray Hill Parkway
East Rutherford, NJ 07073-2316
Phone: 1-800-526-0275
Fax: 1-800-227-9604

To Leslie "Papa" Neely

The Past

You have to know where she came from to figure out why she is the way she is.

Chapter 1

"Where the fuck is my pumps? YaYa! You better not have your little hot-to-trot ass in my shoes! Mama gon' light fire under your behind. If I done told you once, I've told you twice about being in my shit," Dynasty yelled as she walked into her daughter's room. When she saw her daughter standing in the full-length mirror wearing one of her black sequin dresses and a pair of her designer high heels, she had to smile. All of the anger left her face as she admired her only child's curly, untamed hair and beautiful green eyes.

Dynasty didn't know where her daughter got those damn eyes from. She always suspected that Disaya was really the illegitimate child of one of her clients, but Buchanan Slim, her pimp and lover, would never hear of it. He loved Disaya the minute she came bursting out of Dynasty's pink pussy and had laid claim to the child despite the speculation of his other hoes and business associates.

Having Disaya was like a blessing to Dynasty. When she had given birth she had immediately been upgraded. She went from a street-walking, dick-sucking ho to a high-paid, dick-sucking ho; not that it made a difference, but in her world, where pussy was worth more than gold, there was distinction between bitches who got on their knees for fifty dollars and those who got on their knees for thousands. She was the HBIC of Slim's operation, and although their relationship before Disaya was strictly business with pleasure, after her daughter was born Slim and Dynasty quickly fell for one another.

Slim loved Dynasty and worshiped Disaya. He didn't care that Dynasty was a prostitute. In fact, he kept her working purposefully because she brought in more money than any of his other hoes, but instead of servicing regular everyday-type niggas, she began to service Wall Street–working, pulpit-preaching, and moneymaking mogul-type niggas. In simple terms, she became that bitch in the sex game.

Dynasty didn't mind that Slim continued working her, because theirs wasn't a fairy-tale love. They lived the street life in the underworld, where Prince Charmings had never been heard of. Dynasty did not believe in white ponies and happily ever after. All she knew was struggle, and the fact that Slim could provide her security and comfort was all that mattered to her. The way that Slim loved her was the only way she knew of it to be, so she accepted it gratefully . . . pimping and all. Dynasty was a hot commodity in her profession, because she became the woman to see for an amazing night.

"You look gorgeous, baby doll, but Mama needs those shoes," she stated as she approached Disaya and picked her tiny body up and out of the size eight heels. "Why you always pick the most expensive shoes in Mommy's closet to play in? You never go for the old Payless shit. You put your stankin' little toes in the same pair of Prada pumps every time." Dynasty grabbed the side of her daughter's face and shook it gently as she playfully reprimanded her. Disaya laughed and revealed a toothless grin as she exposed her two missing front teeth. She was only six years old, but Dynasty already knew that her daughter would be one of the most beautiful women to ever grace the earth.

"I like Pada, it's cotor," Disaya stated as she watched her

mother slip into the shoes and walk toward the dresser to apply her makeup.

"That's Prada, baby, and you mean *couture*. I see your damn daddy done had you around one of your tacky-ass aunties. Where did you learn that word?" she asked her daughter.

"Auntie Lai taught me," Disaya responded cluelessly.

"Fuck does she know about couture? That busted bitch wouldn't know couture if Donatella Versace personally handpicked her tramp ass for a ho-stroll down the catwalk," Dynasty stated heatedly.

Dynasty and Slim had explained their lifestyle to Disaya by convincing her that all of Slim's hoes were her aunties. Dynasty hated the fact that Slim still had sexual relations with his other hoes, and especially didn't like the fact that he was taking Disaya around them so regularly. *That mu'fucka is definitely gon' hear my mouth about that shit. His slick ass,* she fumed silently.

"Why I can't wear your Prada, Mommy? I can pay you. Daddy gave me a lot of money," Disaya stated naively, the innocence of her youthful voice filling the room and making Dynasty look at her daughter with love.

Dynasty remembered when her own view of the world had been so vague. It was before she had known anything about bills and eviction notices . . . about cockroaches and mice . . . or about debt and taxes. Now her viewpoint was much more cynical.

Dynasty sat down on Disaya's bed and patted her knee. "Come here, baby doll," she stated.

Disaya climbed onto her mother's lap and began to play with her hair. "You're so pretty, Mommy," Disaya said as she pretended to fix her mother's hair.

"Yeah, Mommy's pretty, YaYa, but you are beautiful, baby doll. You like fine things. You like to walk around in six-hundred-dollar shoes, huh?" Dynasty asked her daughter.

Disaya just nodded her head as she continued to play in her mother's hair.

"That love for the finer things in life ain't gon' ever change.

You like Mommy's things, but Mommy won't always be here, baby doll. You have to learn to get it on your own. You have to have a plan, YaYa," Dynasty preached.

"A plan for what, Mommy?"

"A plan to survive, baby . . . to go after the things in life that you want. One day you are going to be a beautiful, beautiful woman. You have been blessed, girlfriend. You will have the type of beauty that makes grown men stop dead in their tracks to look at you. You are rare, YaYa. You can get whatever you want in this world, but you have to use your blessings to your advantage. Have a plan, baby. Have a hustle and use what you have to get exactly what you want in life . . . including all that Prada you love so much," Dynasty stated.

"If I make a plan then you and my daddy will buy me Prada?" Disaya asked ingenuously as she wrapped her arms around her mother's neck and hugged her tightly.

Dynasty laughed and replied, "Little girls don't get Prada, but when you're a little older you'll understand what I'm trying to teach you."

"What are you trying to teach her?" The baritone of Buchanan Slim resonated through the room as his tall, lean frame leaned against the doorway. His dynamic presence demanded attention.

"Mommy's teaching me how to make a Prada Plan," Disaya chimed.

"A Prada Plan?" Slim asked as he put his hands in the pockets of his slacks and approached his daughter's bed. "And what exactly is that?"

"It's a way for me to be pretty and wear lots of Prada and have lots and lots of money and make people give me whatever I want," she said happily, revealing her spoiled and materialistic nature.

"Is that right?" he asked as he pulled a black box from his pants pockets. "Well, it looks like your Prada Plan is working already." He handed the box to Disaya and kissed her on the cheek. She eagerly removed the ribbon and opened it to find two gold necklaces with two heart lockets inside. "I wanted to give you my heart, baby girl," he said as he pulled out one and fastened it around his daughter's neck. She opened the locket and saw a tiny picture of the three of them.

"Who is the other necklace for, Daddy?" she asked.

"It's for your mama," he answered as he placed the other locket around Dynasty's neck. "You are the only two women that I'd ever give my heart to. If anything ever happens to me, the two of you will always have my heart." He leaned over and kissed Disaya on the cheek. He then turned to Dynasty and said, "Hurry up and finished, getting dressed, ma. We've got to make this move. Time is money and you know I don't waste either, baby."

Dynasty nodded and blew her daughter a kiss before leaving her room. It was the last time that Disaya would ever see her parents again, and *the Prada Plan* would be the last words of wisdom that her mother would ever give her.

Chapter 2

"How many times do I have to tell you to keep that bitch Lai away from my daughter, Slim?" Dynasty fussed as she opened the car door and plopped down in the passenger seat. "You know that jealous bitch doesn't like me. She's probably putting all types of shit in YaYa's head about me. I swear if one hair on my daughter's head is missing, I'm going to beat the brakes off of that bitch."

"First of all, you need to check that mu'fuckin' tone, Dynasty, and remember who the fuck you addressing," he replied. one finger pointed sternly in her face. He then turned that same menacing finger into a gentle hand that rubbed the side of her face.

Slim had been a pimp for more than twenty years and was seasoned in the art of intimidation and manipulation. It was not hard for him to keep women in line. He had a finesse that exuded confidence, and if he had been in any other profession there was no doubt that he would have been the best at it. In another lifetime he could have easily been the CEO of a major corporation. Many poor decisions had led him down the train-wreck path that he was on, and it was too late for him to pursue anything else. There was no turning back. He couldn't see himself doing anything different. He had become so accustomed to using women for his personal gain that he felt there was no other avenue for him. He never thought of the women he steered wrong, or of the lost souls that he helped to breed. Even the woman before him, Dynasty, did not cause him to change his perspective. Yes, he loved her but he did not know how to respect her, so therefore she remained one of his hoes.

"Why do you let her get under your skin? Lai is just like every other one of my hoes . . . a means to an end. I don't give a damn about her."

Dynasty knew that under the hypnotic spell of Buchanan Slim she would let him get away with murder. She loved him, and he could tell her that the earth was indeed flat and she would have believed him. Since having Disaya, her priority had been her family and she had never known that she could love anyone other than herself, but having a child had changed her. It was the most selfless act she had ever committed, and she loved her daughter dearly, valuing each moment that they spent together. It was the only type of emotional attachment she had ever felt, and she was grateful for Slim for accepting the role as Disaya's father, even though physically it was so obvious that the child wasn't his. The fact that Slim loved Disaya without doubt or regret made her trust him with every fiber of her being. If he said that there was nothing going on, she would force herself to believe him, even though her intuition told her otherwise.

"Fine, Slim. Just please keep her away from Disaya. I don't trust her with my daughter and I've been hearing the shit she been talking about her kids being yours. You better check her ass, because, if I see her, I can't be held responsible for my actions," she stated.

"I already told you, I ain't her baby daddy. Those boys don't belong to me. I'd never deny my seed. You should know that," he said with a tone that let her know the conversation was over.

Slim parked his car up the block from the Benjamin Hotel and got out with trademark finesse that only he could possess. His patent leather gator shoes were symbolic of his slick personality, and his Kool-Aid smile was all he needed to talk any woman out of her panties.

From the looks of the couple, one would never guess that they were prostitute and pimp. Outwardly they appeared to be among the wealthy. They always dressed the part when they entered the five-star establishment, because they wanted to blend in. The clientele that Dynasty attracted was of a high social ranking, and Slim never wanted her to feel out of her element. She played the role like a pro too, eating it all up and enjoying the pedestal that Slim had placed her on. It was like her throne and she wore her crown as his queen proudly.

Dynasty glided through the lobby with Slim's hand placed gently on the small of her petite back as they approached the elevators. Riding to the twelfth floor, Dynasty was ready for business. She closed her eyes and went through the mental preparation that she had mastered over the years.

It took a confident and strong woman to turn a trick. A simpleminded ho would have looked down on herself and let what she was doing alter her perception of herself, but Dynasty was a bad bitch and she knew what was up. She always made the money, and never let the money make her. Her self-worth was not defined by what she possessed between her legs, but rather what was in her heart, and she had always held herself in high esteem. Therefore, no matter how many different inhabitants took turns in the dwelling she called a pussy, none took ownership. She decided who, when, where, and how, and if a nigga didn't pay the rent, then he got evicted quickly. She was about her money. Her motivation was no different than the street hustlers that lived on the block . . . they were all chasing a dollar, trying to get a piece of the pie and solidify their own American dream.

This is business, she thought to herself as she deeply inhaled and then exhaled in meditation. *What I do does not define who I*

am. This is about the money . . . about my livelihood and the liveli-
hood of my family. The ring of the elevator bell caused her to open
her eyes and end her mental psychology.

"You ready?"

"Of course, Daddy," Dynasty answered before placing a wet,
sensual kiss on his lips.

"Hmm," he complimented as he enjoyed the taste of her
honey-dew lip gloss. Slim felt himself growing excited. Being a
pimp, he was around pussy every day, all day. He could have it
anytime he wanted it, but sex with Dynasty was his weakness. Her
ripe, wet flesh made him weak in the knees, and he knew why she
was able to charge so much for a taste of her pie. She was a neces-
sity, and he made sure to partake in her goodness whenever he
could. "Let Daddy get some of this before your first client arrives."

Dynasty never broke their kiss as Slim picked her up and carried her the rest of the way to her room.

Slim laid Dynasty on the bed and stood up as he removed his
shirt. He admired her curvaceous body. He watched lustfully and
stroked his stiffening manhood as Dynasty removed her dress
slowly. Her long blood-red fingernails contrasted against her skin.
He lay down on top of her. "I love you," he whispered as he entered her.

Bam! Bam! Bam!

"Open up this door! Slim, I know you're in there!" they heard
someone scream through the door.

"Who the fuck is that?" Dynasty asked. "I know that ain't who
I fucking think it is!" Dynasty yelled as she pushed Slim off of her.

Slim quickly threw on his boxers. He opened the door so hard
that the doorknob put a hole through the wall. "What the fuck
are you doing here?" he asked Lai as he snatched her inside of the
room so hard that her arm popped out of the socket.

"What am I doing here? What are *you* doing here, Slim?" the
girl asked him as she shot a hateful glare at Dynasty.

Slim could smell the liquor on Lai's breath and knew that she was drunk. It was the only way she would have the balls to boss up against him. The liquid courage she had consumed had her in another element. The girl was determined to come and claim her man from Dynasty.

"Bitch, he's recuperating from that rotten-ass pussy you've been giving him," Dynasty said.

"Sit down. Let me handle this," he said.

"Well, handle it then," Dynasty shot back. She rolled her eyes as she leaned back on the bed and lit a square, intentionally keeping her composure, to show Lai that she was the queen B around here and that the little intrusion hadn't ruffled one feather. She blew the smoke from the cigarette out of her mouth seductively as she looked Lai up and down, shaking her head in disgust. "Obviously if you got to chase him, he don't want you, bitch," she mumbled.

"You were supposed to leave her! You promised me," the girl shouted hysterically as tears came to her eyes. "Why are you doing this to me? I thought you loved me?"

Slim was losing his patience with the young girl before him. He faulted himself for playing with her emotions. He had made her promises that he never intended on keeping. He had crossed the line with her and had gotten into her heart instead of her head. Now he was dealing with the drama of a woman scorned.

Dynasty began to chuckle to herself, which infuriated the girl. "Loved you? Leave me? Maybe if you were rocking some of that couture shit you're teaching my daughter, you could find your own man, bitch, 'cuz mine ain't going nowhere. So you and that bastard-ass baby need to find another sponsor," she stated, her words being absorbed like poisonous venom.

"He doesn't love you!" the girl screamed. "Don't you wonder why he's always in the street? Where do you think he is when he stays out all night? I'm the one cooking his meals and sucking his dick every damn day! He's leaving you!"

* * *

Dynasty stood up and walked toward the girl until she was within arm's reach. "I'm not the help, bitch. I don't have to lift a fucking finger. He has bitches like you come and clean *our* house and cook *our* meals. The spit you're putting on his dick is only cleaning off the cum I left there, you trick-ass ho. How does it taste?" Dynasty was lethal with her quick tongue and was known for putting chicks on blast and making them feel stupid.

"Like fish, bitch!" Lai shot back.

Without hesitation, Dynasty slapped the shit out of her, but the girl was not easily intimidated. She snatched Dynasty's necklace clean off her neck, but not before Dynasty hawked up a huge gob of spit and deposited it on the girl's face.

The smirk of satisfaction drawn across Dynasty's face disappeared instantly when she saw the chrome handle of a small handgun emerge from beneath the raincoat that the girl was wearing.

"No!" Slim screamed, as he lunged for Lai and muscled the gun out of her hands.

Pow! Pow!

"Bitch, what have you done?" he asked as he slapped her across the face with all his might. "What the fuck did you do?"

Two bullets were all it took to end a life.

The deafening blasts seemed to echo its vibrations into space as the entire room seemed to stand still.

The girl shook uncontrollably as she snapped out of her fit of rage and the realization of her actions hit her. "Oh my God! What did I do?" she asked as her gloved hands shook with terror and regret. She watched in horror as blood leaked from Dynasty's body and soaked into the light carpet beneath her. "Oh God. I'm so sorry. I'm so sorry," she mumbled as she backed out of the hotel room, gun in one hand, necklace in the other. Before she had time to think she bolted from the room, her legs barely strong enough to carry her away.

Slim rushed to Dynasty's side as he tried to plug up the holes and stop the bleeding. It didn't matter what he did. His efforts were futile. One of the bullets had pierced her heart, killing her instantly before she even got the chance to feel any pain. "Don't die on me, baby girl. Damn it, Dynasty, breathe for Daddy!"

"Somebody call an ambulance!" he screamed frantically.

Slim heard a crowd forming in the hallway, but he ignored it and tended to Dynasty as best as he could. He covered up her body with the bedsheet, desperately trying to respect the body that he had disrespected for so long. He didn't leave her side until he was forced to.

"Drop the weapon! Put your hands in the air!" he heard a police officer scream as he pointed a department-issued 9 mm in his face.

"I didn't do this. I would never do this to her," he said calmly as he used two fingers to close Dynasty's eyes. She was the mother of his beloved daughter and the only woman who had ever been able to capture his heart. His foolish infidelity had gotten her killed and he knew it.

He looked at the gun that he had taken away from Lai. It was still in his left hand, and he shook his head as he realized how the scene must have looked. "Fuck!" he muttered as he put the pistol down. He knew that his fingerprints would be the only set on the gun. "Bitch wore gloves," he whispered as an odd chuckle tickled his throat. "The bitch had on gloves!" he shouted.

"Sir! Step away from the body and put your hands in the air! If you do not comply, we will shoot you."

Buchanan Slim stood to his feet like a man and turned his back on the officers with his hands placed behind his back. He didn't resist his fate. He did what every black man dreaded, and assumed the position, making sure that he did not look threatening. He gritted his teeth as he held his head high. If he was going to go to jail, he was going to do so just like he had done everything else in his life: with pride and with style.

They escorted him out of the building and disregarded everything Buchanan Slim told them about what had led to Dynasty's death. In their minds he was already guilty . . . the case was closed and another little black girl was to be tossed into society without anyone in the world to turn to for help.

Disaya had the worst possible background. Her father was a pimp, her mother a whore . . . she was the product of a dysfunctional home. From the very beginning she was expected to fail. Nobody could ever understand her struggle. It was official. Disaya was on her own.

Chapter 3

When Disaya awoke the next morning she was surprised to see that her mother and father had not yet come home. They had never left her this long before. Usually they would tuck her into bed, and before she opened her eyes the next day they would be over their daughter, showering her with hugs and kisses. This time was different, however, and she knew in her young heart that something was dreadfully wrong. Today they were nowhere to be found.

She wandered from room to room, but the fact that her mother's bed was still made and there was no scent of incense burning meant that no one had been home since last night. One of the perks of living in Marcy Projects was that everybody knew everybody. Most of Disaya's "aunties" were only a building or two away, yet she was reluctant to go and ask for help. Dynasty had always drilled that privacy was important. Disaya had been taught that family business was for family only and that whatever happened underneath their roof stayed there. She didn't want to get in trouble if she made the wrong decision, so she went into her parents' room, crawled underneath their bedspread, and balled into a fetal position as she patiently waited for Slim and Dynasty to return.

The first few hours passed by quickly. She watched cartoons and tried to keep her mind off of the fact that she was home alone, but as daylight disappeared and the everyday creaks and noises of the house began to frighten her, she realized that her parents may not be coming back. Too afraid to move, she lay there silently with her eyes squeezed tightly shut. Her tiny breaths were erratic from fear of the unknown and there were knots in her stomach. She was hungry, and all she really wanted was to hear her mother yelling at her or her father's deep, soothing voice. She tried her hardest to stay awake, but eventually the fatigue shut her body down.

Disaya didn't move for days. She waited obediently and patiently for Dynasty and Slim's return. By the third day, her body was weak. She was dehydrated and starving. She had wet the bed several times out of fear alone, and the stench had begun to reek throughout her parents' bedroom. There had been so many times she had wanted to run for help, but her six-year-old logic told her to stay put. She didn't want to leave and miss Dynasty and Slim if they came home while she was gone, so she played the waiting game. The tiny child didn't know that she was waiting for a resolution that would never come.

When she finally heard the knocks at the door, she jumped up with urgency and sprinted toward the front door.

She pulled open the door with excitement and relief as she cried, "Mommy, Daddy, I thought you left me!"

Her disappointment was evident when she was greeted by a total stranger. A white woman stood before her.

"Disaya?" the woman asked as she kneeled in front of the small child.

Disaya didn't respond, but looked at the woman as if she had an infection that Disaya didn't want to catch.

"Disaya, your father sent me to come and get you," the woman stated. "My name is Mrs. Thomason."

"You know my daddy?" Disaya asked hopefully as she wiped her eyes.

"Yes, I know your daddy. He sent me to come get you. You have to come with me, okay? Something bad has happened to your mother. She died, sweetheart," the woman stated.

She died . . .

She died . . .

She died . . .

The words hit Disaya like a ton of bricks, and she ran into the woman, swinging as hard as she could. "No . . . no. You liar . . . my daddy doesn't know you. You don't know my mommy!" Disaya stated as she swung and cried hysterically.

The social worker had seen this scenario one too many times, and her sympathy was waning. She grabbed the little girl firmly, but without force, and dragged her out of the home.

Disaya kicked and screamed for dear life as she fought to stay in the only home she knew. She could feel that her world was getting ready to change, and somehow she knew that it was a transition that she was not ready for.

Disaya was placed into temporary foster care, with the provision that next of kin would be able to take her. To Disaya's dismay, no one ever came. She didn't have any family besides her mother and father. None of Slim's hoes ever even considered taking the child in. They all felt that Dynasty and Slim had gotten what they deserved. They felt it was payback for being treated second-rate next to Dynasty for so many years. Nobody thought twice about the young life that hung in the wings.

Her foster mother was an older woman who was fifty-four years young. As soon as she opened her door, she could see the lost look in Disaya's eyes, and she opened up her arms wide to the child into her home.

For some strange reason, Disaya felt no hesitation when she ran into the woman's arms. She cried heavily on her shoulders. "They're gone. They took my mommy and daddy!"

"Oh, sweetheart, everything is going to be okay. Go ahead, let it out," the woman said as she rubbed Disaya's back gently with a motherly touch. The old woman looked at the caseworker and nodded her head. "She'll be fine here. I'll keep her until you can find permanent placement."

Mrs. Thomason nodded and said, "Disaya, this is Ms. Jacqueline. You are going to stay here with her for a while. I'll see you in a couple days, okay?"

Disaya was numb. She didn't care who took her in. It didn't change the fact that she was on her own. She watched as Mrs. Thomason got into her car and drove away.

"Now, what is your name?" Ms. Jacqueline asked.

"YaYa," she whispered with her eyes on the floor and her chin on her chest.

"Well, YaYa, let me show you where you're going to sleep."

Disaya followed Ms. Jacqueline down a set of stairs into a finished basement. There were three beds set up down there. It was obvious that two of them were already occupied, so Disaya got in where she fit in and took the empty bed.

"I'm going to fix some lunch. Make yourself comfortable. The other girls are out back. If you'd like to meet them I'll introduce you."

Disaya did not respond. She lay down on the bed and turned toward the wall as she released her tears. Disaya opened up the locket that Slim had given her and admired the picture inside. She gripped it tightly in her hand, until her sobs became whimpers, and whimpers transformed into light snores. Sleep was her only way to escape the harsh reality her life had become, and she welcomed it as she slipped into an unconscious state.

She was roused out of her sleep by the sound of footsteps coming down the stairs. "Hey, new girl!" she heard someone call out to her.

"My name ain't new girl," she replied as she sat up to face a girl who appeared to be her age. She wore denim blue jeans that had been cut at the knee to make boy shorts and a T-shirt. Her hair was pulled back in a greasy ponytail.

"You ain't got to be all smart-mouthed. I was just trying to be nice to you!" the girl stated while standing with her hands planted firmly on her hips. "Why are you on my bed anyway? Get your stuff off of my bed!"

"Ms. Jacqueline told me to put my stuff here, and I don't see your name on it," Disaya replied. She was already angry about the death of her mother. She felt like she had a ball of fire smoldering inside of her chest. The tears that she had cried attempted to put out the inferno of pain, but it was useless; there was just too much emotion pent up inside of Disaya. The fact that the girl was giving her a hard time made her even more furious. On a regular day, Disaya might not have stood up to the girl, but on this day she felt she had nothing to lose.

"You can have it! I don't want it after you sat on it. You look dirty! I don't want to lay on it after you anyway!"

Children's insults could be so trivial, but Disaya took it to heart.

"You're dirty!"

"Your mama's dirty!" the girl spewed.

Hearing the girl disrespect her mother, Disaya got tears in her eyes. "Don't talk about my mama, bitch!" she yelled. It was the first time a curse word had ever left her mouth, but slowly it gave her a feeling of control. It released some of the built-up pain that was inside of her. It made her feel a little bit better, and from the look on the girl's face, Disaya knew that she was shocked.

"You be cussing?" the younger girl asked in a low whisper, as if she was amazed.

"Yep, sho'll do," Disaya lied. She had never said a dirty word a day in her life, and she knew that if her mama or daddy ever heard one grace her lips they would have taken a belt to her behind with a quickness, but it didn't matter. Right now, at this moment, they were not there to protect her, and cursing made Disaya feel strong and less afraid. "I'll cuss any bitch out, especially for talking about my mama," Disaya said. She had heard her mother use plenty of bad words, and she made herself sound like Dynasty when she talked. If she was going to start cussing, she wanted to sound just like her mother because she was almost positive that Dynasty had a master's degree in swearing.

"What other cuss words you know?" the girl asked, intrigued. She was the same age as Disaya, and to a six-year-old swearing was like forbidden fruit. She had heard many adults use bad words, but when she attempted to say them she always got in trouble. She couldn't believe that the little scrawny girl in front of her was so seasoned.

"Shit, damn, bitch, whore, bitch," Disaya said as she listed the words out on her fingers.

"Uh-uh, you already said the *B* word," the girl pointed out. "That's all you know?"

"How many do you know?" Disaya asked.

The girl shrugged. "I don't know. I've never said none before."

"Then I know more than you," Disaya said matter-of-factly.

"What's your name?" the girl asked.

"YaYa," she answered shortly. "What's yours?"

"Mona," the girl replied.

They didn't speak after that, but they respectfully stayed out of each other's space for the rest of the night.

Disaya kept to herself, speaking only when she was spoken to. She slowly withdrew into a personal shell. She was consumed with thoughts of her parents. She felt like she was in a bad dream, but this was her reality. There was no waking up from it. Night fell upon her too quickly, and as the house settled down for the night, she closed her eyes and fell into a haunting sleep.

Disaya felt something wet between her legs and instantly thought she had peed on herself. The uncomfortable feeling awoke her, and she opened her eyes to find that she was spread-eagle on her bed. The wet feeling between her young thighs was caused by the boy that was on top of her, his head between her legs and his tongue moving a mile a minute. She gasped and attempted to close her legs and push the boy off of her, but he got on top of her, the weight of his body silencing her as he put his hand over her mouth.

"Stop it!" she cried. Her fearful screams were muffled by the boy's fingers.

"Shh!" he whispered. "Shut the fuck up." He wrapped one hand around her tiny neck. "You don't want me to hurt you, do you?"

YaYa shook her head as hot tears wet her cheeks.

"Okay, then shut up and open your legs back up. I promise this won't hurt. I'm not gon' fuck you. You're not old enough. I just want to eat you out."

His hands pried her thighs back open, and she trembled uncontrollably as he lowered his head and licked at her young peach, stripping her of the innocence of her childhood. She knew what was happening was wrong, yet she still felt the tingling that erupted each time he licked her down there. It felt good and nasty at the same time, but she still cried because she knew that it wasn't supposed to be happening. A physiological response to stimulus caused her to feel pleasure and sent sparks flying through her body, but an emotional and mental response caused her to reach her hand out for Mona, silently begging for help.

Mona pretended to be asleep, but she saw what was happening. She knew that it was going to occur before it even did, because before it happened to Disaya, it had happened to her every night. Ms. Jacqueline's seventeen-year-old son, Mark, came to her room every night to molest her. The only difference was, he had advanced way past the point of oral sex with Mona. He had penetrated her, destroying any possibility she would ever have in life to form a healthy male-female relationship.

Mark ate YaYa out and masturbated simultaneously, completely ignoring the damage that he was doing to the young girl beneath him.

YaYa closed her eyes and prayed for it to be over.

A few minutes later she felt wetness splatter all over her nightgown, but she didn't open her eyes until she felt him get off of her and heard his footsteps ascend the basement steps.

She felt ashamed, embarrassed to be in her own skin, and as she stood to wipe the wetness from in between her legs she wept.

Mona went over to Disaya and wrapped her arms around her. "Shh, don't cry too loud. Ms. Jacqueline will hear you," Mona advised. "Don't worry, he does it to me too. You will get used to it."

"I don't want to," YaYa cried hysterically. "I'm telling."

"No, you can't." Mona lifted her shirt and turned around so that YaYa could see the welts on her back. "I used to tell, and this is what Ms. Jacqueline would do to me. She called me a liar then punished me. You can't tell her, YaYa. It has to be a secret. If you tell anybody, they will take you away to a group home, and it just gets worse there."

YaYa nodded her head. "He does it to you too?" she asked.

"Every night, except for tonight, because he did it to you," Mona admitted.

"We can run away," YaYa said.

"Where?"

"Anywhere, just to get out of here," YaYa replied. She heard her mother's voice in her head telling her to survive. She had to have a plan to survive. "I'll think of something. I'll make a plan, and then we will run away from here."

Mona thought about it and replied, "Okay, but until then you have to keep quiet." She stuck out her pinkie. "You promise?"

Disaya nodded. "I promise," she replied as she wrapped her pinkie around Mona's.

It was on this day that they began to look at each other as allies rather than enemies. It was this vicious secret that bonded them together for life. Each other was all they had, and that alone forced them to depend on one another. Their friendship was built on that common rape, but it was one that would last them a lifetime.

Chapter 4

Within a week Disaya was robbed completely of her childhood. Mark frequented her room every night, sometimes prying her legs so far apart that she could barely walk on them in the morning. The throbbing ache of sexual abuse made her feel dirty and unwanted, almost as if it was her fault . . . as if she had invited it. Her tiny body rejected the unnatural act of sex, and she began to bleed between her legs, but she still didn't tell. She hid her bedsheets in the closet for fear that Ms. Jacqueline would discover them and send her to a group home. Mona had already planted the seed of terror in Disaya's head about the group home, and if it was any worse than where she was now, Disaya knew she couldn't handle it.

She started developing a plan. Her mother's last words of advice were the only thing she had to hold on to, and her survival skills were the only thing she had to rely on. She knew that if she could just hold out until her mother's funeral then she could find one of her family members or aunties to take her home with them. Once she was safe and away from the foster-care system she would ask her auntie to come and get Mona out. That was her plan. As simple as it seemed to her, she had no idea that it was much more complex.

She and Mona clung to each other. From the outside looking in, it appeared as if both were happy young girls, but they were both terrorized and terrified daily by the fate that awaited them at night. She dreaded the nighttime, and each evening when the sun retreated behind the clouds they trembled until the inevitable occurred. They were enduring what no child should have to experience, and together they yearned for a way out. They were desperate for one, and YaYa was hopeful for the light at the end of the tunnel, while Mona remained cynical and unbelieving. She had hoped for too long and received nothing but sexual abuse in return. She had given up, but in a strange way she was glad that Disaya was going through it with her and that she no longer had to keep her secret alone. The burden seemed less heavy and she felt less dirty because it was happening to someone else as well.

The days crept by despondently slow, and their silent torture became unbearable, until finally the day of the funeral arrived. Mona stared at Disaya with tear-filled eyes. Disaya was dressed in a dark blue ruffle dress with cute little white ruffle socks and bows all over her head. Ms. Jacqueline had purchased the dress for YaYa in an effort to make the little girl feel wanted.

Mona's heartbeat was like galloping horses, racing toward the finish line. She was afraid for YaYa to walk out of the door. She feared that if her newfound friend left, she would never look back, and as Disaya walked out of the door, Mona crossed her fingers and let a solitary tear fall down her cheek.

Dynasty's funeral was crowded with associates who whispered in speculation. Everyone wanted to know what went down and how the royal couple of the hood had met their demise. Disaya was escorted into the funeral home by her caseworker. Seeing her mother lying in the front of the church did something to her . . . a part of Disaya died that day, but she didn't cry. Looking on in disbelief, she could feel her tiny chest cavity contracting, as pain squeezed a vise grip on her heart.

After viewing Dynasty's body she turned to look for her father.

He wasn't in attendance; because he had never married Dynasty he wasn't allowed to be present. A state validation didn't define the love of her family. She refused to believe that her father was responsible for her mother's death. No matter how many times it was explained to her, she knew better. She cried for the loss of her mother, the arrest of her father, and the drastic way in which her life had been forever changed. She watched as people stood in her mother's honor, some gave speeches, some testified by telling half-truths about how much they loved Dynasty.

Most of the bitches hooping and hollering were the same ones that Disaya had heard her mother arguing with over Slim. Dynasty had even busted a few of the bitches up, but they were still there clucking like chickens over her loss.

Disaya's eyes searched desperately across the familiar faces. She reached out for them, but most of the women didn't even look her in the face. She spotted her Auntie Lai. Her mother never liked Lai, but Lai was always nice to Disaya.

"Auntie, auntie," Disaya yelled as she sprinted over to Lai with her arms open wide. She noticed that Lai had tears in her eyes. "Auntie, please don't let them take me." Disaya was so frantic that she was bouncing up and down in frightful anticipation— the idea of going back into the system haunting her young mind. "They're hurting me," she admitted in a hushed tone. Her eyes were begging. A young soul was crying. In her own way YaYa was begging to be saved. "They're doing things to me, Auntie," Disaya whispered frantically.

Lai's tears were relentless as she absorbed the little girl's pleas for help. Disaya was the daughter of the man she loved and the woman she killed. She simultaneously loved and hated the little girl in front of her. She knew that Disaya was the only reason why Slim had chosen Dynasty over her, and she secretly despised the little girl for that, but Disaya was such a lovely young girl. She was gorgeous with green emerald eyes and long, wavy hair. She couldn't help the guilty feeling that tugged at her conscience. Lai hugged Disaya tightly and whispered, "I'm sorry, sweetheart. I'm so sorry, but I can't take you." She stood and walked down the center aisle of the church while YaYa ran behind her.

"Please! Auntie Lai, I'll be good!" Disaya screamed. She couldn't help but feel deserted. It felt like a million eyes were on her as the attendees of the funeral turned and gasped at her show of emotion. "Please! Don't leave me! Please!" she cried. She knew that all of the people in attendance were phony. They all professed their dedication and love for her mother, but none of them was willing to lend a helping hand.

After the funeral, Disaya took one last look at Dynasty's lifeless body and then reluctantly walked away with Mrs. Thomason. She desperately tried to make eye contact with the women she had come to love as family. Tears fell as she watched her aunties purposely avoid eye contact. The same women who had combed her hair, babysat her, jumped rope with her, and sometimes whooped her little behind when she got out of line . . . these same women were now turning their backs on her, and it only intensified the stabbing twinge of loneliness she felt. She didn't know if she could make it on her own, but she didn't have a choice but to try.

As Mrs. Thomason loaded her into the car, Disaya said goodbye to the life she once knew. She turned around in the backseat of the car and stared despondently out of the window. She pressed her hand against the rear windshield, as everything she knew grew smaller as the car moved on, carrying her back to a fate worse than death.

Once the church disappeared from view, she threw a fit in the backseat of the car. She kicked and screamed and cried and demanded that Mrs. Thomason take her back, but her efforts were in vain. She was trapped, and no matter how big of a commotion she caused, the car never stopped moving. She threw a tantrum until she was too tired to do anything other than breathe. She lay her head on the backseat and wept. She wept for the life she was leaving behind and dreaded the one that awaited her ahead.

Chapter 5

Six years passed under the watchful eye of Ms. Jacqueline and her pedophile son. Growing up without a mother or even a father to guide her had been hard for Disaya. She never really knew what love felt like because she was beginning to forget the love that her parents showered her with daily. She felt incomplete. She was forever lost in a world of deception, abuse, and confusion. Her heart was empty, and she instinctively grew cold on the inside while getting hard on the outside. She disconnected herself from her existence because it hurt too badly to think about everything that she lived through. She sometimes wished that she had died too, because the day that they took her away from her parents' home, living became harder than dying. Tearing her away from the only home she knew did permanent damage to her psyche. Her calloused outlook on life hindered her from trusting anyone or loving anyone besides Mona.

The only reason Disaya had even let Mona into her world was because Mona reflected the same amount of hurt that she felt. They were so much alike, alone in a cold world . . . trying to make it together while being violated every day in every possible way. Disaya and Mona remained silent about the treatment because they didn't want to be separated and sent away to different group homes, but at the tender age of twelve YaYa wised up and realized that she was the one with the power. Her looks had never failed her.

Over the years she had grown up quite nicely. She was constantly reminded of how cute she was and grown-ups oohed and ahhed over her beauty every day, as if something so beautiful didn't belong in the hood. She was as foreign as a concrete rose, and she knew it. Although she still had a child's body, she was beginning to come into her young adult years. Her tiny breasts had begun to sprout, and instead of becoming a stick figure, she was rounding out in her hip area, not too much but enough to form a young curve. If her twelve-year-old figure was any indication as to how she would develop, she would be what a man would call a brick house.

Mark was now twenty-three and couldn't contain his urges to sex the young girls, but Disaya wasn't stupid. She now knew that what he was doing to them was wrong and used it to her advantage.

"Have a hustle and use what you have to get exactly what you want in life . . . including all that Prada you love so much."

She now knew what her mother meant by those words and was beginning to understand that wasn't shit in this world free. Mark was going to start paying her for what he took from her. It was her Prada Plan . . . to get what she wanted, by using what she had.

That night Disaya lay in bed, the darkness of the room enveloping her as she stared at the clock radio on her nightstand. The red illuminating numbers cast a haunting glow as she counted every second in her mind.

"You awake?" Mona asked.

"Yeah, I'm up," Disaya replied, her voice bleak and dejected.

"How much longer do we have?" Mona inquired.

Disaya already knew what Mona was referring to. For six excruciating years Mark had come to their bedroom at the same time every night. They had timed him down to the second.

"About three more minutes," YaYa whispered.

"I'm tired of this shit, YaYa," Mona stated, her voice cracking. "I don't know how much more of this I can take. My body hurts every day. He doesn't treat me the same way he treats you. He hurts me. He's rougher and meaner with me."

"We have to take it. You're all I have, and if we say anything we're getting shipped away from each other," YaYa said.

The door creaked open, sending an eerie chill up YaYa's spine and hushing them both into submission. Footsteps descended the staircase.

YaYa held her breath as she felt the weight of Mark's body as he sat on the side of her bed. She pretended to be asleep, but that didn't stop Mark's pursuit. He touched her budding breasts, squeezing them so hard that they throbbed tenderly.

To a grown woman it may have felt good, but she wasn't a grown woman. She had barely reached adolescence. She was still a child. Immature. Underdeveloped. Not sexy in any way. Yet still he molested her. Her body was not ready for the trauma that it had been receiving for the past six years. Even if she managed to survive the physical exploitation, the mental and emotional trauma that was caused were wounds that she and Mona would carry with them for the rest of their lives. The curse that they shared would remain beneath the surface of their being and would help them harbor insecurities for the rest of their lives. The damage was already done, and it was irreversible.

"Disaya, wake up. You know what time it is," he whispered as his slimy tongue ran across her breast.

She flinched and sat up. Inhaling, she took a deep breath as she prepared to stand up for herself. "You touch me again, I'm going to scream," she said, her voice shaking as she squirmed away from Mark's touch and pressed her back firmly against the wall.

"What did you say?" Mark stated in surprise.

"You heard me. If you want us to keep quiet about what you've been doing to us, you are going to have to pay us," YaYa stated.

She saw the look of panic that formed in his eyes, and it caused her courage to build a little more.

Mona sat up in her bed in astonishment and fear. She didn't know what was going to happen next. She waited to hear a struggle, a slap, something, but what she least expected occurred.

"You's a cold little bitch, huh?" Mark asked with amusement in his voice. "A'ight, I'll pay you, but since I'm paying for this pussy, you better not ever give my shit away. Even when you get older, you better tell these little niggas your shit is taken." He pulled out a wad of money and peeled off two twenty-dollar bills.

Disaya's eyes lit up, but she contained her excitement, not wanting to tip her hand to her enemy. Although it wasn't much money, to Disaya it symbolized respect. She knew that Mark was going to have his way with her whether she wanted him to or not—now at least she was benefiting from the arrangement. It was a fucked-up train of thought for a twelve-year-old child, but it was her reality. There was nothing that she could do to stop it, so she made sure the abuse was done on her terms.

She took the money and then said, "Mona too."

Mark reluctantly peeled off more money and placed it on Mona's bed. Disaya's attitude and sudden feistiness made him even hornier, and his grown-man's penis couldn't wait to get inside of her little-girl essence. He leaned into her, and his weight forced her onto the bed.

Her body tensed up, and she instinctively struggled against him. A tear came from her eyes as she felt his hands part her shaking legs.

"I'm paying for this now. You better not fight me," Mark threatened as he gripped the sides of her face tightly with one hand.

YaYa let the tension go away from her body, and she took her mind back to when she remembered happiness, as Mark did whatever he wanted to her. Her body was there, but mentally and spiritually she was somewhere else. She had learned over the years that becoming detached from her abuser and his horrid acts of

abuse was the best way for her to survive, and as he had his way
with her, she let her mind wander back to when she was happy
with her family. It drifted in the past to when she felt safe and
loved, and secure with the ones she cherished most. Her mental
vacation was the only thing, besides Mona, that helped her make
it through.

A nagging pain awoke Disaya the next morning. It felt like
lightning bolts were going off in her stomach, and the feeling was
intense enough to cause her to double over in pain. She pulled
back her sheets to get up, but froze when she saw that her crisp
white linens were covered in crimson. There was blood everywhere. She was used to being sore and bleeding a little bit after
Mark took advantage of her, but the amount of blood on her bed
today made it look as if someone had been murdered.

"Mo! Mona, wake up," YaYa whispered, shaking Mona out of
her sleep.

"What, YaYa . . . what's wrong?"

"I'm bleeding. I think something is wrong," YaYa said, panick-
ing.

Mona looked at the amount of blood on the sheets. Neither
girl knew what a period was. Ms. Jacqueline had never explained
it to them. It was something that was learned from a mother, and
both were without one, leaving them ignorant to the most basic
feminine functions.

"Aghh," YaYa cried out as she doubled over again from the un-
familiar pain. "I think something's wrong."

"I'm going to get Ms. Jacqueline," Mona said in panic before
racing up the stairs.

YaYa didn't even get a chance to protest. The next thing she
knew, Ms. Jacqueline was coming down the stairs. She stopped
dead in her tracks when she saw Disaya sitting on the ruined
sheets.

"Lord, you had me thinking she was dying down here, Mona.
Disaya, you just started your period, baby. All women have them

. . . once a month. Go get washed up, and I'll take you to the store to get some products."

YaYa nodded, relieved that nothing was wrong, and ascended the steps. She was embarrassed but was grateful that the bleeding was normal. She wasn't prepared to tell Ms. Jacqueline what her son had been doing to them. She had never received any beatings from Ms. Jacqueline, but she wasn't naive enough to believe that it could never happen.

The old woman seemed to take a liking to Disaya more than any other foster child that came across her way. She fed YaYa, purchased her the best clothes, and liked to spend time with her, yet she treated Mona poorly, feeding her scraps and getting her hand-me-downs. YaYa had peeped the difference from the very beginning, but she had grown to look at Mona as a sister and so shared whatever Ms. Jacqueline gave her. She was glad that no questions were asked and the problem was diagnosed and solved before the cat was let out of the bag.

After cleaning herself, she and Mona met Ms. Jacqueline in the driveway.

"Where do you think you're going, Mona? It don't take two of y'all to buy no damn pads. You still have chores to do. Ever since Disaya got here, you've been like her shadow. Gone git in the house. We'll be back in a few," Ms. Jacqueline stated harshly as she shooed Mona away dismissively.

Mona looked up at the house in fear. Mark was still inside, and without Disaya nearby he terrified her. She looked back toward the car.

YaYa instantly recognized the expression on Mona's face, but there was nothing she could do, so she mouthed, *It'll be okay,* then climbed into the car. She didn't allow herself to look back at Mona because she too was afraid of what may happen to her once she was alone in the house with Mark.

Mona stood on the front porch and with dread watched Ms. Jacqueline's car disappear up the street. Her stomach felt as if there were a million butterflies fluttering around inside because she knew what was about to go down as soon as she stepped foot inside the house. She thought about running away. She wanted to run as far as her legs would take her, but she couldn't leave YaYa. They had forged a sisterhood so deep that without each other they felt lost. Without any family they leaned on each other for support, for companionship, for security. They were the only constant in each other's life.

Mona was conflicted. She wanted to save herself, but her conscience refused to allow her to desert YaYa. Yes, they were in hell, but they were in hell together. *No, I can't leave without her*, Mona thought as she crept back into the house, her heart beating frantically . . . the intensity inside of her almost choking her, making it hard for her to breathe.

She crept through the house until she reached the stairs to the basement, descending the steps one at a time. Her nerves were so bad, it felt like she was walking through a haunted house instead of what should have been her home.

She stopped dead in her tracks, one foot hanging in midair; she was about to step down to the next step, but something made her cease. She could smell him. She knew his body scent better than she knew her own, and he had already come down the stairs. He was somewhere in the basement . . . in her bedroom. Lurking. Waiting. Preying on her.

She turned around slowly. She didn't want to make too much noise. She looked at the open basement door. Desperation filled her eyes. She was halfway from the bottom and the top. *All I have to do is make it up those steps. I can run outside and wait for YaYa to come home. Just go.* Her body began to shake uncontrollably.

She turned on her heels and attempted to ascend the steps, but before she could even lift her legs, a hand reached in between the stairway and pulled her down with such force that she fell face first, her head hitting the corner of a step with such impact, she felt the blow beneath her skull.

"Are you trying to run from me?" Mark asked. His sadistic tone was angry, almost punishing. "You know what I want. All you have to do is give it to me and get it over with."

Mona was disoriented from her fall, and before she could get up, he was over her, pulling on her clothes.

"No! Stop it!" Mona screamed as she swatted at his hands and punched into the air, hoping to connect with his face.

"Oh, you gon' fight me, huh?" he asked through clenched teeth. He brought his hand up and slapped her across her face. Then he grabbed her summer shorts and ripped them off her body. He pulled so hard that he dragged her down three more steps. Her head bounced off of each one as if it were a plastic ball.

"Don't!" Her cries were futile and only enraged him more.

"Shut!" He pulled her pants completely off. "The fuck—" He smacked her again, this time causing a fireworks display to erupt behind her eyes. "Up!" he screamed as he put his hand over her mouth and nose. His hand was so big that he was smothering her.

"Hmm! Hmm!" she screamed. She couldn't breathe, and she kicked and fought furiously as she felt her lungs struggling for air. "Hmm! Hmm!" Her insides burned and she knew that she was dying.

"When I let go of your mouth, you better shut the fuck up! If you scream, I'll kill you, bitch. Walking around in this tight shit, teasing me all day . . . now you don't want to give it up," Mark stated as if he was obsessed.

He finally removed his hand, and her lungs gratefully welcomed the oxygen. She gasped greedily in an attempt to feed them. Mark grabbed her by the wrists and forced her down the remainder of the stairs then shoved her toward her bed. Her bottom half was completely exposed, and she trembled as she stared at his erection. Her eyes searched the room for something she could defend herself with, but she saw nothing. She was helpless and didn't have a choice but to submit to him. She could feel her face swelling, and a knot formed on her temple, causing her head to throb.

"Please don't," she whispered.

He removed his jumbo-sized penis and turned her around. She was confused. He had never done this before but he had always inflicted pain upon her, so she braced herself for what was about to occur.

She felt him lubricate her bottom with spit, and she began to jerk against him. "No! Don't!" she screamed.

"Shut the fuck up and bend over before I break your fucking neck," he demanded in a sinister tone that told Mona she'd better comply. "I want to take this ass."

He pushed her neck down into the pillow and positioned the tip of his thick shaft on her anal entrance, and just as he was about to defile her, she heard YaYa yell her name.

"Mona!"

"YaYa! Help me!" Mona screamed just before Mark punched her in the back of the head, then flipped her around and punched her in the face. Her bottom lip burst on contact, causing blood to pour all over her shirt.

"Mona!"

Mona heard YaYa's voice getting closer, and Mark scrambled to put himself back together.

YaYa and Ms. Jacqueline had come back from the store, and YaYa heard the screams as soon as she stepped foot inside the house. She took off for the basement, Ms. Jacqueline on her heels.

As soon as she saw her best friend bloody and swollen she attacked. "Why did you do this to her? We never did anything to you! I hate you! I hate you!" YaYa yelled as she swung with all her might, hitting Mark in the head as he curled up to avoid her blows. Her hits did little damage, but it got her point across. "I'm going to kill you! I hate you!"

Ms. Jacqueline pulled YaYa off of her son. "That's enough." She then turned her attention toward Mona. "I done told you about being fast, haven't I? You little fast ass, little heiffa you! Setting my son up! I should beat your fast ass myself!" Ms.

Jacqueline grabbed Mona up by the collar, practically lifting her from the ground.

"Yeah, she was walking around here talking nasty to me, opening and closing her legs. She asked me to do it, Ma. She the one talking about she wanted to see what dick felt like. I swear, Ma, she's been asking for it. I thought she could handle it," Mark stated.

"You fucking liar!" Disaya screamed. She turned to Ms. Jacqueline. "Mona didn't do anything! He's been raping us! He's been coming to our room every night since I've been here. You have to do something! Why are you punishing us? Punish him!"

"Just shut your mouth!" Ms. Jacqueline yelled, and for the first time she smacked Disaya in her mouth. "You both are getting too grown. You can't live here anymore. Them damn checks ain't worth it. I'm going to call Child Services tomorrow and have them come and get you. Ungrateful little heiffas! Come on, Mark. Bring your stupid ass upstairs," she fussed as she pulled him by his ear up the stairs. Before she slammed the door she yelled, "And don't bring your asses up these stairs. Ain't nobody tried to rape your hot asses. You're just grown as hell. Stay down there and don't make a fucking sound! Pack your shit! You both are getting out tomorrow!"

"YaYa, I didn't do anything!" Mona cried.

YaYa rushed to her side and hugged her tightly. "I know, Mo, I know you didn't. I didn't want to leave you here. I had Ms. Jacqueline stop at a gas station, so we wouldn't have to go far. I'm sorry I left you by yourself! It's okay. Everything will be okay!"

YaYa's fury was like an inferno burning inside of her chest, and all she could see was red.

"They're going to split us up!" Mona cried hysterically as she sobbed uncontrollably, snot, blood, and tears making a hideous combination on her face.

"No, they won't, Mo. Fuck this. If they can't find us, then they can't split us up. We're getting out of here. Nobody should have to live like this. Don't nobody want us, but we got each other. That's enough. We'll be okay."

"How?" Mona asked. "We don't have anywhere to go."

"We'll figure it out. Before my mama died she told me to have a Prada Plan."

"A what?"

"A hustle plan to get what I want in life. We can do this, Mo. It has to be better than this," Disaya argued. Mona nodded and Disaya continued. "Pack your stuff. Whatever you think you might need. We're getting out of here tonight, and we're going to make that grimy nigga pay for everything he's done to us."

The digital clock read 3:57 AM as Disaya slid out of her bed. She was already dressed to go. She had slept in sweatpants and a hoodie in anticipation of their escape. She had stayed up all night and waited until the perfect time for them to leave. Mona had passed out from pain and exhaustion hours ago. Disaya didn't disturb her, because after what she had gone through she knew Mona needed her rest.

She grabbed her bookbag full of clothes and slung them over her back. She walked over to Mona's bed. "Mo!" she whispered. "Wake up. We've got to go!"

Mona sat up and saw YaYa leaning over her with a finger pressed to her lips, letting Mona know to be quiet. Mona nodded and then eased out of the bed. After slipping into sweats too, she grabbed her bookbag and was ready to go.

Disaya led the way up the stairs, and when they opened the basement door, a pungent smell hit their nostrils, causing them both to cover their mouths and noses.

"What's that smell?" Mona asked.

"I turned on the gas stove but didn't light the burner. It's been on since they went to sleep. I knew it wouldn't seep into the basement," Disaya responded.

"What are you going to do?"

"Get payback," Disaya replied. "If the gas hasn't already killed them, then the fire will." Disaya made her way to a pack of New-port cigarettes that was sitting on the kitchen table. She picked up the entire pack, along with the lighter that sat nearby. She then made her way to the back door. "Hold open the door and be ready to run," Disaya whispered.

Mona did as she was told, and YaYa lit the cigarette. She puffed it to get the nicotine burning nice and steady, coughing as the foreign nicotine entered her virgin lungs. She forced herself to suck on the cancer stick until the tip was glowing red, and then she tossed it onto the gas stove. She could hear the ignition of the flame, but she didn't look back as she raced out of the door.

Amber flames arose instantly as both girls ran away from the scene. They watched from a couple houses down, their hearts beating like an African drum. They held onto each other as the cold night air nipped at them, but the heat in their hearts kept them warm as they watched flames engulf the house. They waited to hear a scream or a voice coming from the house, but they heard nothing. All they saw was the flickering flames jumping to and fro inside of the house.

"YaYa, do you think they're dead?" Mona asked as neighbors began to come out of their homes and crowd around the burning house.

"I hope so," she replied.

"Do you think anyone will look for us?" Mona asked without any remorse.

"It doesn't matter. They won't be able to find us," Disaya stated matter-of-factly. "Forget Ms. Jacqueline, forget Mark, and forget the state. We're on our own. Nothing can tear us apart."

They heard the distant sound of sirens, and they turned and walked away casually so that they didn't look suspicious. They had just committed arson and murder, but to them it was the only way to survive. Living under Ms. Jacqueline's roof had murdered them in many ways. In their eyes it was payback. It was karma for Ms. Jacqueline turning a blind eye to what her sick son was doing. It was get-back for Mark taking away what little childhoods they had left after the untimely separation of their real families.

As they walked into the night, they had no idea what types of struggles they were about to face. They had just become products of the streets. Their destinies were in their own hands, and the game that they were now playing was one where the winner took all and the losers lost everything. It was the game of life. And before they were even teenagers, they had the responsibility of taking care of themselves.

"The Prada Plan, right?" Mona asked out of the blue. "That's what your mama said to use to get what you want. That's what we are going to do to take care of ourselves out here?"

"Damn right. The Prada Plan is all we got."

The Present

She's got to eat today, fuck a tomorrow.

Chapter 6

Nine Years Later

A tear graced Disaya's face as she thought about how far she and Mona had come. It wasn't easy growing up in the streets, but they had made it. Many nights they went hungry, many nights they went without a roof over their heads, but her mother had equipped her with hope when she had invented the Prada Plan, and somehow Disaya and Mona always seemed to come up on a lick. Whether it was stealing, conning, or just plain struggling, the two girls always seemed to make it through.

As YaYa pulled up to her job, she realized that this was the first time she had been stable since the death of her mother. No, she wasn't balling, but she was bartending at one of the hottest clubs in the city, she had a decent one-bedroom apartment, and she wasn't worried about where her next meal was going to come from. Considering everything that she and Mona had been through, she had to give herself props . . . she was doing pretty well.

Disaya stepped into the club and smiled when she noticed how packed it was that night. *Tips gon' be on point tonight,* she thought to herself as she made her way toward the bar. Her skintight

Seven jeans and gold halter only added to her sex appeal, which she knew would increase her value that night.

"Hey, YaYa, where you been? You been missing crazy money tonight," Mona stated.

YaYa hopped onto the bar and twirled her legs around so that she could get to work. "Straight? These niggas working with deep pockets tonight?" Disaya asked.

"Shit, deep enough. I've already made a buck fifty and it ain't even eleven o'clock," Mona bragged as she flipped a tequila bottle in the air before filling two shot glasses with the liquor.

Mona was a tall, high-yellow girl with sandy hair that cascaded down her back. She was average in the face, mostly because of the scar above her right eyebrow from that tragic day so many years ago, but most dudes were willing to look past what she lacked in beauty because she made up for it with a set of perky D-cups that she always kept on display. She was in no way comparable to Disaya, however.

With her caramel-colored skin, green eyes, and shoulder-length layered hair, Disaya made sure she stayed fly. Her five-feet-seven frame was perfectly proportioned, and she had a figure that most women would kill for. Disaya always seemed to demand the attention of the room, and tonight in the club was no different.

"Yo, let me get a bottle of Mo-mo, baby girl," a dude stated as he repeatedly slapped his hand on the bar counter. He had walked straight up to the bar, disregarding the people who were waiting in line for their drink orders to be filled.

Disaya kept taking orders from the rest of the line, while Mona went to take care of the man.

"Nah, ma, I was talking to ol' girl. I want her to hook me up," he stated with an intoxicated slur.

Disaya overheard the guy and turned around as she continued to work the entire bar. "Yo, my man, my girl here gon' get you right. Just give her your order, and she'll take care of you," Disaya said with a smile. "That'll be six dollars," Disaya stated to another customer as she continued to serve her clientele.

"That's all right, I'ma wait for you," the dude said with a slick smile.

Mona walked up to Disaya and whispered, "You might want to take care of him, girl. That's Ronnie B."

"Ronnie B?" Disaya repeated in confusion.

"Bitch, Ronnie B . . . Elite Management. Word is he throwing this party to scout for more models for his company. I hear they be getting crazy paid too," Mona replied.

Disaya didn't give a damn who the dude was. She had heard about his entertainment company, though, and word on the streets was that anybody associated with him was getting paid. She strutted over to the dude sitting at the end of the bar and peeped him from head to toe as she approached. She could tell by the Audemars Piguet that he sported on his wrist that he was working with more chips than the average dude.

"What can I get for you?" she asked him.

"What's your name?" he inquired, completely ignoring her question.

"YaYa," she replied as she shifted her weight to one side.

"YaYa . . . what is someone as attractive as you doing working behind a bar?" he asked.

"Paying the bills," she replied with a quick tongue.

YaYa was not the type of chick to front like she had more than what met the eye. She was a real chick and wouldn't claim to be anything more than what she was. She knew she was a Rocawear ho, but she was looking to be upgraded and was determined to get her paper up so that she could graduate from hood-rich clothing lines to high-end designers. She knew that most niggas in the hood had hustle plans, but she wasn't trying to compete in their games.

Disaya wasn't built for the coke game, but she did have all the right assets to get what she wanted. She had a seductive and natural beauty that was so rare in the hood. That was the advantage that she had on all of the other girls from her neighborhood. She was strikingly gorgeous and she knew it. She flipped the game and turned what a dude would call his hustle plan into her Prada Plan, which was to use what she had to get what she wanted.

The man sitting before her was about to become her meal ticket and he didn't even know it. She was still on the grind and wasn't going to stop until she reached the top. She had an insatiable appetite for money and wouldn't stop chasing it until she was at the top of her game.

I'll be rocking Prada in no time if I can get down with his company, she thought to herself.

"Your man ain't taking care of home?" he asked.

"Is that your slick way of asking me if I have one?" she replied as she placed one hand on her hip. Her arched eyebrows frowned as she waited for him to reply.

"I guess that wasn't all that smooth, huh?" he asked with a smile.

YaYa smiled too. She could tell that he was embarrassed from the wack line he had just thrown her way.

"You straight. Your game just need a little work, that's all," she replied with a laugh.

He nodded his head, lifted his glass and said, "Blame it on the liquor."

"Well, you're running a little low on that, so what can I get you?"

"Have one of the waitresses bring a couple bottles of Mo and Cris up to VIP," he said as he went into his pocket and pulled out a wad of money and a business card. He placed them both on the countertop.

Disaya picked up the green and the card then counted out a thousand dollars as he began to walk away. "Hey, you gave me way too much!" she shouted after him as he continued to maneuver through the crowd.

He stopped in his tracks, turned around and said, "That's your tip! Come to the address on the card tomorrow if you trying to make more," he replied.

YaYa looked at the card that she held in her hand. She was about to respond, but when she looked back up, Ronnie B had already disappeared into the crowd. Disaya looked back at Mona, who had been eagerly watching the entire encounter.

"What he say?" Mona asked eagerly when Disaya returned to her side.

Disaya passed her the card and replied, "The nigga gave me a five-hundred-dollar tip and told me to get at him if I wanted to make more."

"What!" Mona yelled excitedly. "YaYa, do you know how hard it is to get down with Elite? He just up and told you to come through. You going, right?"

"Hell yeah, I'm gon' go, but you got to come with me. I ain't trying to be up in there by myself."

"You know I'm down. If I can get with Elite, I can finally make some real cash and stop fucking with these cats with shallow means," Mona muttered while thinking about her current situation. "I'm tired of messing with these niggas with play money."

Disaya burst into laughter. "What the hell is play money?"

Mona began to laugh too as she replied, "You know . . . play money. Niggas be walking around here with twenty-two's and chromed-out cars, but don't have no real cash. They be parking them shits at they mama's crib at the end of the night because they grown as hell still living at home."

"Or they be wrapping rubber bands around a stack of ones with a hundred-dollar bill on top to make it look like they balling," Disaya added through her laughter.

"Hell yeah! Them fronting-ass, no-money-getting niggas be talking about . . . 'Girl, I will keep your hair done.' I be wanting to say, 'Nigga, please, I can do that myself!" Mona continued.

Disaya couldn't stop herself from laughing because she knew her girl was telling the truth. "All jokes aside, though, I'm not fucking with no more broke niggas. If he can't buy me that brownstone in Manhattan, I ain't fucking with him. It's time to step into the big leagues," Disaya said confidently.

"Well, it doesn't get any bigger than that," Mona stated as she nodded her head toward the VIP balcony where Ronnie B was.

Ronnie B's eyes were glued on Disaya, and he lifted his glass in the air and nodded to her. Disaya smiled seductively as she returned his stare.

"Excuse me! Can I get a rum and Coke?" a girl asked, snapping Disaya out of her daze.

She turned around and got back to work. She thought to herself, *I'm about to get this money. These niggas getting they grind on. It's time to pull out the Prada Plan and make this cake.*

Chapter 7

Disaya tossed clothes all over her apartment. as she debated with herself about what to put on. She had seen some of the girls that worked for Elite Management and they were all model-type chicks. She didn't want to walk into the place half-stepping. She knew that whatever she wore, she had to be on point, and none of the clothes inside of her closet was going to get the job done.

"Damn!" she yelled in frustration as she picked up her phone. She quickly dialed Mona's number.

"Hello?" her friend answered in a whisper.

"Bitch, why are you whispering?" Disaya asked in confusion.

"I'm shopping on West Thirty-first," she replied, still whispering.

"You must have read my mind," Disaya replied. "Meet me at Saks in an hour."

Disaya quickly threw on her Seven jeans, a Bob Marley T-shirt, and some Force Ones.

An hour later she met Mona in front of the store.

"You bring your bag?" Mona asked.

"You know I did. This is more valuable than a Visa," she joked as she patted the black bookbag that she carried in her hand.

"You want to create the distraction or you want me to?" Mona asked.

"You do the distraction, I'll take care of the rest."

The girls walked into the store and headed their separate ways. This was a routine that they had gotten used to, so they were both confident that they would be in and out in less than twenty minutes.

Disaya pulled out a red pen and marked stars on the tags of the clothes that she liked the best. They both knew that they needed to look fly for the night. Ronnie B wouldn't even look twice at them if they weren't dressed to impress. She peeked over at Mona, who was a couple aisles down. The two girls didn't even speak to each other, they were so busy concentrating on the task at hand.

Once Disaya had marked all the clothes that she liked the best, she asked for assistance from one of the salespeople. "Excuse me, do you have this dress in white and a size eight?" she asked the white redheaded woman who was trying to keep tabs on Mona.

The woman's eyes cut low in the corners as she watched Mona closely.

"Excuse me?" Disaya stated again, this time with a little more attitude.

"Oh . . . umm, let me check in the back for you," she said as she reluctantly turned her back on Mona.

The saleswoman walked to the back of the store, and in less than two minutes flat, Mona had walked around the entire department and boosted all the clothes that Disaya had tagged. She discreetly stuffed them into the black bookbag and then walked into the restroom, where she proceeded to remove the alarm sensors from the clothes.

The woman came back with the dress just as Mona was exiting

the bathroom. The woman ran behind the cashier's counter, picked up the phone, and called security. She didn't even think to hand Disaya the dress. "Hey! Excuse me, miss! I'm going to have to check your bag!" she yelled across the store just as Mona reached the exit.

"What!" Mona yelled out. "Bitch, I ain't got to steal from your store!" She made sure to raise her voice so that she would attract the attention of the other patrons in the store.

Disaya smirked as she watched the entire scene. Security arrived with the manager.

"Excuse me, miss, we are going to have to check your bag," the manager stated.

"What, because I'm black I can't afford to shop in this store? You think I got to steal!"

"I saw her putting clothes into the bag, sir," the saleswoman reported to her manager.

As Mona continued to argue with the staff, Disaya walked into the restroom where Mona had swapped bags and picked up the black bookbag full of designer clothes. Disaya had tagged everything from Dior to Fendi, which would cause the store to take a hell of a loss. She carried the bag at her side as she walked right past Mona and the group of people.

Mona winked her eye and gave her a quick smile before Disaya strolled out the front door, merchandise in hand. They had just gone on another one of their shopping sprees. They never spent a dime, yet they always made it happen and stepped out fresh.

Disaya waited outside and burst out laughing when she watched through the window as the manager opened Mona's bookbag to find nothing in it but an old quilt. The look on the saleswoman's face was priceless.

When Mona walked out of the store she met Disaya up the block. She had three large Saks bags in her hand.

"What is all that?" Disaya asked.

Mona was laughing hysterically and replied, "I raised so much hell, they gave me store credit just for accusing me." She handed one of the bags over to her girl. "Here are the shoes you were looking at."

"Bitch, those were some seven-hundred-dollar shoes! How much store credit did they give you?" Disaya asked in astonishment.

"Twenty-five hundred dollars," Mona replied in a nonchalant tone.

"You's a bad bitch," Disaya said as she slapped hands with her friend.

"No, *you's* a bad bitch," Mona replied. "We about to put this Prada Plan of yours into action."

Disaya could feel the butterflies fluttering in her stomach as she approached the large warehouse. She knew that Ronnie B used the warehouse to host some of his infamous parties. She was fly in her cream Dolce & Gabbana jacket. The cropped style of the jacket stopped just at her waist and matched the cream knee-high leather Margiela boots she was rocking. Her designer jeans suffocated her wide hips and thick thighs, allowing her voluptuous derrière to become the focal point of her appearance.

Can't nobody tell me shit, she thought as she stepped seductively into the building.

There were girls scattered throughout the lower level of the building, and a group of dudes mingled on the second level of the loft-style warehouse.

Disaya turned toward Mona and said, "What the fuck is all this about?"

Mona shrugged her shoulders and continued to follow Disaya through the room.

Before she could answer, one of the girls made her way upstairs and clapped her hands to get everybody's attention. "Excuse me!" she stated loudly.

Disaya looked up at the chocolate-colored girl. She had the beauty of a super-model. She was slim, and her long, jet-black hair was held off her face with a pair of Dior sunglasses. The girl's

shit was official too. She wasn't rocking no shades from China-
town; she was clad in an original head-to-toe hookup straight
from the designer's Manhattan store. Disaya knew this because
she had just drooled over the ensemble hours earlier while out
boosting with Mona.

Ronnie B stood behind the girl, one hand wrapped around her
waist.

"Ladies, welcome to Elite Management. All of y'all are here
for the same reason . . . y'all are trying to get down. As you can
see, you have to be perfect, or damn near close to it in order to
get down with us. We don't need no simpleminded, stuck-up-ass
bitches in here either. I'm gon' tell y'all the truth right now. You
will fuck, suck, and please whoever you are asked to. It don't matter if the nigga is fat, ugly, white, black, whatever. If he got that cake
to put up . . . we will take care of him. The cut will be seventy-
thirty. Don't get bigheaded and think that you can do this on
your own, because you can't. Some of the most hood-rich niggas
in New York request our services. We deal with niggas so big, you
can't even get them to look your way, let alone become wifey. So
drop them gold-diggin'-ass tactics that y'all have been using. If
you ain't afraid of money and you trying to get it with us, I need
y'all to get in line one by one so we can start the interviews."

"Fuck this bitch think she is?" Mona whispered in Disaya's ear
as she looked up at the landing where the girl stood.

"Ain't no telling, but I don't know if I'm down with this. I didn't
know Ronnie B was getting down like this. I was thinking he was
on some model-management-type stuff. Seventy-thirty split. I
know this nigga didn't ask me to come here so he could pimp my
ass," Disaya attested as she frowned.

Her perfectly arched eyebrows showed her distress, and Ronnie B noticed her disposition as he approached. "What up, Mama?"
he asked as he looked her up and down while licking his lips in
lust.

Disaya didn't respond. She crossed her arms and looked at him
with an attitude before turning her attention toward Mona.

"You ready?"

"Whoa . . . hold up. What up? I thought we had a good conversation the other night. You're getting ready to bounce just like that. You ain't been here ten minutes."

"Look, this ain't for me. I'm not one of your little groupie broads. I don't get pimped. If I sell my pussy, believe me, I better be profiting a hundred percent." Disaya walked away.

Ronnie walked after her and grabbed her arm lightly. "Yo, YaYa, just hear me out, okay. I need you, ma. You got everything I'm looking for. I only fuck with the baddest bitches in New York and you one of 'em. I'm not trying to pimp you, ma, I'm trying to feed you. Working with me, you'll get money. Yeah, I'll be taking a cut . . . but that's simply a small finder's fee. You'll be caked up and living like you want to be living, you feel me?"

"Come on, YaYa, the Prada Plan, remember?" Mona said, trying to convince her friend to at least give it a chance.

Ronnie B picked up on the comment and said, "Yeah, YaYa, the Prada Plan . . . see, your girl down . . . now all I need is you on the team and I'm good. Money gon' flow like water."

"Fine, but I ain't standing in this long-ass line," Disaya added as she gave in.

Ronnie B took her hand, and she grabbed Mona's as they maneuvered their way to the front. Disaya could hear the smart comments and smacking lips of the other girls waiting in line.

"You're next," Ronnie whispered in her ear as he opened the door and walked inside.

Disaya waited in line for a half an hour, and finally the door opened. She stepped inside and strutted into the room. Her body language displayed confidence as she stood in the middle of the room. She stood in front of a table of six people, one of them being the dark-skinned girl who had addressed the group of wannabes earlier.

"I'm Leah . . . and you are?" the girl asked.

"I'm YaYa," Disaya answered as she shifted all her weight on one leg, giving her hips an enticing shape.

"Turn around, ma," one of the dudes that was sitting at the table instructed.

A half-smile crossed Disaya's face as she turned around slowly, pausing so that they could take all of her in.

"Damn, baby girl, you hurting 'em," the guy commented as she clapped her cheeks together discreetly, showing she could work her ass muscles.

Ronnie B just sat back and observed Disaya. He wanted to see how she handled herself under pressure.

"So tell us about yourself, YaYa," Leah instructed.

"Ain't too much to tell. What you see is exactly what you get."

"Well, why do you want to be down with Elite?"

Disaya frowned and replied, "I don't. I was asked to come here. I'm just trying to see what y'all got to offer."

"We ain't offering shit. You got to show us why you should be down," Leah replied smartly. She got up and walked over to Disaya and circled her while she eyed her up and down. "Are you down for whatever?"

"I'm down to make money," YaYa replied with a smart tongue.

Leah stopped in front of YaYa and stood directly in her face. She stood so close to her that Disaya could smell the peppermint scent on her breath. Leah kissed her softly on the lips.

YaYa was hesitant at first, but decided to see where the kiss would lead. She knew that Ronnie and his crew were testing her to see if she was really ready for the lifestyle that they led. She realized that if she joined Elite Management she'd have to do a lot more than kiss another woman, so to prove herself, she tongued Leah back passionately.

To YaYa's surprise, she felt her pussy get wet. She wasn't bisexual and had never experienced a sexual encounter with a woman, but just the fact that she had a roomful of men lusting after her while she kissed another girl made her body tremble in curiosity.

"Damn, shorty right," one of the dudes said to Ronnie B as they slapped hands.

"That's why I chose her," he replied.

The girls ended their kiss, and Leah nodded her head in approval.

"She's in," Leah said as she switched back to her seat and sat down.

"Here you go, baby girl," Ronnie B said as he held out a Sidekick for her. She walked toward him and accepted it. "Keep this on you at all times. Only use it to contact one of the Elite members. All of our numbers are programmed in there. I'll hit you up when I need you."

Leah pulled an envelope out of her purse and passed it to Disaya. "Go get yourself fresh . . . I can see by the way that you're dressed that you don't really need the help in the clothes department, but buy yourself something new anyway. Consider it a signing bonus."

Disaya began to walk out of the room, and before she opened the door Ronnie B yelled, "Send your girl in."

Chapter 8

Disaya couldn't wait to make that fast money. She knew that this was her chance to come up in a big way. Her clientele was about to shoot through the roof. Now that she was down with Elite, she would be introduced to some of the most hood-rich niggas the East Coast had ever produced, and she hoped that she would be able to find a nigga to take care of her.

She counted the money that Leah had given her. It was five stacks, and she planned on using that to put a down payment on a new whip. She was currently driving a 2003 Mazda and decided that it was time for an upgrade. She knew that she couldn't really afford the car, but she figured that she should treat herself. YaYa had champagne tastes with beer money and was tired of riding around in her five-year-old car.

She drove her car down to the dealership and as soon as she stepped out of the car she was surrounded by the different dealers. They thought that she was a naive woman that they would be able to swindle. They had no idea that she planned on hustling them out of the best car on the lot. She had on a short jean Az-zure skirt and a knit sweater that hung loosely off one shoulder. Her stiletto heels clicked on the pavement as she made her way into the dealership. She had a trail of salesmen following behind her, but she was looking for a specific dealer. She didn't even want to waste her time with the employees; she wanted to deal with the owner. She walked directly to the rear of the building and opened a door that had the name *Bill Perkins* engraved on it. An attractive, older black man sat behind the desk with a pair of reading glasses on.

"Hello, Bill, I need a car," she said.

He looked up at her and then at the swarm of salesmen standing idly in the hallway, watching her every move. His eyes then did a once-over of the beautiful girl that stood before him. "Excuse me," he said as he got up and walked past her. "All right, gentlemen, get back to work!" he instructed the group of lusting men. He turned around to see that Disaya was sitting on the edge of his desk with her legs crossed. Her skirt was so short that he could see her black lace panties underneath.

"What can I do for you, Ms . . ." he paused as he realized he hadn't caught her name.

"Jessica . . . Jessica Simpson," YaYa said with a smirk, giving him a ridiculously false name.

"Well, Jessica, what can I do for you?"

"I need a car," she repeated.

"Is there a specific price range that you're trying to stay in?" he asked.

"No, sir, I want the best car on this lot," she replied.

He raised an eyebrow at the young woman. "The best car on my car lot is a dark blue Dodge Magnum with a HEMI engine. That's a big car for such a small, pretty young lady like yourself. It also has a big sticker price to go along with it."

"Well, Mr. Perkins, I like riding on big things, if you know what I mean. I've got five thousand dollars cash and an '03 Mazda to use as a trade-in."

The man laughed at her as he shook his head. "That's not going to get you a forty-thousand-dollar car, young lady."

Disaya leaned back on his desk and spread her legs seductively.

"We should be able to work something out. I've got something that's worth more than gold."

Bill Perkins shut his door and closed the blinds to his office window.

When he turned around, Disaya could see the bulge in his slacks. *I'm getting ready to start tricking niggas for a living anyway. I might as well start with him,* she thought to herself.

The dealer actually wasn't a bad-looking man. He appeared to be in his early fifties, and his graying facial hair gave him a mature look.

She stuck one finger in her pussy and then lifted her finger to his lips. "Come taste me," she said as she licked her sweet, glossy lips.

He licked her wetness off of her fingers as he grinded his hardness against her body. "Hmm," he moaned as he began to nibble gently on her neck.

The man's hands sent a tingle up her spine. He moved like a man who had the expertise of a Casanova, and Disaya knew that he had seduced many women in his day. He knelt down on one knee and slipped his tongue into her pussy, twirling it in circles inside of her. She moaned so loudly that she was sure the entire establishment knew what was taking place inside the office. His head game was on point, and she couldn't help but to enjoy it.

The man inserted two fingers into her opening, as his tongue tap-danced on her clitoris. She moved her hips like a belly dancer as she pressed her vagina firmly against his mouth. He was giving her so much pleasure that she couldn't help but to grind back.

Bill put his hands underneath her skirt until both of them gripped her ass cheeks. He massaged them as he helped her grind her pussy on his tongue. He reached down with one hand and began to stroke himself while he pleasured her.

Disaya looked down and saw the thick eight inches he was working with. It wasn't all that long, but it was thick and juicy.

Damn, I should've brought some condoms, she thought as she watched his hand move up and down his shaft. The pleasurable look on his face brought her to her climax, and she felt herself cum. He didn't seem to mind, and seconds later he grunted loudly as he erupted.

Disaya stood up and fixed her skirt. "Is that payment enough for you?" she asked.

The man looked up at her and then climbed to his feet. It had been a long time since he had done something freaky. His wife was an older, more reserved woman and had surpassed menopause. He was sexually suppressed, and Disaya had no clue how much joy she had just given him.

"Just let me draw up the paperwork. I do have to warn you—I can get you off the lot today with, say, half of the bill taken care of. You will still have to make payments on the car every month until the remaining balance is taken care of."

Once I roll the car off the lot it's mines anyway. The repo man won't be able to find my ass, let alone my car, she thought. "I understand," she said aloud.

Bill Perkins gave her a credit of twenty-five thousand dollars for the Dodge Magnum and then drew up the paperwork in Jessica Simpson's name. Disaya couldn't help the smile that spread across her face when he handed her the keys.

He walked her to the car and opened the door for her. "Don't hesitate to stop by if you ever need a tune-up," he offered with a wink as he wiped his beard.

Without responding, Disaya put the car into drive and peeled out of the parking lot.

> *I got grands in this bitch, ma*
> *come and get you some*

Disaya and Mona sat in the Magnum with the windows down as they sang along with Rick Ross and bounced in their seats to the beat of their anthem. The parking lot of the car wash was packed, as everyone pulled up trying to show off what they were riding in. It was the middle of August, and everybody who was anybody in Harlem knew that this was the place to be on a Friday night. Disaya's new car sparkled underneath the streetlights that illuminated the lot. She was proud of herself because she knew that she was hanging with the big boys, as far as her whip was concerned. The girls stepped out of the car, dressed to impress, and they both hopped onto the hood of the car.

"Bitch, don't fuck up my paint job with them stilettos," YaYa warned as she eased her body onto her hood. Her factory speakers were turned up to the max, and both girls grooved to the mix CD that was pumping from the car.

There were people everywhere getting their smoke and drink on. Half-dressed girls walked from one end of the parking lot to the other, trying to grab attention from the local hustlers, and dudes were falling for the bait. Everybody was chilling, though, having a good time.

Disaya and Mona sparked up a blunt and then fell into a rotation of puff, puff, pass, as they let the weed take their minds to another level.

"Yo, let me get some of that?" a familiar voice shouted out as a car pulled up beside them.

Mona looked over at the black-on-black Lincoln Navigator, and a smile spread across her face.

"What up, Bay?" she said loudly as she hopped off the car and stepped to his window.

He nodded his head at YaYa. "What up, YaYa, girl? Don't be acting all new like you don't know nobody," he yelled playfully.

YaYa threw up the peace sign as she leaned back on her hood and continued to get blunted.

"I see you shining, baby girl," he yelled with laughter in his voice as he noticed her new car. Bay owned the car wash. He was a hustler and was getting big money around town. He was smart, though, and opened up several front businesses with his dirty money; the car wash was one of many.

"Just a little bit," she replied with a smile. She inhaled the smoke and held it down for a minute before blowing it out.

"Y'all trying to get into something?" he asked.

"Hell no, Bay. Every time we chill with you, y'all mu'fuckas be all hugged up and shit, leaving me feeling like the ugly friend and shit. I ain't no damn third wheel," YaYa said.

Mona and Bay had been fucking around since forever. They were each other's jump-off, and YaYa always felt out of place when she was around them.

"Come on now, YaYa, you know you far from ugly. You got these chickens beat by a mile. Besides, I'm supposed to be meeting my mans at the spot, so we can all just chill. I got some Goose at the crib. Baby, you know that's your juice."

Disaya smiled at Bay. She shook her head from side to side. She had to admit that the nigga knew her well. They had grown up in the same hood together and had always been cool. She had taken her first sip of alcohol with Bay when she was fifteen. He had gotten her pissy off of Grey Goose and she was hurling for days.

"Whatever, Bay . . . you and Mona, go do y'all thing. I can't mess with y'all tonight," she said as she continued to lean back on her car.

"YaYa, come on, girl," Mona pleaded as she gave her best friend the sad face. She knew that YaYa would not be able to tell her no.

"All right, damn. You know you ain't right for pulling out that fucking face either, bitch. I'll follow y'all over there. Bay, this nigga better not be ugly!" she said as she got down off her car and threw the roach onto the ground.

Ya Ya was feeling the effects of the weed as she followed closely behind Bay's car. When she pulled onto his street, she noticed a pearl white Cadillac STS sitting in front of Bay's crib. *At least the nigga riding right*, she thought to herself as she stepped out of her car. She wore long khaki gauchos and a peach-colored strapless top. Her heels tied around her ankles and showed off her perfectly French manicured toes and defined calf muscles.

She watched as a tall, brown-skinned dude stepped out of the vehicle. He wore light denim Evisu shorts. They were baggy, but not to the point where his ass was showing, and matched the white Bape polo shirt he was rocking. He was fly, and the way he wore his fitted NY Yankees hat low over his eyes gave him a mysterious look.

"He ain't ugly," Mona whispered to Disaya.

"Nah, he definitely ain't that," she agreed as he approached.

The girls watched as Bay slapped hands with the dude. They both walked over, and the introductions began.

"Yo, this my dude Indie," Bay announced as he unlocked his door and pulled Mona's hand, practically dragging her into the house.

Before she fully disappeared into the house, she yelled, "It was nice to meet you, Indie. I'm Mona, this is my girl"—Before she could even finish her sentence, she disappeared up the steps, headed to Bay's bedroom.

Disaya shook her head. She knew that they were going to leave her hanging like that, which was why she didn't want to come.

"And you are?" Indie asked as he looked down at Disaya.

"I'm YaYa," she replied as she stepped inside the house. She walked straight into the kitchen and went for Bay's liquor cabinet.

Indie sat down at the kitchen table and watched the beautiful girl in front of him.

"You want something to drink?" she asked as she stood on her tiptoes, trying to reach the top shelf.

Indie came behind her. He reached up and grabbed the bottle with ease.

"Thanks," she stated. She looked up at him and thought, *Damn, this nigga is fine.* She grabbed two glasses and took the Grey Goose bottle into the living room.

Bay's place was decked out with a seventy-two-inch big screen and Italian leather furniture. Indie followed behind her and took a seat next to her on the couch. They were both silent as they sat side by side, not knowing what to say to one another.

Disaya wasn't normally the shy type, but for some reason she was at a loss for words. "Okay, this is awkward," she said with a laugh.

"We need to do something about that," he replied with a smile that was so gorgeous, he should've been on toothpaste commercials.

"Okay, I'm gon' keep it real with you. Bay and Mona are always hooking me up with these ugly, crazy mu'fuckas, so I'm a little reluctant to fuck with you," she admitted. "It's obvious that you ain't ugly, but I got a couple questions for you."

Indie smiled at her blunt nature and sat back. "Shoot," he said.

"You got kids?" she inquired.

"Nah, no kids." Indie leaned back on the couch while he extended one leg out to make himself more comfortable.

"Is that your mama's car you driving?"

When Indie started to laugh, Disaya hit him softly with one of the couch pillows. "I'm serious. Answer the question."

"Let me just clear this up for you right now, ma. I don't know what type of niggas you used to fucking with, but I'm not one of 'em. I'm a good dude. I don't drive nothing I don't own. I don't have any kids or crazy baby mother running around here. If I did have a shorty, you would know it, because I'm a man, and when I do have kids, I plan on having them with my wife. I handle my business, I don't lie, and I'm not for the bullshit. I'm straight up with everybody that I encounter."

Disaya nodded her head in approval. "Okay, I hear you. Let me ask you this, though. If your shit is tight all like that, why you ain't got a girl?"

Indie smiled and replied, "Because I'm looking for a woman. Now can I get to know the beautiful woman that is sitting in front of me?" he asked her as he took a sip from the Grey Goose.

"I think I can make that happen," she replied. "But can I ask you one more question? I promise this will be the last one."

"What up?" he asked with a sexy smirk.

"Are you gay? Because you seem to be too perfect," she said with a laugh. It was his turn to throw a pillow at her and she burst out in laughter.

"Nah, I'm a hundred percent. That's something you will learn in time, if you're lucky," he said.

"If I'm lucky?" YaYa asked flirtatiously.

"Yeah, ma, *if* you're lucky," he repeated seriously as he stared into her eyes. Most men were intimidated by Disaya's take-charge personality, but the way that Indie was penetrating her soul with his stare made Disaya turn away first. She blushed and quickly turned her head.

Indie and Disaya sat in the living room talking all night. They practically cleared out Bay's liquor cabinet. Disaya was impressed with Indie. He seemed to have his shit together. He was a real dude and she enjoyed being in his company. They even pulled out Bay's Monopoly game and got it popping. For the first time Mona and Bay had hooked her up with somebody she was actually interested in. They chilled until four in the morning until they both became tired.

"This bitch is still upstairs with this nigga. I'm about to go home before I pass out," Disaya said with a slur in her voice. She stood up and grabbed her keys. She was tipsy and her balance was off, causing her to stumble.

"Yo, ma, you can't drive anywhere tonight," Indie said. "Come here." He motioned for YaYa and she grabbed his hand so that he could pull her onto his lap.

"I got to get to the crib," she said as she laid her head on his shoulder.

"We'll crash here for tonight. In the morning we'll grab some breakfast and then I'll make sure you make it home safely. That's okay with you?" he asked her as he rubbed the top of her head.

"Yeah," she replied as she closed her eyes.

Indie chuckled at her as she curled her legs up on the couch. She reminded him of a child, as she fell into a light sleep. She was gorgeous and he could tell that she was a little rough around the edges, but he liked her feistiness. He was going to make sure that he saw her again.

Bay and Mona came downstairs the next morning and saw their friends laid up together on the couch.

"Looks like she liked him," she said as she noticed all the empty liquor bottles on the floor.

"This mu'fucka get all the hoes." Bay chuckled, amazed that Indie had been able to charm YaYa.

"YaYa, girl, get up," Mona called out.

"Umm, I'm up. And who you calling a ho, Bay?" she asked drowsily as she began to stir out of her comfortable sleep.

"You know I ain't mean it like that," Bay stated sincerely as he slapped Disaya hard on her thigh, waking her up fully.

The commotion awakened Indie as well. He gently stroked the top of her head and asked, "You feel better?"

"I feel worse," YaYa moaned. Her stomach was queasy and her head felt like it would explode from the pounding headache.

"You ready to go?" Mona asked.

"I don't think I can get up right now, Mo . . . my shit is really banging," YaYa replied.

"Yo, YaYa, you can crash here for a couple hours until you get yourself together. From the looks of it you drank yourself into the grave last night. I got to make a couple moves, but you can let yourself out once you straight," Bay offered.

"I'm a little fucked-up myself. I'll crash with you if that ain't a problem," Indie added.

"Nah, that ain't a problem," Disaya replied with a smile. She tossed her keys to Mona and pointed a finger at her, then said, "Mo, don't fuck my shit up."

"Whatever, YaYa," Mo replied with a dismissive flip of the hand. "Ain't nobody gon' fuck up your car, girl. Call me when you make it home," she said as she kissed Bay on the cheek.

"Don't do anything I wouldn't do!" she yelled as she walked out the door.

Bay left shortly after her, leaving Indie and YaYa alone.

"How you feel?" Indie asked her. She was still lying on his chest and it felt good to be in the arms of a man.

It had been so long since she was seriously attracted to someone. Most niggas she simply tolerated because their pockets were on swoll. Niggas these days were idiots. Everybody wanted to be a drug dealer, and half the time they didn't have what it took to be a real hustler. She had encountered all types. There were the ones who liked to hit on her because they were insecure with their own manhoods. She disposed of them quickly and most times made the niggas pay for any wrong treatment they had given her. Then she had encountered the niggas that worshipped the ground she walked on.

"You're gorgeous, sweetheart."

"I'll give you the world."

"I just want to be around you, ma, you're beautiful."

Yada-Yada-Yada . . . it was always the same shit with those types of men, and although the compliments were flattering to the ear, she would never take a dude home if he seemed too eager. Needy niggas were headaches. Their clingy and suffocating ways worked her last damn nerves to no end. She had made that mistake once and dumped that chump before he even knew what hit him.

Disaya needed a challenge. She needed a man that could put her in check without making her feel like less than a woman for playing the game by his rules. She needed a man, not a boy, who she felt safe with and who provided security. She wanted someone who was stimulating to both her body and mind. Most dudes she met, she could out-hustle and that was the problem.

She couldn't read Indie yet, but out of all the men she had ever messed with he seemed to be the closest to her mark. He was a hustler . . . a hood nigga. You could tell it from his swagger, and it was confirmed when he didn't brag about his hood status. Real niggas don't need to talk about what they do. They move at their own pace and get money low-key.

Disaya was almost positive that she had met her match in Indie. He was fine as hell, and his swag was so on point that he made her panties moist just from his stare alone. That was hard to find nowadays. She was open and hoped that they could get to know each other better.

Indie didn't have to hit Disaya with lines or game because his personality was magnetic and she was drawn to him without all the extras. Extra niggas came with extra problems, but Indie was different. There was something about him and Disaya wanted to know more.

"My stomach is killing me," she admitted. "What about you?"

"I'm good. I don't get too fucked-up. I can handle my liquor," he said. "I just wanted to make sure you were straight."

She sat up and looked at him in the eyes. "You seem like you're a good dude," she said.

"Why do you sound surprised?"

She shrugged her shoulders then replied, "I don't know. Niggas ain't built right these days. You just seem different."

"I'll take that as a compliment," he said. "You hungry?" he asked.

She nodded and then slowly rose to her feet. She excused herself and went to the bathroom.

Damn, I look tore up, she thought to herself as she stared in the mirror at her disheveled appearance. She opened Bay's medicine cabinet and squeezed some toothpaste on her finger. She tried her best to get her teeth clean without a toothbrush. She didn't want to be all in Indie's face with stank breath. She straightened her hair with her fingers. It wasn't that bad. It had a wild look to it, but she figured it would have to do. *Let me go back downstairs before he think I'm up here shitting or something,* she thought as she hurried back to the living room.

"You ready?" he asked.

"Yeah, we can go," she stated. She followed him to his car and to her surprise he opened the door for her. *Yeah, this dude is definitely different than most. His game is nice. I might have to give him the goodies.*

They drove to IHOP and ate breakfast together. Disaya ordered an omelet and pancakes to soak up some of the liquor from the night before.

Disaya was tearing into her food when she noticed Indie laughing at her. "What is so funny?" she asked with a mouthful of food.

"You killing that omelet," Indie teased her.

"Oh what, you thought I was one of them girls that don't eat?" she replied with a laugh.

She looked at Indie and wondered what it would be like to be his woman. She knew that he would treat her right. She could just vibe with him. They clicked in a major way, but she knew that at that moment in her life there was only room for one love and that was the love for money. She had just gotten down with Elite. She was trying to get her paper up and that was her first priority.

After breakfast he dropped her off at her apartment. She was reluctant to get out of the car because she was having such a good time with him. "Thanks for breakfast, Indie. I had a good time with you," she admitted.

"You ain't got to thank me, ma. Get at me if you want to do it again," he said.

"I just might do that," she replied in a seductive tone. He got out of the car and opened her car door. "Why do you do stuff like that?" she asked in a sincere tone.

She had never met a man like Indie. His swagger was hood. He dressed like a hood nigga, walked like a hood nigga, and it was obvious that he was getting money like a hood nigga, but he was not the average dude. The way that he treated her had her open.

He was a gentleman and that's something that she had never encountered.

"Because you deserve it," he said as he touched her chin. She wanted to reach up and kiss him, but she knew her breath was foul. Instead she put her arms around him and stood on her tiptoes to hug him.

"Thank you, Indie. I had fun." She pulled a pen out of her purse and wrote her number on the inside of his hand. "Call me," she invited as he made eye contact with him. She walked away, letting the natural sway of her hips hypnotize him. She turned around just before she disappeared through the doors. He was watching her just as she knew he would be. She smiled and waved before the door closed behind her.

Disaya was on cloud nine as she walked into her apartment. She couldn't stop thinking about Indie. He was perfect and she was feeling him to the fullest. She reluctantly took a long, hot shower. She didn't want to rinse the smell of his Issey Miyake off of her, but she knew that she had to.

She crawled into bed and drifted into a mind-numbing sleep. Just as she began to dream she felt the vibration of her Sidekick. She thought that maybe it was Indie, so she jumped up to answer her phone. She saw that she had a message from Ronnie B, and her mind quickly refocused on money. *Hell yeah, it's about damn time*, she thought. She had expected to get right to work, but it had been almost a week since she had linked up with Elite. She flipped up the Sidekick and read the message.

I got a job for you.
Come to the Marriott on Lexington and 51st tonight at 11 P.M.
It's time to get this money.

Chapter 9

Disaya and Mona stepped into the building. Each girl had their own thoughts racing through their minds. They didn't know what to expect and they were silent as they made their way to the top floor of the hotel. Nervousness ate at their bellies. Anticipation halted their breathing. They did not know what to expect and their thoughts consumed them. Were they getting themselves into something they weren't ready for? Was Elite dangerous? All of these questions were swarming through their minds, but they buried their insecurities under their cashmere dreams and kept it moving.

"I'm nervous, YaYa," Mona admitted as they watched the numbers to the elevator slowly ascend.

"Me too. We'll be all right, though. Let's just go in here and make the money. Don't let the money make you. You don't have to do anything that you don't want to. If you start getting uncomfortable we'll dip, okay?" Disaya said, reassuring Mona just as much as herself.

"Okay," Mona replied nervously as she took a deep breath to calm her nerves.

Disaya stepped off the elevator first and was amazed when she saw that the entire top floor of the hotel was one huge, presidential suite. She was even more shocked to see the Miami Heat basketball team lounging around the room. The first familiar face that she noticed was Leah's. She was chilling with the star center for the team. She walked over to them and smiled. "Y'all ready?"

Mona and Disaya didn't respond verbally, but they nodded their heads to signal yes.

Leah chuckled seductively as she looked them both up and down. She recognized the nervous energy that they had. "Calm down. This is easy. These are the easiest clients to please. Professional ballplayers can't get too freaky because they are in the spotlight. They are only in town for the night. They just came back from the Garden, so they are really just trying to kick back. All you really have to do is be good company. You know, show them a good time," Leah instructed. "Mona, you start over there with some of the other girls. YaYa, you can come with me."

Disaya followed Leah over to the sectional sofa where the starting five players were. Disaya fit in nicely with the group as she joined in on the casual conversation that they were having. The longer she was there the easier it got. She began to feel like she was having a good time with close friends instead of a group of people she barely knew. Disaya noticed that one of the players was distant. He didn't talk much and when he got up and headed out to the balcony she decided to follow him. She got up and slid open the glass door that led to the balcony. She walked over to him with two champagne flutes in her hand.

"You look like you need this," she said as she handed him one of the glasses. The midnight air was cool against her skin, and the atmosphere on the balcony was much quieter than inside the suite.

He turned around and looked down at her, "Thanks," he replied as he guzzled the expensive champagne.

"I'm a big fan, Mr. MVP," she said with a smile. He looked her up and down as he licked his lips.

"I wouldn't expect someone like you to follow sports," he replied in a husky, low tone that melted the seams on YaYa's panties.

"I don't follow sports, just you," she responded as she slid her body between him and the railing to the balcony.

"I heard about y'all New Yitty chicks," he said with a smile.

"Oh yeah? Well, what exactly did you hear? I can tell you if it's true or not," she said as she sipped at her champagne, obviously flirting.

"You don't have to tell me. I can see that it's true just by looking at you," he replied.

"Oh, you really got to tell me what you heard now . . . since you claim I fit the description," Disaya replied with a sexy laugh.

"It's nothing bad. I just hear that y'all some go-getters up here. Y'all see what y'all want and y'all go after it. I hear it ain't nothing like a New York woman. Y'all know how to put it down," he explained.

"That's true, at least in my case," she admitted arrogantly.

"See, you trying to get me in trouble," he whispered in her ear as he showed her his wedding band.

"I would never do that. I'm not trying to come between that. I just want to show you a good time. Let you know that you've got something warm to get into when you come to such a cold city," YaYa replied. Seduction oozed off of her every word and she could feel the bulge grow in his Armani slacks. "You know you want to," she whispered in her ear, letting her tongue wet his earlobe as she pulled away. "If you didn't, you wouldn't be here." He put his arms around her waist and palmed her ass tightly. He pulled her into his crotch and a small moan escaped his lips. He lifted her onto the railing of the balcony and her heart began to pound frantically as she felt her womanhood cream in anticipation.

"What are you doing?" she asked nervously as she looked at the twenty stories below her.

"Shh, trust me," he said. He began to kiss on her neck and massage her breasts, making her pussy instantly drip with wetness.

She couldn't believe she was getting ready to have sex with one of the most talented players in the NBA. She spread her legs and he put his hands underneath her Prada dress. She unzipped his pants and pulled his manhood out of its confinement. *Damn,* she thought to herself as she looked down at his length. She pulled a condom out of her bra and gently slid it onto him. "See, I'm not trying to trap you. I just want to please you, Daddy," she moaned as he maneuvered himself into her.

He easily filled the space between her legs with his nine inches and he pushed her head back as he moved in and out of her, using deep, passionate thrusts.

Disaya's upper body hung over the balcony and seeing how high up she was filled her heart with fear. The fear added to the erotic fact that she was having sex out in the open on a balcony where people could see her. The situation caused her body to tremble uncontrollably. She rotated her hips and threw the pussy back at him with a vengeance as he fucked her proper. The streetlights below had her in a daze as their lustful encounter took place under the stars.

Oh my God! she thought to herself. She hadn't known that dick could be so good. She could feel every muscle in his body working as his athletic frame moved in and out of her.

He pulled her up and stayed inside of her as he put her against the balcony window. Her back hit the glass with a thud, causing everyone on the inside of the presidential suite to focus their attention on the couple outside.

Disaya didn't give a damn who was watching her, though. The nigga was fucking her so right, she was losing her mind. Every time he entered her, he paused deep inside her and rotated his hips, creating friction against her clitoris. She rolled her hips furiously as she wrapped her arms around his neck to keep her balance.

Leah looked on in lust at the scene that was taking place on the balcony. She had definitely underestimated Disaya. She had thought that YaYa would be afraid to get down for hers, but it was obvious that she had what it took to be down with Elite. Disaya's ass cheeks were pressed against the balcony door and everyone in the room was in awe of her voluptuous body. *Damn,* Leah thought to herself as she discreetly slipped her hands between her crossed legs. Leah watched in lust as she subtly slipped her middle finger into her pussy while she rubbed her clit with her thumb. "Ohh," she moaned quietly as she looked on at the sexual escapade that was taking place on the balcony. She couldn't take her eyes off of them, and everyone in the room was watching intensely. The way Disaya moved her hips was enticing, and no one could take their eyes off the couple outside.

Mona stood in the middle of the room watching her friend get down on the balcony. She had wanted to get busy with the player she was chilling with all night, but she didn't want Disaya or anyone else to think that she was a ho. By witnessing Disaya in the act, she figured it was okay to get it popping.

"Damn, do you get down like your girl?" one of the players asked Mona while gripping himself through his pants.

Without saying a word she grabbed his hand and led him into the bedroom.

"Right there," Disaya moaned as she felt his dick begin to throb inside of her. He pumped in and out of her so hard that she came harder than she ever had in her life.

He finally put her down and kissed her on the lips. "Aww shit, we got an audience," he said as he turned her around.

Disaya's mouth fell open as she realized that she had just put on a show. She hid her face in his chest as they both stepped back inside the room. Hoots and hollers erupted throughout as they entered. "Oh my goodness," she mumbled.

"Don't be shy. You're a celebrity now," he praised.

They enjoyed the rest of the night with each other, and as promised Disaya made him feel like he had someone in New York who he could call on the next time he visited. She had to admit he was mad cool and the sex was on point, so she honestly wouldn't mind if he did get at her the next time he came up.

At the end of the night he walked her to her car. "How much do I owe you?" he asked her as he pulled out a checkbook from his pants pocket.

"How much was it worth?" she replied.

He shook his head in amazement. He had never encountered a chick like her and knew that she was worth the twenty-thousand-dollar check he was about to write her. He handed it to her and then took off his number three chain and put it around her neck. Her mouth almost dropped to the floor when she felt the weight of the many karats that sat around her neck.

"Make sure you get at me if you ever come to Miami," he said. He opened her car door and she got in.

"I will, Mr. MVP." She closed the door and pulled up to the entrance of the hotel where Mona, Leah, and some of the other girls were standing around saying their good-byes.

Mona and Leah approached her car. Mona hopped into the backseat, and Leah sat in the passenger side. "I didn't drive here tonight. You mind if I ride with you?" Leah asked.

Without responding, Disaya sped out of the parking lot, leaving tire tracks on the pavement.

Leah turned toward YaYa and said, "What the fuck? Bitch, you got game, I gots to give it to you. You put it down in there for real," she said as she nodded her head in approval. "I've got to admit, I'm impressed."

"Yeah, and you got that nigga to give you his chain," Mona added as she noticed the bling around her girlfriend's neck.

Leah looked over at the necklace and said, "Just a word of advice, don't wear that shit when we go into the spot to meet Ronnie. He'll want a cut of that too. I always keep it a hundred percent when it comes to the cash, but as far as I'm concerned the extra shit is my tip, feel me?"

Disaya nodded as she pulled into the warehouse's parking lot. The two-story loft-style warehouse served as the office space and meeting spot for Elite. Disaya removed the chain from her neck and put it in her glove box before stepping out of the car. They all walked into the building. Some of the other girls had already arrived. Disaya did the math in her head and concluded that she would get six stacks of the twenty-thousand-dollar check that she had in her hand. She frowned when she realized how small her cut actually was, but it didn't matter because the chain in her car was worth at least thirty large.

She walked up the steps to the top of the loft and the three girls entered Ronnie's office. He had the money that he had made that night neatly sorted out in thousand-dollar stacks on his desk.

"What's good, baby? How'd it go?" he asked Leah as they sat down across from him.

"Everything was everything. Same shit, different day. We got a new superstar on our hands, though," she said enthusiastically.

He looked over at Disaya and smiled. "So how much did you pull in?"

Disaya put the check in front of her face and replied, "Twenty gees."

Ronnie B nodded his head as excitement filled his eyes. "That's what the fuck I'm talking about!" He took the check and gave her six of the thousand-dollar stacks that was sitting on his desk. He collected his cut from Mona and Leah, then they all got up to leave.

"I'm coming to your crib," Mona told YaYa as they walked out of the building.

"What y'all bitches getting ready to get into?" Leah asked.

"Nothing. Mona's ass practically lives at my house. We don't really be doing shit, though, just chilling. Why? You coming through?"

Leah didn't usually chill with females. Especially chicks that were from Elite, but she had to admit that YaYa and Mona were on her level. She didn't have a problem chilling with them because their hustler's mentality was similar to her own. "Yeah, I'll roll," she said.

The girls headed back to Disaya's and they instantly vibed. It was weird because Disaya and Mona had never let another chick into their circle, but Leah seemed to fit right in.

"Girl, that nigga had you assed out on the balcony," Mona teased.

"Hell yeah, everybody got a peek at that fat ass," Leah added.

Disaya was so embarrassed she didn't know what to say. "I couldn't help it. That boy had me in the zone. The dick was so right. I didn't even realize everybody was watching. Do you think I went too far?" she asked Leah.

"Hell no! I wish I had a damn camcorder. We could've taped that shits and then sold them bitches for like ten dollars a piece."

"Girl, please, I'm not trying to be out here on nobody's tape." She waved her hand, dismissing the thought.

They all stayed up clowning and joking until they passed out on the living room floor.

The ringing of Leah's Sidekick woke them up the next morning.

Leah flipped up her screen and read the message that Ronnie B had just sent her.

Leah I got a job for you and YaYa. This nigga out of D.C. coming up and he want a ménage à trois with two of the best. I don't know if Disaya is down with that girl-on-girl action, but he gon' want to see a lot of it. He's paying big money. Make sure that she's ready. Be at the Benjamin in Manhattan tonight at 9.

"Where's Mo?" Disaya asked as she looked around the apartment. There was a note on the couch.

Leah reached over and grabbed it. "Bay called me after y'all went to sleep so I bounced with him. I will catch up with y'all later," she read aloud.

Disaya flipped her hand and said, "I should've known."

"Who's Bay?" Leah asked.

"This dude we grew up with. Him and Mo been fucking around for a minute, and every chance they get, they hook up." Disaya could still smell the sex on her body and got up and began removing clothes. "I'm about to hop in the shower," she announced.

"You mind if I take one after you?" Leah asked as she realized that she hadn't taken a shower after last night's escapades.

"Nah, girl, make yourself at home, but unless you want to take a shower in ice water, you better just jump in there as soon as I get out. I'll make sure I make it quick," she said.

Disaya removed the rest of her clothing. She had never been shy about someone else seeing her body, so she left the pieces on a pile in the middle of the floor, even though she had just met Leah.

Leah watched Disaya as she walked into the bathroom. "Girl, your body is banging. I wish I wasn't so skinny," Leah complimented, shouting loudly so that Disaya could hear her from the bathroom.

"Leah, please, your ass look like a model. You ain't got nothing to worry about. I wish I was your size. Everything I eat goes straight to my ass and hips." Disaya opened the shower curtain and adjusted the water temperature before stepping into the stream of water.

"So how long have you been down with Elite?" YaYa asked, yelling over the sound of the loud shower pipes as she lathered her loofah and spread the suds all over her body.

"A couple years now," Leah responded as she walked into the bathroom and stood in front of the mirror.

Leah looked through YaYa's clear shower curtain, and the silhouette of her body made Leah moist between the legs. Disaya's curves were perfect and Leah sat down on the toilet and enjoyed the enticing view. She removed the dress that she had worn the night before and couldn't stop her hands from making their way to her pussy. She played with her clit with one hand, rolled her nipples between her fingers with the other, while she watched Disaya wash her naked body. She loved playing with herself. No one could make her cum the way she could make herself cum.

The feeling mounting inside of her finally became too much to bear and she had to see what Disaya's skin felt like. She stood up and pulled back the shower curtain slowly as she stepped inside.

"Whoo!" Disaya yelled out in surprise. "Girl, you scared the shit out of me. What you doing?"

"You said the water gets cold quick," Leah stated nonchalantly.

"Here, I'll step out. Let me rinse off," Disaya said.

"Wait a minute, girl; here, let me wash your back," Leah offered.

Disaya handed her the loofah and Leah rubbed her back gently. Disaya's breath became shallow as she felt Leah's soft hands caress her back.

"YaYa, you are tense, girl," she commented. She started at the top and rubbed the soap lower and lower until she reached her ass. Leah dropped the loofah and began to rub her hands all over Disaya's back. "I give killer back rubs. This should loosen you up," she said.

The feeling of Leah's hands on her body made Disaya's nipples hard. A sensation of pleasure went off in her ass cheeks and traveled up her spine. She wasn't sure what was going on between the two of them. *Is this bitch gay?* she thought to herself. Disaya didn't say anything; she simply allowed Leah to massage her back.

Leah's hands traveled south and she ended up massaging her caramel mounds. Leah's fingers melted into skin as if her bottom was made of soft marshmallows.

"What are you doing?" Disaya whispered as she felt her pussy get wet.

"Relax, girl, I'm just loosening you up," Leah replied sweetly. Her hands moved around the front of YaYa's body and caressed her breasts. Her nipples were on point and Leah pinched them gently, causing tingles to shoot up and down YaYa's spine.

"You want me to stop?" Leah asked.

"No," YaYa admitted. She didn't know what the hell had taken over her. She was far from gay, but Leah did something to her. Her touch felt different than any man's ever had.

Leah turned her around and they stood breast to breast and shared a kiss as the water from the shower sprayed down on them. Leah's mouth found Disaya's nipples and she suckled on them slowly, rolling her tongue over Disaya's breasts. Leah put her hand in between YaYa's legs and felt that her clitoris was hard and began to grind her own clitoris against YaYa's.

"What are you doing to me?" YaYa moaned in a pleasurable tone.

Leah didn't respond. She simply got on her knees and tantalized her love button with her tongue until YaYa had an explosive orgasm.

YaYa rinsed her body and hopped out of the shower. She anxiously wrapped a towel around her body. She was a little embarrassed by what had just taken place.

Leah, on the other hand, could not have been happier. She was bisexual and had been attracted to YaYa since the first day she stepped foot in her presence. Ronnie B just gave her an excuse to seduce her.

"Are you gay?" YaYa asked her, finally breaking the silence between them.

"No, I'm not gay. I love, dick, YaYa, but every once in a while I do like to get my pussy licked right. The only people that I find can do it like I like it is a woman. Have you ever felt anything like what I did for you in there?" she asked.

"No," YaYa admitted.

"Did you like it?" Leah asked.

"Yeah, I did," YaYa admitted again in an unsure tone.

"Well, then, that's that. What we just did don't make you gay. You love dick, but every once in a while I'll get you right and eat your pussy for you. Truthfully, I had to break you in. There is a lot of girl-on-girl stuff that goes down in Elite. In fact, tonight we are going to the Benjamin for a threesome with this D.C. cat. He gon' want to see me and you doing our thing anyway, so just consider what we just did practice. Ronnie B couldn't have you going in there looking like an amateur, so he asked me to make sure that you're ready. This is the business, baby. I just happen to be good at it." With those words Leah walked her naked body over to Disaya and unwrapped the towel from around her body. "Now let me get you ready for tonight," Leah said as she lifted one of Disaya's breasts and devoured it in her mouth. She pushed Disaya down on the bed and climbed on top of her. She smiled when she felt YaYa's clit get hard once again. She rubbed their clits together and kissed Disaya on the lips.

"Wait," Disaya moaned, unsure of what she was doing.

"It's all in the game, YaYa," Leah whispered in her ear as they continued to bump coochies.

"It's just business?" Disaya asked as she grinded back.

"That's it. Just business, YaYa. Now just lay here and let me make you cum like you never have before."

YaYa and Leah stepped in the lobby of the luxurious Benjamin Hotel wearing nothing but trench coats. Their stilettos clicked across the floor as they made their way to the elevator. They took it to room 222 and knocked. A fat, sloppy-looking dude opened the door and invited them in. He was already pissy drunk and Disaya could smell the 151 reeking from his pores.

They walked in, and he immediately pounced on them. He tried to kiss Leah in the mouth, but she felt as if she would gag from the nasty smell of him. He was sweating profusely and she wanted to get him as far away from her as she could. She pushed him off of her and told him to lie on the bed and enjoy the show.

Disaya had a disgusted look on her face as she looked down at the drunken mess that lay on the bed. He had stripped off his clothing and had nothing on but a pair of boxers. He had his penis pulled out of the slit in the front and was stroking himself in anticipation. *This big fat, nasty-looking . . .* Disaya thought to herself as she looked at the dude in disgust. "What type of shit is this?" YaYa mouthed to Leah.

Leah shrugged in a state of confusion. She had never encountered a client like this before. She knew that he had to be working with big chips if Ronnie B was messing with him, though.

"Let us freshen up real quick," Leah told the dude. She hurriedly pulled YaYa into the bathroom.

"Call Ronnie right now," Disaya whispered.

Leah pulled out her Sidekick and dialed his number, but received no answer. "He's not picking up," she said nervously. "Look, this dude must have some money, so let's just do the job and get up out of here," Leah suggested.

"Fine by me," Disaya replied.

They headed back into the room.

"Hurry up and show me something," the dude instructed.

Both girls dropped their coats, but before he could touch them they began kissing each other. It wasn't sensual like it had been earlier, but rushed and exaggerated. Both of them just wanted to give him a show so hopefully he would take care of himself and they could get paid then go home.

"Let me join in," he stated as he pulled Disaya down onto the bed.

He prepared to enter her but Disaya stopped him.

"Hold up, dude! You ain't going in me raw. You better put on a condom," she stated.

"What! I told Ron B I don't do condoms. I paid that nigga extra for it too," he said aggressively as he prepared to stick himself inside her.

"Hold up!" Leah said as she pulled the guy off of YaYa. "We don't go without protection, and what do you mean, you already paid Ron B?"

"He asked for twenty stacks up front, ma. He charged me extra to go in raw," the dude said.

"Look, you need to take your problem up with Ronnie B. We don't get down like that. Let's go, YaYa," Leah stated firmly.

They put on their trench coats.

"What the fuck you mean, let's go. I paid cash money for y'all stank bitches. I'm about to get something from somebody!" he yelled.

"Okay, Daddy, fuck it, we game," Leah said, trying to calm the guy down. "Lay down, baby," she told him.

He calmed down and lay on the bed with his dick in his hand.

"You want me to suck it for you. Can I put it in my mouth?" she asked in a seductive, whiny voice.

"Yeah, put it in your mouth, baby girl," he moaned as he closed his eyes.

Disaya threw up in her mouth a little bit when she saw Leah take him into her mouth. She sucked on it seductively while he pushed her head down on him forcefully. His eyes were closed and he was enjoying himself.

Out of nowhere Leah bit down on him with all her might.

"Awww!" he yelled out loud in excruciating pain.

"Oh shit!" Disaya yelled.

"Bitch, let's go!" Leah yelled as they both scrambled into their coats and rushed out of the room.

Before the door closed they heard ol' boy screaming into his cell phone and assumed he was talking to Ronnie.

Both girls were furious as they drove toward the Elite warehouse. "I know Ronnie ain't trying to pull dirty on me," Leah stated. "He knows that the money supposed to go through our hands first."

They slammed their car doors as they arrived and raced up the stairs to Ronnie B's office. "What the fuck is wrong with you?" Leah yelled as soon as she saw him.

Ronnie B didn't say anything, but he did haul off and slap the shit out of her. Blood flew from Leah's mouth from the force of the blow.

"Bitch, you walked out on one of my clients. You damn near

took his dick off! That nigga paid ten large to fuck with y'all bitches and you just gon' walk out. You making me look bad," he said as Leah held her face in shock.

"Fuck you, Ronnie. You already know that ain't no nigga running in me raw. I'm not about to be out here catching AIDS for your ass. Then the nigga paid you. What the fuck he paying you for, huh? You ain't the one opening your legs for the fat, sloppy mu'fucka. You said he paid ten?"

"Yeah, bitch! He paid ten!" Ronnie yelled back at her.

"You lying, dirty-ass nigga, he already told us he gave you double that."

"I'll pay y'all bitches what I want to," he informed her as he walked away from her and sat back down at the table.

"No, Ronnie, you gon' pay us what you owe us. The cut already seventy-thirty, which is some bullshit for what you do. As a matter of fact, fuck you. I don't need you. I know half of your clientele personally anyway. I don't need you pimping me, I can get my own gwop!" Leah stormed out of the room, leaving Disaya standing there, staring at Ronnie B.

"So what you gon' do, YaYa? We don't need her. That bitch pussy drying up anyway."

Nah, her pussy far from dry, Disaya thought to herself.

"You can take her place as the HBIC," Ronnie offered.

Disaya shook her head and walked away. She couldn't believe that she had thought being down with Elite was where the money was at. Leah was right. They could branch out on their own and make 100 percent of the profits. They didn't need Ronnie B.

Mona was standing at the bottom of the stairs with a couple other members of Elite when Disaya came racing down the steps.

"YaYa, you okay?" she asked in concern.

"Yeah, I'm good. Get your stuff, we out," Disaya told her as she looked behind her to see Ronnie B standing at the top of the loft.

"What you mean, we out?" Mo asked.

"We don't need this nigga. We can get this money on our own."

Ronnie B came down the stairs and stood next to Mona. He put his arm around her. "Come on, ma, don't listen to these hoes. You can run all of this. You can take Leah's place at the top. You the head bitch of Elite now. You gon' give all that up to go back to how you used to live?"

"Mo, don't listen to him. He's grimy," Disaya pleaded.

Ronnie B pulled out a wad of hundred-dollar bills and handed them to Mona. "Can you get this much money anywhere else?" he asked her.

Mona took the money and said, "I'm staying, YaYa."

"Mo!" Disaya yelled out to her friend.

Mona never looked back as she ascended the steps with Ronnie, and for the first time since knowing Disaya she chose someone else over her best friend.

Chapter 10

Six Months Later

Disaya decided to treat herself to a day of shopping. She had been stressing out over Mona for the past few months. Leah found out that Ronnie B was messed up behind them leaving, and to prevent any of his other girls from leaving, he became violent and controlling.

He was making all of his girls pop ecstasy on the daily so that they would be even freakier for his clients. Some people didn't think anything was wrong with that. A lot of people don't even view X as a real drug, but Disaya knew better. That shit was just as addictive as crack or crystal meth, because it was a combination of a whole bunch of bullshit. It was dangerous, it was addictive, and in a lot of cases it was deadly.

Disaya didn't fuck with drugs. That shit was for chickens and bird bitches who didn't value themselves enough to say no. She was livid that Ronnie B had her best friend turned out. He had gotten into her mental something serious, and now there was no reasoning with Mona. Ronnie B's word was gospel, and she took it as truth every time. He even decreased their cut to eighty-

88 *Ashley Antoinette*

twenty, so a lot of his girls, including Mona, began to turn tricks
on the side.

Leah had even told YaYa that she had seen Mona walking the
ho stroll just to make extra money.

Ronnie B was having a hard time competing with Disaya and
Leah. Money was indeed flowing like water. They discovered that
word of mouth was the best marketing scheme, and they also
took advantage of the Internet. They set up their own Web site
called www.pradapanties.com and they became a hot commodity
online. They were getting thousands of hits each day, and everybody, from rappers, hustlers, and ballplayers, was recruiting their
services. They took professional pictures in seductive poses and
posted them on their site. They also had live chats for twenty
minutes for $19.99. They were making bank for real and living
the life.

In a matter of months she had been upgraded and was now
making more money than she could have ever imagined. She had
fucked with all the hip-hop heads. They all knew who she was,
and whenever they were in town they requested her services personally. She knew how to have a good time and how to give a
good time. She never thought that she was disrespecting herself,
because she had been molested at such a young age. She disconnected the emotional part of sex from the physical part, so it was
simply about a dollar with her.

Disaya's Prada Plan was actually coming true. She now had
money coming in consistently, and she stayed laced in her favorite designers. It sometimes bothered her that she had to
spread her legs and drop her morals to achieve her dreams, but
the constant flow of money clouded her judgment and made
everything that she was doing seem worth it.

Disaya walked out of her house and got into her Magnum. She
drove over to Fifth Avenue and Fifty-seventh Street to her favorite jewelry store, Tiffany's. She was getting ready to lace herself in diamonds because she felt like she deserved it.

She walked into the store and stopped at the first display. It displayed dozens of diamond engagement rings. She traced her hand over the top of the display as she admired the beautiful jewelry.

"Shopping for that special ring?" a blond-haired salesman asked. He had a feminine tone to his voice, and Disaya immediately noticed the gay swagger he possessed.

"Oh, no . . . I was just looking," she said.

"Would you like to try one on?" he asked. Before Disaya could reply, the salesman had taken out the yellow canary, two-and-half karat diamond ring. "Is this the one that you had your eye on?" he asked.

Disaya nodded as she held out her finger. He slid it on for her, and she admired it as she saw the flawless quality of the stone. "Damn!" she exclaimed in a whisper. She could see herself rocking that ring one day.

"It's almost as beautiful as the woman that's wearing it," a voice behind her said.

She turned around and smiled when she saw the familiar face. She hadn't heard from him since they had chilled together at Bay's house, but he looked just as good as the last time she had seen him.

"It looks like I'm too late, huh?" Indie said as he nodded toward the ring that she was trying on.

"What? Oh, no! I was just trying it on," she said, embarrassed, as she took it off and handed it back to the salesman.

"How have you been?" he asked. He still had the same gangster swagger and was fresh in Sean John jeans and a black button-up with a matching fitted cap.

"I've been all right. Don't be acting like you interested now. You never called," she said sweetly, but seriously.

"Nah, ma, it's not even like that. I've had a lot to handle, you know? Business first, shorty."

They walked out of the store, and she noticed that he was gripping a different car this time. He was riding in a Silver Nissan Maxima.

"Well, it was good to see you again, but I got business to take care of," she stated smartly as she walked toward her car, with a sway in her hips that would make the average man dizzy.

"Whoa, whoa!" he said as he grabbed her arm gently, stopping her from walking away. "Okay, I deserve that. Let me make it up to you," he offered.

"I'm straight; I don't fuck with niggas that don't put me first. I'm high-maintenance, and it takes a lot of time to please me. I got to be a priority," she said as she folded her arms across her chest and moved her neck with every word.

"You know, you sexy when you mad. I noticed that when I first met you. When you're upset about something you chew on your bottom lip," he said.

Disaya rolled her eyes, but smiled slightly because he was telling the truth. It was a habit she'd had since childhood.

"I don't want to be the reason why you hot, ma . . . let me take you out."

Disaya smirked and peered at him intensely as if to say, *Nigga please*, but she couldn't help but to forgive him. *The nigga got an A game, I got to give him that*, she thought. "Okay," she agreed. "You can take me out, but you got some making up to do."

She parked her car in a parking garage around the corner and then hopped into the car with him. They continued their day of shopping along Fifth and Madison Avenues.

She purchased so many clothes and shoes that she had a hard time carrying everything. Indie kept up with her and she quickly found out that he loved to shop just as much as she did.

She was clocking his pockets too. He was working with major chips and a part of her wondered how he made it. The nigga even had the audacity to whip out a black card to purchase his items. *Those joints are invitation only, this nigga is definitely paid*, she thought to herself as she admired the sexy man in front of her.

"So what is it that you do?" she asked him as they walked down the block.

Indie didn't respond right away. She could tell that he was in deep thought. He stopped walking and looked down at her, "I peep your style, YaYa. I know you ain't new to game. You not one of these little naive chicks out here, so I'm gon' keep it real with you. I'm not proud of what I do, but it's all I know how to do. I'm getting money. You know, me and Bay, we doing our thing right now. I don't plan on being in this spot forever, but right now it is what it is."

"You don't have to explain that to me, Indie. I'm not exactly where I want to be in life either. I understand you doing what you got to do to stay on top. I respect that," she told him.

They continued walking until they got back to his car. He put all of her bags into the trunk and she couldn't stop staring at him.

"What you looking at?"

"You," she replied as she reached up to kiss him.

He put his arm around her waist and pulled her close as they continued to kiss.

"Indie, I like you, but you ain't ready for a girl like me," Disaya stated as she pulled away from him.

"You something else, you know that, right?" he asked. "Let me get to know you . . . come away with me for the weekend. We'll fly out to Vegas and do it big."

"What's in Vegas?" she said skeptically.

"The De La Hoya-Mayweather fight," he confirmed. "You don't have to worry about money or nothing. I got you. Just come with me."

Leah lay across Disaya's bed as she watched her girl pack her clothes. She was jealous that she was going to Vegas without her.

"Who is this dude you going with?" she asked.

"His name's Indie. I met him a while back," she replied.

"Well, how long are you going to be gone? You know the website is popping. We got dudes lined up to fuck with us," Leah reminded.

"We'll only be gone for a couple days, so I'll be back in time."

"All right, girl. Well you want me to tighten you up before you go?" Leah offered as she licked her lips seductively, thinking about how sweet YaYa tasted. One of the reasons why she loved being in business with Disaya was because she loved the way her pussy tasted. Disaya didn't know it, but Leah was becoming attached to her in a big way, and she didn't like the fact that Disaya was so geeked over her weekend getaway with Indie. *I'm gon' have to get rid of this nigga*, she thought to herself.

"He's a real dude, Leah. He doesn't bullshit or try to game me. He keeps it one hundred with me. That's why I like him," she said.

"You think he's feeling you the same way?" Leah asked, pretending to be happy for her. On the inside she was steamed. Even though YaYa only let her get the goodies when they were making money, Leah still didn't want to share it with some dude. *Especially if he ain't paying*, Leah thought.

"I don't know, but we'll see this weekend," she replied.

Disaya stepped off of the plane and fell in love with the city of Las Vegas almost instantly. There were palm trees and slot machines everywhere, and it felt good to be in a completely different atmosphere.

"You wait for the bags. I'll go grab a rental," Indie said. He kissed Disaya softly on the lips before leaving her side.

She couldn't believe she was here with him and couldn't wait to get out of the airport. She waited for twenty minutes and their bags finally arrived. She picked them up and then stepped outside where Indie was waiting curbside.

He had rented a Hummer for their stay and she jumped into the passenger seat. They drove up the strip and arrived at the Encore Casino and Resort.

"Are you serious? This is where we're staying?" she asked in disbelief as she looked up at the gorgeous hotel. The fountain was lit up and sprayed straight into the air as she admired it in awe.

Indie laughed at her and replied, "This is it, shorty. What, this ain't good enough?"

"Hell yeah, this good enough. I've never stayed in anything better than the Holiday Inn, so I'm in heaven right now," she admitted.

They made their way up to the deluxe suite, and Disaya collapsed onto the bed. "Oh my goodness, I love Vegas. I love this room. I love this life. . . ." She sat up and looked at him. "I could live like this for real," she said.

Indie made his way over to her and sat next to her. He opened one of his suitcases, which contained nothing but money.

"Indie! You brought all that money for four days?" Disaya asked in disbelief.

"Yeah, it's only a hundred stacks. You got to do it big while you're in Vegas. Ain't no half-stepping. Besides, half of it is yours."

"Don't lie!" she yelled.

"I don't lie. I want you to have a good time." He pulled stacks of money out of the suitcase and sat it in front of her. "This is yours."

She reached over to him and kissed him passionately on the lips. He kissed her back, but when she tried to ease in between his legs he stopped her.

"You don't have to do that. I'm not trying to buy you, YaYa. I brought you here so that I could get to know you better. I'm feeling you, and I'm at a point in my life where I'm looking for one chick to be with," he explained.

"You think that chick is me?" YaYa asked as she blushed.

He cleared the hair from her face and said, "I don't know. That's what I'm trying to find out." He got up and opened a door that led to another room. "This is your room; I'll be right next door if you need me."

"You're not sleeping in here with me?" she asked with a pout.

"Nah, ma, you ain't just a jump-off to me. I respect you so I'm gon' treat you like a woman. Let me ask you something. Could you see yourself being with me?" he asked as he walked back over to where she was sitting.

"I don't know. I want to see myself being with you. I want to be with you. It just seems like your expectations are so high," she responded. She could feel the tears welling in her eyes because she knew that if Indie knew what she did to get by, he would never mess with her.

"Let me give you some game, Disaya. You are beautiful, but you don't respect yourself. You flaunt your sexuality, and believe me, ma, I see you, but I also want to get inside your head. I don't want to fuck you. I fuck hoes. I want to get to know you, and I want to learn to love you. Yeah, I want to know your body, because you were definitely blessed in that department. But if you gon' be wifey one day, I got to respect you first. You a little rough around the edges, and I'm willing to groom you, yo, but you got to let me know that this is what you want to do." He wiped the tears from her face and kissed her on the lips. "These tears let me know that you want to change," he said.

"You don't know how badly," she mumbled to herself.

It was the first time that she had actually begun to regret how she was living her life. Indie pulled out strange emotions from within her. Being around him, a man who respected her so much, made her want to respect herself.

Indie stood up and headed for the door. "Get gorgeous, shorty. There is a dress for you in the closet. I'm about to hit the casino. The fight starts at nine. I'll meet you downstairs, all right?"

Disaya nodded her head and watched him as he walked out of the room. He had given her a lot to think about. His words almost made her fill with shame. It was almost like Indie could see right through her. *If I tell him about what I've been through, will he be able to look past it?* she thought to herself as she got up to get dressed.

She put on a black Valentino baby doll dress. It flowed when she walked and gave a subtle view of her Coke-bottle figure. She put on matching heels and added her Tiffany accessories to accent the beautiful dress. She had never dressed up like that before and she was in awe of herself as she stood in front of the mirror. She actually felt like a lady. She pulled her hair up in a loose ponytail that was held up by a diamond-studded clip. She applied a light bronzer to her face and a neutral-colored eye shadow to her eyes. Her appearance was striking, and a tear slipped down her face as she turned around in the mirror.

She stepped out of the room and made her way down toward the casino. She was eager for Indie to see her like this. She hoped that she could change his perception of her. She stepped into the casino, and as she walked toward the craps table, all the men standing around it focused their attention on her. She sparkled underneath the dim lights.

She smiled at the way he shook the dice close to his ear as he prepared to toss the ivory. She stood at the opposite end of the table from him, and when he finally looked up, his jaw dropped in surprise.

He paused for a second as he admired her transformation. A sly smile spread across his lips. He finally threw the dice, and the dealers yelled, "Yo! Eleven winner!"

She walked over to him and he pulled her in front of him. He stood behind her and wrapped his arms around her waist. "This is how I want my wifey to be," he whispered in her ear as he kissed her neck.

The dealers brought the dice back toward Indie. "Shoot something, lil' mama," he challenged her, whispering the words in her ear.

She picked up the dice and tossed them onto the table.

Leah lay in her bed and played in her pussy while she held the phone to her ear. She was talking to Nanzi, a go-getter in Harlem who was getting money. Leah had contacted him a couple days ago to see if he was interested in what she and Disaya had to offer him. He was game and was willing to pay big money for a night of fun with the two girls. He had heard that they were skilled in the art of seduction and was trying to see how they got down. Leah couldn't go through with the meeting without Disaya. She needed her to be there. Her plans for him wouldn't work if Disaya wasn't there. She was trying to keep the nigga at bay until YaYa got back into town, so she gave him her number so that they could talk.

"You got my pussy wet with all that you talking," Leah said seductively over the phone. She had been having phone sex with Nanzi for a couple days, trying to keep him interested in her proposition. She wanted him to know that she was a freak, and had promised that she would turn him out as soon as Disaya could join in.

"Why don't you let me come handle that for you?"

"Nah, I got to wait for my girl. Don't worry, though; she comes home in a couple days. It's gon' be worth the wait. Her head game is on point, believe me, I know," she replied.

"Y'all get down like that? With each other?" he asked, intrigued.

"Yeah, daddy, we get down however you want us to get down," she stated.

She couldn't wait until Disaya came back from Vegas. She knew that Nanzi was the answer to all of her problems. She was about to get paid.

Disaya and Indie were having a great time at the casino. Indie was infatuated with her and made her feel like she was worth something.

"Can I tell you something?" Disaya asked.

"What up, baby?"

"I think I want to change for you," she admitted.

"Show me, ma, that's all I ask. A lot of people talk, and I hear what you're saying, but actions speak louder than words. Now can I tell you something?"

She didn't respond, so he took it as his cue to continue speaking. "I'm feeling you, and if you let me, I want to take care of you."

Disaya smiled graciously as her heartbeat sped up. She was speechless. She really didn't know what to say.

Indie changed the subject as he looked at his phone and noticed that it was almost time for the fight to begin.

"You ready to see a mu'fucka get knocked out?" Indie asked as he led her through the casino and out onto the busy streets.

The Las Vegas strip looked like a carnival. The lights and attractions from the different casinos were quite a sight.

"I heard Fifty Cent supposed to be walking Mayweather out," Disaya shouted as they entered the MGM. She could barely hear herself above all of the chatter in the arena.

"Yeah, I heard that too. You know that's a flashy-ass nigga. He about to give it to De La Hoya," Indie commented as they found their seats.

Disaya noticed how close they were to the ring. She looked to her right and noticed that they were seated among the stars. She knew that Indie had broken bread for the seats. They would have a perfect view of the fight.

Disaya didn't really care for sports, but just the fact that she was sitting next to Indie made her night enjoyable. She tried to imagine what life would be like if she chose to take him up on his offer. *He wants to take care of me*, she thought to herself as she looked at the gorgeous man that was sitting to her right. She tried not to think about anything but the present as she enjoyed herself.

After the fight, they resumed their casino antics and did it real big at the craps tables.

Indie and Disaya retired to their room at 4 A.M. She stopped in the hallway because she was unsure where he was going to sleep.

"Will you sleep with me tonight?" she finally gathered the nerve to ask him.

He opened the door for her and they went inside. He unzipped the back of her dress and eased it off of her shoulders. With his arms wrapped around her waist, he kissed the nape of her neck and guided her to the bed. He stripped until he wore nothing but his boxers and then lay onto the bed. He grabbed YaYa's hand and pulled her down next to him.

Disaya's head found a comfortable place on his chest and she closed her eyes as he stroked her hair until she fell asleep.

Disaya woke up the next morning and found Indie sleeping soundly beside her. He was so damn fine to her, and she really hoped that he could see a future with her. He made her feel so special the night before. He made her realize that she was worth so much more. She was selling her soul to the devil just to make some quick cash and without even knowing it, he had given her the strength to change her life. For that alone she was in love with the man. All she had to do now was get him to love her back.

She kissed his chest and worked her way down until she reached his manhood. He had that morning hard-on, and she took him all into her mouth.

He stirred in his sleep and awoke to the pleasure that she was giving him.

"Yo, what you doing?" he asked groggily.

His protests quickly turned into moans as she put her professional head game into effect. His muscular frame tightened up as she pleased him, and he felt like he would explode at any moment. He curled his toes, trying to stop the pressure that was building up in his body. He told her to hold up as he switched into the sixty-nine position. He stuck his tongue in between her legs and licked her pussy gently, almost like a cat drinking milk.

Disaya moved her hips and head in unison as she sucked him like a lollipop. He slipped his tongue into her asshole, causing her to cum instantly. She was always disgusted by dudes who wanted to play with her ass, but Indie was the exception. He made her feel so good that she was throwing her ass back on his tongue like it was a hard dick.

Disaya got up and rode him backwards so that he could get a view of her ass. She bounced up and down on him, grinding slowly as she rode his shaft.

He licked his fingers and stuck one in her ass. The feeling was so erotic she lost her mind.

She massaged his balls and rode him while he fingered her ass with one hand and rubbed her cheeks with the other. She was feeling so horny that she invited him to do something that she was terrified of. She got on all fours and said, "Fuck me, Indie."

He got on his knees and stuck the tip of his long, thick dick in her wet pussy. He then removed it and wet her ass with it. She braced herself for the pain that she expected to feel. "Relax, ma, I won't hurt you," he whispered in her ear.

Disaya tried to relax her muscles, but when he eased himself into her ass she felt like he was ripping her apart. *Oh shit,* she thought as she closed her eyes and gritted her teeth. He began to grind slowly, and once he was inside of her, the pain subsided, and the orgasms came one after the other.

He fucked her slowly and reached around to finger her at the same time. His thumb danced on her clit while his middle finger ventured inside her pussy walls. He maneuvered his dick in and out of her ass, and it felt so good, she was speaking in tongues.

"Indie," she called his name loudly over and over again. He finally pulled himself out of her ass and stuck his dick into her pussy. His pumps grew more and more powerful until he erupted inside of her.

She turned around and laughed lightly as she saw his eyes roll in the back of his head.

"Damn, girl," he exclaimed. "You got that wet wet," he complimented.

"I know, and I'm ready to let it be yours if you want it," she said.

He touched the side of her face and replied, "I want it. I want you."

They got up and took a shower together, where their lovemaking continued for another hour. The ringing of Indie's cell phone interrupted them, and they both got out and entered the room.

"Damn, that was Bay," Indie said as he looked at his caller ID. He dialed Bay's number and waited as the phone rang.

"What up, dude?" Indie greeted when Bay finally picked up.

"Yo, is YaYa with you?" he asked.

Indie frowned and said, "Yeah, she right here, hold up." He passed Disaya the phone.

She displayed a look of confusion as she took the cell phone from him. "Hey, Bay," she said.

"Yo, YaYa I'm gon' kill yo mu'fuckin' friend when I see her. That bitch foul! I swear on my mother I'm murking that ho when I catch her," he threatened.

Disaya's facial expression immediately dropped, and fear entered her heart. "Yo, Bay, you need to chill out with all them threats. What the fuck are you so hot for?"

"That nasty bitch gave me HIV. Word is bond, she's dead when I catch her!" With those words he hung up in her face.

Tears of shock, fear, and disbelief formed in her eyes as she looked up at Indie hopelessly. They graced her face as she broke down crying in the middle of the hotel room floor.

"What's wrong? What happened?" Indie asked as he knelt down and wrapped his arms around her in his attempt to comfort her.

"Mona gave Bay HIV. My best friend is dying," she said as she cried into his chest. "I wasn't there for her," Disaya uttered in disbelief as she thought about Mona's fate.

Damn, that's fucked-up, he thought to himself. Mona was so young and was probably one of the last chicks he would've expected to have the virus. Her beauty had been deceiving, and he was disappointed to hear that another beautiful sister had let her promiscuity lead to her death. Mona was lost in her chase for money, and now her recklessness had affected one of his closest friends. He knew that birds of a feather usually flocked together, but he hoped and prayed that Disaya was nothing like her friend.

Chapter 11

Disaya didn't want to ruin their trip, but the news about Mona had ruined her spirits. All she could think about was the fact that Mona had contracted HIV. *That could have been me*, she thought to herself. No matter how hard she tried, she could not get the tears to stop falling from her eyes. She looked out of the airplane window in order to avoid facing Indie. He didn't say anything, and he gave her some space to think. He did, however, hold on to her hand to let her know that he was there if she wanted to talk.

The flight seemed to take forever. All she wanted to do was go check on her friend. *God, please let this be a big misunderstanding. How can she have AIDS? She is a good person. Please don't take her away from me*, she prayed silently.

Disaya had never experienced a relationship with God before, but she desperately felt the need to ask Him for help. She knew that the reason why she was hurting so badly was because she was just as lost as Mona was. They had been leading the same lifestyle and doing the same things. She realized that the shoe could have easily been on the other foot.

When they finally arrived back in New York, Disaya rushed to get her baggage.

"I have to get to her," she said as she quickly located her bags and headed for the car.

"Tell me what you need me to do," Indie gently instructed as he opened the car door for her. She dropped her chin to her chest and closed her eyes.

"I just need you to take me home. Right now that's all you can do," she said sadly.

"Okay," he said. He could see that she was hurting and he wanted to help her, but he knew that she wasn't ready to let him in. He drove her to her apartment, and they sat silently in the car.

"I'm sorry about the trip," she said in a low tone.

"Don't worry about that. You go do what you got to do. Call me if you need me," he told her.

She nodded her head and opened the door to get out. She didn't even bother going up to her apartment. She headed straight to her car and drove away.

She walked into the Elite warehouse and immediately noticed how much it had changed. The smell of stank pussy was everywhere, and it looked more like a crack house than a place of business.

"Mo!" she yelled as she rushed up the stairs. There were girls spread throughout the building and they each looked worn-out. Disaya was shocked. Some of the hottest chicks in New York had been members of Elite, and now they looked like used-up prostitutes.

"Mo!" she stated as she knocked on Ronnie B's office door.

Ronnie pulled open the door and licked his lips when he saw Disaya standing there. "So you finally came back to Daddy, huh?" he said.

"Not hardly, nigga. Where is Mona?" she asked him as she pushed past him and entered his office. She saw Mona laid out on

Ronnie's desk. She was naked, and another girl was in between her legs licking away.

"Mona! Get up! Do you even know what you're doing?" YaYa yelled as her sadness quickly turned into rage. She looked around at the X pills that were scattered all over the desk. It was no wonder Mona had contracted HIV. Ronnie had turned her out on X and had turned Elite into a sex shop. Girls who had been high-paid escorts had been converted into low-class prostitutes. There was no telling what type of dudes he had Mona tricking with. She pulled Mona up by her hair and said, "Put on some clothes and let's go!"

Ronnie harshly snatched Disaya's arm and pulled her away from Mona.

"She ain't going nowhere. This my bitch. She's good right here," Ronnie stated.

"Don't put your fucking hands on me. I don't give a damn what you say, she's leaving here with me," Disaya said. She pulled Mona up off the desktop.

"Why are you tripping, YaYa?" Mona asked.

"Shut up, Mona, let's go," Disaya yelled as she dragged her into the hall. Mona held onto the rail of the loft. Disaya could hear the girls at the bottom of the loft talking shit.

"She don't want to go. You ain't her mama. Let the bitch go! I told you that she wasn't leaving up out of here!" Ronnie shouted.

"Fuck you, Ronnie! She already done caught HIV fucking around with you. I'm not about to let you pimp her until she's too sick to make you money."

"HIV? Bitch, you got HIV!" Ronnie shouted. "I been fucking you and you infected?" he questioned as he grabbed Mona by the face.

"Stop it!" Disaya screamed as she clawed at his arms, trying to get him to release her friend. Ronnie had Mona leaned over the edge of the railing.

"I don't, Ronnie, I swear I don't!" Mona pleaded.

Disaya looked in her friend's eyes and saw that she really believed herself. *She doesn't even know she's infected,* Disaya thought. Before she could do anything to stop him, Ronnie B violently shoved Mona over the edge of the railing.

Everything seemed to move in slow motion, as Disaya watched Mona fall three flights down to the concrete floor below. "No!" she screamed.

The frightened screams of the other girls were deafening and Disaya took off down the stairs. "Mona!" she yelled as she ran to her friend's side. There was blood leaking from the back of Mona's head.

"YaYa?" Mona called out to her. There was so much blood around Mona that Disaya was afraid to go near her.

"I'm here, Mo," she yelled to her from a couple feet away.

Mona couldn't move her body and an excruciating current was flowing through her entire body. The pain was so great that tears built up in her eyes. "Is it true? Do I have AIDs?" she asked.

"Don't think about that right now, Mo," Disaya said in a panic as she pulled out her Sidekick. She frantically dialed 9-1-1. "Please help me! My friend was pushed over a ledge. There's blood everywhere," she cried.

The building quickly cleared out as everyone scrambled to get away from the scene. After giving the operator the address to the building, Disaya looked down at her friend. "Mo, hold on, girl. The ambulance is coming."

"YaYa, I want to see you. I don't want to die alone," Mona begged as tears flowed freely down her face.

Disaya's heart was pounding from the fear of contracting Mona's deadly disease, but she knew her friend needed her. She walked over to her and knelt down beside her. Disaya was horrified of touching Mona. She was sure that it was probably in her head, but she could smell the infectious blood as it poured from Mona and soaked through her jeans. Disaya tensed up as she felt her skin become moist from the contact. She was terrified of the disease that Mona was harboring, but she was even more afraid of losing her best friend in the world. She gripped Mona's hand tightly as she rubbed her hair softly. "Just hold on, Mo. You's a bad bitch, Mo. Come on, Mo. Bad bitches don't die," Disaya cried.

Mo chuckled halfheartedly as she felt her eyes close. "I'm sorry," she replied before her eyes shut against her will.

Leah arrived at the hospital to see Disaya sitting on the floor in the hallway, still covered in Mona's blood.

"Is she okay?" Leah asked as she rushed and hugged her friend. She could see that YaYa was distraught, and a twinge of jealousy ran through her as she realized how much YaYa truly cared for Mona. The feeling quickly passed, and she sat on the floor next to her and held Disaya as she cried hysterically in her arms.

"I knew I shouldn't have left her with Ronnie B. If she would've just left when we did—"

"This is not on you, YaYa. Mona is a grown woman. We couldn't control what she did. She chose to stay down with Elite," Leah said. "This is not your fault. The only thing that we can do is be here for her now."

Disaya nodded her head and replied, "I know you're right, but I still can't help but to feel guilty. She got that shit, Leah."

"What shit? AIDs?" Leah asked in disbelief.

"HIV," Disaya confirmed with a thick sadness in her voice. Disaya noticed that Leah had cut her hair into a shoulder-length wrap that was similar to her own. With the change of a hairstyle their resemblance was uncanny. YaYa didn't know what was up with the mini-me impersonation. She had never been the type of chick to dress like her friends. She valued her individuality, but she knew that now was not the time to trip on little stuff.

"Damn, that's fucked-up," Leah mumbled in disbelief. She had heard of different chicks getting caught up by the virus, but she had never been this close to the disease. She always thought that she protected herself enough not to worry about catching HIV, but now that Mona had contracted it, she wasn't so sure. If she had stayed down with Elite, she could have easily fucked behind

Mona or even had sex with Mona, which would have put her life on a permanent countdown.

There was a long silence between the two girls. They were both lost in their own thoughts.

Disaya was concerned for her friend. *I should have been there for her,* she thought. *If she would have left Elite when I did, none of this would be happening.*

"See, that's why we need to hit it big one time. We need to quit fucking with all these different niggas. We need to do it big one time. I got the perfect dude lined up too."

"What?" Disaya asked in disbelief.

"Look, just hear me out. This dude named Nanzi hit us up on the site, and he is working with some major money. He wants to get down with us. He wants to do it at his crib because he don't trust anybody. The payoff is large too. More than we have ever made before. We can do this one last time and be set for a minute," Leah urged.

"I can't believe you're even thinking about that right now," Disaya said as she shook her head in disgust.

"Excuse me, Ms. Morgan," a nurse said as she called Disaya by her last name.

"Yes?" Disaya responded eagerly as she and Leah stood up.

"There is a social worker here to see you regarding your friend's condition," the nurse stated as she motioned to a black woman in a blue pantsuit. The woman looked uncomfortable in the hospital as she approached Disaya.

"Hello, I'm Ms. Tillman," the black woman introduced. She didn't even wait to hear Disaya's name before she continued. "Your friend is injured very badly. Upon running some blood tests the doctors also discovered that she's very sick."

"Is it true—does Mona have AIDs?" Disaya asked. She desperately wanted to hear the word no come out of the woman's mouth, but the distressed look on the lady's face told Disaya that all of the rumors were true. Although Disaya already knew, hearing it confirmed broke her heart. She covered her mouth as tears welled in her eyes. She shook her head from side to side. "No," she whispered.

The sympathy in the social worker's face was evident. The woman sighed heavily and put her clipboard down on the counter of the nurses' station. "I'm so sorry that you and your friend have to go through this. I can't imagine what you must be going through, but you have to pull yourself together for the both of you. Now, I'm not supposed to be asking you this, but does your friend have any medical coverage?"

"No, I don't think so," YaYa replied.

"The treatment she needs is very expensive. The fall that she took damaged her spinal cord and she is hemorrhaging. The pressure from the blood is putting strain on her damaged spinal cord. If the doctors don't operate in the next couple days, she will be paralyzed."

"How much are we talking?" YaYa asked.

"The surgery and estimated recuperation costs that were listed in her file will be around three hundred thousand dollars. She only needs a ten percent down payment in order for the hospital to put her on the operating table. If there are any relatives or a church family that you can reach out to on her behalf for donations, you should. Like I said, you didn't hear this from me."

Disaya nodded her head in understanding.

"Thirty thousand dollars will get everything started," Disaya said as she thought about the money that Indie had given her in Vegas. She had left it in his car. She didn't even think about taking it with her because she was in such a rush to get to Mona.

"One last time and we can pay Mona's down payment. After that, you'll still be set for a minute," Leah whispered in Disaya's ear.

"I'll come up with the money. I'll have it by tomorrow." She didn't want to do it. She wished that she could be the woman that Indie wanted her to be, but her friend needed her. *I have to get this money*, she thought.

* * *

Disaya sent Indie to voice mail for the fifth time that night. She closed her eyes and leaned over the sink as she dreaded what she was about to do. Indie had made her realize that she needed to respect herself. While they were in Vegas he had made her feel something that she had never felt before . . . love. She felt love from him, but also for the first time in a long time she loved herself. What she was about to do went against everything that he wanted her to be. A part of her wanted to walk out and run to him, but she knew that she needed to do this for Mona. Mona had always had her back and she couldn't leave her hanging without at least attempting to help her.

Disaya walked out of the bathroom wearing a black lace camisole and saw Leah standing across the room behind Nanzi.

Nanzi had a camcorder in his hand and had it aimed at Disaya's body. He got excited as he zoomed in on the curves of her body, and he lusted for her when he focused on the fat lips between her legs.

"What is he doing? You didn't say shit about being on tape," Disaya protested.

"Yo, just chill, ma," Nanzi instructed.

"Do a dance for me," he asked as he put the camcorder on the tripod stand. He ran over to his surround sound stereo system and pressed play. Young Jeezy bumped throughout the room.

"Fuck that, I'm not dancing on no fucking tape," Disaya replied adamantly.

"Your girl is tripping," Nanzi stated to Leah, who was standing behind the camera.

"Look, she said no camera. Let's just turn it off," Leah said as she winked at YaYa. "You will still get your money's worth, baby. I promise you. I've tasted that pussy. It's the best in the world."

Disaya inhaled deeply and tried to make the tension seep from her body, but it was useless. She closed her eyes as a tear slid down her face. *"You got to respect yourself, ma."* She heard Indie's words playing over and over in her head as she moved her body to the beat of the song. She felt cheap, and for the first time in her life, she felt like a ho. She kept her eyes closed as she felt Nanzi's lips on her neck.

Nanzi wasn't a bad-looking dude, and it was obvious that he was caked up. A year ago, Disaya would have been all over him, but she had grown up since then. She now realized that everything that glittered wasn't gold.

She opened her eyes and saw Leah watching her behind the camera. She felt dirty and cheap, but she continued with the thought of saving Mona on her mind.

"Why I got to pay for this pussy, ma? A bitch like you supposed to be taken care of," he whispered as he stuck one finger in her pussy. He brought it to her face and pushed his finger forcefully in her mouth.

Indie's face flashed in her mind. "I can't do this," Disaya whispered as she pulled her straps back onto her shoulders and rushed out of the room.

"Yo, what's up wit' ya girl?" Nanzi asked impatiently.

"Nothing, she's cool. I'll be right back," Leah stated. Leah rushed after Disaya and grabbed her arm when they got into the hallway.

"What the fuck is up?" Leah asked.

"I can't do this, Leah," she admitted.

Leah put her hands on her face and kissed her. She stuck her tongue down her throat sloppily. "Save this pussy for me, YaYa. I'll take care of him," she whispered.

Disaya backed up from Leah and pushed her off. "Leah, gone with that shit! I can't do this anymore. This ain't for me. I'm better than this."

"Look, just calm down. I'll go and take care of Nanzi, then we'll get what we owed and bounce. Just work the camera," Leah instructed.

Both girls walked back into the room. Disaya stayed behind the camera and watched as Leah stripped. Her mouth instantly found its place around Nanzi's shaft. Her head was in his lap and her ass was in the air, facing the camera. She clapped her fat ass cheeks together and fingered herself as she gave Nanzi the best head job of his life.

Once her pussy was good and wet, she climbed on top of Nanzi, who was rock-hard, and began to ride him slowly.

Disaya frowned when she saw the pink butterfly tattoo that was on Leah's right ass cheek. *What the fuck? This bitch got her hair cut like mines and she got the same tattoo as I do.*

Nanzi looked like he was in heaven. His eyes were closed, and his hands were planted firmly on Leah's ass as he picked her up and pounded her down onto his shaft. Disaya noticed Leah reaching for something at the headboard of the bed. *What the hell is she doing?* she thought to herself.

Disaya was clueless, but Leah knew exactly what she was doing. She had planned that night perfectly. She knew what her purpose was and was determined to get what she had come for.

Disaya's eyes bugged out as she saw the chrome handgun that Leah pulled from behind the pillow.

Boom! Nanzi never saw it coming.

Blood as red as wine poured onto the white sheets, and Disaya couldn't stop the scream that escaped from her throat.

Leah walked backwards to where Disaya was standing and shut the camera off.

"What did you do? What the fuck did you do?" Disaya asked.

"What I had to. This is our only way to hit the safe. This dumb nigga been flashing his cash all in the streets, talking about his safe . . . talking about he untouchable because he sleep with his pistol underneath his pillow. I knew he would have that mu'fucka right where I needed it to be. He didn't expect me to use his own gun on him. Now we can go somewhere away from all this, YaYa. Just me and you," she said as she rubbed the side of Disaya's face.

"Bitch, are you crazy? You just fucking killed somebody!" she yelled.

"I did it for us. So we could take the money and be together.

Now come on, help me unload this safe," Leah said as she quickly put her clothes back on.

Leah went over to the safe and shot the steel lock off. The powerful force of the .45 in her hand did the trick, and she opened it up.

This bitch is nuts, Disaya thought as she watched Leah unload the money.

"It's like two hundred and fifty thousand dollars in here," Leah said excitedly as she divided the money into two different duffel bags. She wiped the room down and eradicated any trace that they had been there. She swiped the camcorder off the tripod then tossed Disaya one of the bags.

"One hundred and twenty-five thousand dollars. Tell me this wasn't worth it," Leah said.

Disaya was in shock and felt horrible for the man that lay slumped inside the room. She hurried and ran out of the house into the car.

"Disaya, now we can be together," Leah said again.

"Why you keep talking this be-together shit, Leah? I'm not gay. I don't want to be with a woman! That shit is never going to happen, so kill that noise you talking. You are fucking loony! I thought it was just business to you, but your ass is really obsessed with me."

"I'm not, YaYa. I just want us to have the best of everything. Now you can stop messing with that nigga Indie. I know you were with him because of the money. Now we have money," Leah stated. "You and me, boo." There was a crazed look in her eye.

This bitch has lost it, Disaya thought. "Bitch, there is no *we*. There is only me. I'm not fucking with you like that. As a matter of fact, I'm not fucking with you at all. I love Indie. I've never loved you. We were girls who got money together, that's it! Yeah, we had to do some freaky shit in order to get paid, but that's all it was about to me . . . the money."

"You don't mean that," Leah replied. "You just tripping right now."

"Yeah, I am tripping. Bitch, you just blew that nigga brains out. I'm not fucking with you, Leah. Now let me out the fucking car, you fucking dyke," she replied harshly.

Leah pulled over the car in a rage. "Fine, bitch, get out!"

Disaya stepped out of the car and began to walk in the opposite direction.

"Where would you be without me, Disaya? Nowhere! You wouldn't be shit, but a broke bitch with some good pussy!" Leah shouted as she walked away.

I should've never fucked with her like that, she thought as she gripped the bag of money that Leah had just killed for. *This money ain't worth it.*

Chapter 12

Disaya walked for miles until she finally located a cab and took it to the hospital. Her face was so pale that she looked like a zombie as she walked in a slow daze. She kept seeing the look on Nanzi's face when he was shot. The guilt was eating at her, and she tried to convince herself that his death was worth Mona's life. She dropped the thirty gees that Mona needed for her surgery off at the nurses' station, and just as quickly as she had come, she left.

She picked up her phone and called the only person that she knew could make her feel better.

"Hello," Indie answered.

"I need you," she said desperately.

"Where are you? You sound like something's wrong," he replied.

"I'm at the hospital," she whispered. She didn't have the energy to speak loudly. She was drained mentally, physically, and emotionally.

She hung up the phone and stood outside of the emergency room doors. She didn't know if he would show up. She just sat on the curb and waited hopelessly as she thought about all the foul shit she had done.

Indie finally pulled into the parking lot and jumped out when he saw Disaya sitting on the curb. Her face was stained with white ash from her dried-up tears. He ran up to her and said, "What happened to you?"

She didn't respond. Her hair was disheveled, and her eyes were red and puffy from crying.

"YaYa, talk to me, ma. Who did this to you?" he asked her.

She wrapped her arms underneath her legs and balled up as she placed her head on top of her knees.

The sound that erupted from her body expressed true pain, and it broke Indie's heart to see her like that. He picked her up from the ground and placed her gently in the passenger side of his car. He pulled off and took her to his condo on the Upper East Side of Manhattan.

She didn't speak the entire way there. He didn't know what had happened to her, but whatever occurred had traumatized her. He carried her into his home and laid her down on his bed.

"Who hurt you?" he asked.

"The world," she replied in a whisper. She told him about Mona and how Ronnie B had thrown her over the top floor of the warehouse. She left out the rest of the events that had taken place that night, but that alone made him enraged. He knew what type of business Ronnie B ran. He pimped chicks because he couldn't pimp the streets. He didn't have the heart to take on the streets like the real get-money niggas, so he recruited bitches to make money for him. Ronnie B festered on lost souls so that he could feel like a man.

"Don't worry about that. I'll handle that," he told her. "You shouldn't have been around that nigga in the first place. If he had hurt *you*, I would've had to kill him."

He took her clothes off and went and got a sponge and a large bowl with hot, soapy water in it. He rubbed her body down and then kissed her passionately as he lay beside her.

"Don't leave me," Disaya said out of the blue.

"I love you, ma. I'm not going anywhere," he whispered in her ear.

"I love you too."

It had been weeks since Disaya had spoken to Leah, and she was glad that she didn't try to contact her. Leah didn't have it all, and Disaya wanted nothing to do with her. She had been staying over Indie's house for almost a month, and they were getting along well. He had practically moved Disaya in with him. Most of her things were at his house, and he made her feel at home.

The more time she spent around Indie, the deeper her love grew for him. She wanted to tell him the full story of what had happened to her the night he picked her up from the hospital, but she didn't know how he would react. She wasn't willing to risk his love by telling him the truth.

She walked from his kitchen with a plate fit for a king. She had got up extra early just to fix him breakfast. As she walked back toward the room she heard him talking in a low tone on the phone. His back was toward her, and he didn't see her standing in the doorway to his bedroom.

"Ma, it's not like that. I got company, so that's why I haven't been over in a while. I promise you I'll be there tonight. I got something special planned anyway. Look, I got to go. I don't want her to hear me. I'll see you later," he said. He hung up the phone, and when he turned around he was surprised to see her standing there. Her feelings were hurt more than anything, but all he saw was anger in her eyes.

She stood there with a look that said, *Yeah, nigga, I heard you.* Her eyebrows were arched as she waited for an explanation.

"It ain't what you think, yo," he explained as he walked toward her. "Is this for me?" he asked as he kissed the side of her face.

She dodged his kiss and replied, "It depends on who that was on the phone."

"That was my mother, yo."

"Your mother?" she replied with her lips twisted up in a disbelieving smirk.

"Yeah, what, a brother can't talk to his mama?" Indie asked.

Disaya realized she was tripping and handed him his food. "I'm sorry," she said, embarrassed.

"What did I tell you? Huh? I would never hurt you," he said with a mouthful of food.

"I know," she said with a smile.

"Trust me. Oh yeah, and we going to my parents' crib for dinner tonight. My moms want to meet you," he said.

"Meet me for what? How does she know about me?" Disaya asked.

"Don't worry about all that. I got some shit I need to take care of today, so you on your own. Just be ready by six o'clock," he replied.

He finished his breakfast, got dressed, and was out the door, leaving YaYa to entertain her own thoughts.

Disaya hated being left alone. It gave her too much time to think. She tried to block the guilt out of her mind by concentrating on the one good thing in her life . . . Indie. He was everything that she wanted. *Now all I got to do is impress his mama*, she thought as she went into Indie's closet to choose something to wear.

Disaya gripped Indie's hand as she stood outside of his parents' New Jersey home. They lived across the bridge, and the size of their suburban home let Disaya know that they came from money.

A middle-aged woman answered the door and hugged Indie tightly. "My baby!" the woman exclaimed.

"Hey, Ma," he replied. He kissed her on the cheek and then turned to Disaya. "This is—"

"I know who this is. This is the girl that my baby boy can't stop talking about," she said as she embraced Disaya too.

The woman made her feel welcome, and Disaya immediately fell in love with her.

"It's so good to meet you, baby. You are just as pretty as he said you were." Elaine admired YaYa's features. There was no doubting that Disaya was a beautiful girl, but she felt like she had seen her somewhere before. She looked so familiar.

Disaya blushed and replied, "It's nice to meet you too, Mrs. Perkins."

"Chile, please, call me Elaine. Come on in," she said as they walked inside of the house.

"Where's Pops?" Indie asked.

"He's in the den watching that damn football," Elaine said. "Gone back there with him. You know you want to. Your brother ain't here yet. I don't know if he's coming. I've been calling him, but he doesn't like to answer the phone for his old bird."

"He'll probably show up. You know how he is." Indie turned to Disaya and asked her, "you gon' be all right?"

"Boy! Yeah, she gon' be all right. I'm not going to scare the girl off," Elaine said as she hit Indie with a kitchen towel.

Disaya laughed and nodded her head in agreement. "I'm fine."

He kissed her on the cheek and then looked at his mother and said, "Be easy on her, Ma." He made his way into the back of the house, leaving Disaya with his mother.

"Come on, sweetheart, you can help me in the kitchen," Elaine said.

"Call me YaYa," she said.

Elaine and Disaya clicked instantly. Elaine grilled Disaya about everything under the sun, and she seemed to approve of her, but Indie's mother could not stop the nagging feeling that she had seen the young woman before.

Disaya pulled the macaroni and cheese out of the oven.

"Disaya, I want you to meet my father," Indie said as he entered the kitchen.

Disaya turned around, and when she saw the man's face, she

dropped the casserole dish onto the floor. "Oh!" Disaya said as the hot dish crashed at her feet. Disaya panicked as she bent down to clean up the mess. "I am so sorry, Elaine," she apologized. She kept her eyes on the floor to avoid looking Indie's father in the eyes.

Indie bent down to help her. "You okay?" he asked.

"I'm fine," she replied. "The pan was just too hot." She couldn't believe her luck. Indie's father was the car dealer who she had let suck on her pussy in order to get her car. *Perkins, Bill Perkins*, she thought to herself. *Ain't this about a bitch?* A comfortable dinner party had just turned into an uncomfortable situation for Disaya. "Excuse me. I think I burned my hand," she said.

"The bathroom's up the stairs to your right," Indie instructed as he watched her rush off.

Disaya practically ran up the steps, ascending them two at a time, until she found refuge inside the bathroom. She frantically splashed her face with water as she tried to calm down. She shook her hands nervously as she tried to think of an explanation for Indie. An overwhelming nausea overcame her, and she leaned over the toilet and violently heaved up the contents of her stomach. She was sure that her little indiscretion would come out. *Just breathe*, she told herself. She couldn't believe that she had seduced the father of the man that she loved.

She finally made her way downstairs where everyone was seated at the dinner table.

"Are you okay, sweetheart?" Elaine asked.

"Yes, I'm fine," she replied with a weak smile.

Indie stood up and pulled her chair out for her as she sat next to him. "You all right," he whispered to her.

She nodded and grabbed his hand under the table. She was nervous throughout the entire dinner. She could feel his father's eyes on her as she talked. She seemed to charm his mother, however, and she felt extreme guilt for what she had done with her husband. *That was a long time ago. I'm a different person now*, she told herself.

"I think she's perfect, Indie," Elaine stated. "I'd be proud to have a daughter-in-law like her. Plus, I haven't seen you this happy in a long time."

"Daughter-in-law?" Disaya repeated in confusion. She turned toward Indie, but before she could say anything he pulled out a small black gift bag. "What is this?" she asked him.

"Look and see," he told her.

Disaya reached into the bag and pulled out a key. "That's the key to our new brownstone in Harlem."

"What?" she said in disbelief.

"Keep looking," he said.

Disaya pulled out a small Tiffany's box. She opened the box and gasped when she saw the yellow canary diamond that she had tried on months ago.

"You ready to make this official?" he asked.

Disaya looked around the table with her mouth hung open. Her eyes stopped on his father, and she was quickly forced back to reality. Tears filled her eyes. *I can't marry this man*, she thought. To her surprise, Mr. Perkins nodded his head in approval, and Disaya finally answered, "Like a referee with a whistle."

Elaine laughed as she clapped loudly. She was so elated to see her baby boy choosing a woman to spend the rest of his life with.

"It took you long enough, ma. You sure?" Indie asked her as he lifted her chin with one finger. "Will you marry me?"

"Yes. Indie, yes! Yes!" she yelled happily as he slipped the ring on her finger.

"You're a lucky man, son," his father spoke up as he nodded his head in congratulations.

Disaya mouthed the words *thank you* to his father. She knew that he would keep their little secret, and she was forever grateful to him for that.

The doorbell interrupted their joyous occasion and Elaine said, "Let me go get that."

Indie picked Disaya up and hugged her tightly, spinning her around the room. "I love you, girl."

"I love you, Indie. I can't wait until Mona's ass gets better so I can show off my rock!" Disaya said as she held her hand away from her body and admired it.

"Oh, God, no!" they all heard Elaine scream from the front foyer.

Everybody took off toward the front door. Disaya could see the squad car lights in the driveway.

"Fuck is all this?" Indie asked as he joined his mother's side.

"It's your brother, Indie. They say that he's been killed!" she sobbed as she collapsed into her husband's arm.

Disaya saw Indie's facial expression change instantly. A silent rage took over his face. "Indie?" she called out to him as she put her hands on his face.

He pressed his forehead against hers as he shook his head in distress.

"Indie, baby, talk to me," she pleaded as she saw the tears fall down his cheeks.

Indie punched the front door to his parents' house, putting his fist through it. He then rushed out of the house.

"Indie!" YaYa watched helplessly as he got into his car and sped away. The only sound that she could hear was the sobbing of his mother and the breaking of her heart as she imagined how devastated her future husband must be.

Chapter 13

Disaya waited days before she saw Indie again. His parents dropped her back off at Indie's apartment, and the only thing she could think to do was wait patiently until he came home. She blew his cell phone up constantly. She just wanted to know that he was okay.

Disaya cleaned the apartment from top to bottom and made dinner, hoping that Indie would decide to come home that night. She stared restlessly at the clock as she watched the hours pass. Nine became ten, and ten changed to eleven, as she sat at the candlelit table in her Victoria's Secret lingerie. *God, please let my baby be okay. You just brought my soul mate to me; don't take him away so quickly.* Time continued to pass, and eventually she rested her head on top of the table and dozed off.

Indie walked into the house at 5 AM and saw Disaya sleeping at the dinner table. He saw that she had prepared dinner for him. His grief was at its peak, and he wasn't trying to hurt her, but the only thing he could think about was his older brother. He staggered over to Disaya and stood over her for a while, watching her sleep. She was beautiful, and he was lucky to have her by his side. He got down on both knees and laid his head in her lap, holding on to her for dear life, squeezing her as if she might disappear before his eyes.

Disaya woke up and rested her hand on Indie's face as she massaged his tense neck muscles. "Baby . . . oh, Indie, I love you so much. I am so sorry about your brother," she soothed.

"He was my heart, yo," Indie replied through his sobs. "I swear on everything I love that I'm-a murk whoever is responsible for this. Niggas gon' feel it," he threatened.

"Indie, please don't do anything right now. Just think about it. I don't want anything to happen to you. It would kill me if something happened to you," she begged as she saw the vengeance in his eyes.

Seeing him like this tore Disaya up on the inside. He was always so strong and assertive. Now he was hurting badly and needed her support.

Indie didn't respond, but he did stay locked inside his condo until the funeral. He didn't want anyone to see him weak, and the only comfort he got was by seeing Disaya's face. Every time she smiled at him, she took a little bit of the pain away. He almost felt guilty for loving her at a time like this, and sometimes he pushed her away unintentionally.

She was patient with him, though, and understood that he needed to grieve. He didn't talk to her at all. She knew that he was fighting his own battles in his heart and mind, though, so she didn't mind the silence.

He held on tightly to her every time he was around her. He felt like he was underwater and couldn't come up for air. He was drowning in sorrow.

For his entire life his older brother had been there for him and now he was gone. He planned on murdering whoever was associated with the people responsible for his brother's death; he just didn't have the strength to execute his plan. He knew that his heart would be weak for a while. There was a void in his life now that no one could fill. He would give himself time to heal, and then he would hit the streets to find out exactly what had happened to his brother.

The funeral approached and Indie wore a black-on-black Armani suit. He looked like he had stepped off the cover of *GQ* with his VVS cuff links and purple lapel neck accent with the platinum Cartier tie clip. He looked at himself in the mirror and took a deep breath as he prepared to send his brother off.

Disaya sat on the bed in a snug black Prada dress that cut in a low V near her breast line. It also cut low in the back and she wore a huge black hat that covered her eyes. Her satin Prada gloves made her look as if she was born and raised with elegance and class.

"Are you sure you want me to come?" Disaya asked. She felt like she would be out of place at the funeral. "I mean, it's going to be your family and . . . I don't think that I should—"

"YaYa, you are a part of my family now. You're about to be my wife. I need you by my side today," he said.

Disaya felt the flutter in her stomach. She knew exactly what it was. She was pregnant with Indie's baby, but she had been reluctant to tell him because so much was going on with him already. She wasn't exactly sure how far along she was. They never used a condom when they had sex, so she was clueless as to when it happened. She thought that it happened while she was in Vegas with him, but she wasn't exactly sure.

She stared off into space as she thought about the child that was growing inside of her. She was engaged and pregnant. She couldn't believe how much her life had changed in such a short period of time. *I was just trying to hustle niggas out of money. I was chasing a Prada Plan and ended up getting something worth way more valuable than money.*

"You okay?" Indie asked her.

She snapped out of her daze and nodded. *I should wait until after the funeral to tell him.*

"What's on your mind?" he asked.

"Nothing," she replied.

He could tell from the look in her eyes that she was lying. "Don't lie to me, ma. I never want us to keep anything from each other. Promise me that you gon' always keep it real with me."

A tear slipped down her face. "I promise," she replied.

"Now tell me what's wrong?"

"I'm pregnant," she said with her head down.

"You're what?" he asked loudly. He lifted her chin and said, "For real?"

She nodded as tears flowed down her cheeks.

"What you crying for, baby? You just made me the happiest man on this earth. You just gave me a reason to keep living. I'm having a shorty," he said in excitement and disbelief.

Seeing him that excited made her smile. "Is this really okay?" she asked with uncertainty in her voice.

"You ain't got to worry about nothing, YaYa. You're about to be my wife. You're carrying my child. You gon' always be taken care of. My family will never want for anything," he assured her. "I just need you to do one thing."

"What's that?" she asked.

"Help me through my brother's funeral. I need you to be strong for me today," he said weakly.

"I can do that," she replied as she kissed him on the forehead.

Indie's parents walked into the sanctuary first, followed by Indie and Disaya. Disaya felt out of place, but she wanted to be there for her man. She held on to him as she walked down the long aisle of the church. An ivory and gold casket sat at the head of the aisle. The entire room was covered in lillies. The funeral was packed. Family members and friends all showed up to pay their respects.

The closer they got to the casket, the tighter Indie gripped her hand. He hadn't shed any tears yet, and she knew that he would never do it in public, but she knew that he was hurting inside. She placed his hand on her stomach to remind him that he still had two people who loved and needed him. He rubbed it gently before he pulled his hand away.

Elaine broke down to her knees when she saw her son's body lying there. Her sobs were so loud that they silenced everyone else. Bill picked her up from her knees, and helped her to the first pew. It was their turn to view the body and Indie couldn't move his feet.

"It'll be okay," Disaya whispered as she stepped forward with him. She walked up to the casket, and her heart stopped when she saw his brother's face. *Nanzi?* she thought to herself as her breaths became shallow. *Oh my God . . . I did this to him. I did this to Indie. Leah killed Indie's brother.* She couldn't suck enough air for her lungs. *Oh my God,* she thought over and over again. Disaya felt the room spin underneath her, and her legs became weak as she collapsed onto the floor.

"Somebody call nine-one-one! She's pregnant!" The sound of Indie calling for help was the last thing that she heard before the lights in her head went out.

When Disaya woke up, she saw the IV that was sticking from her arm. Indie and his parents sat in chairs around her hospital bed.

"Indie, baby, she's awake," Elaine said as she patted her son's shoulder.

Indie jumped up and rushed to her side. "Don't do that to me, ma. I thought I would lose you too," he said as he kissed the back of her hand.

If you knew what I did to your brother, you wouldn't care, she thought to herself as she began to cry.

"What happened up there?" he asked.

Disaya didn't know what to tell him. She was at a loss for words. Thankfully, one of the doctors walked through the door and overheard the question.

"Stress, fatigue, and pregnancy is not a good mix. Her body is tired, and dealing with the death of a loved one can take its toll on you. You fainting is a sign that you need some rest," the doctor said.

"You don't have to worry about that, Doc, because I'm not gon' let her lift a finger," Indie said. "You might have to flip a couple pages in magazines, though, so you can pick out your new furniture for our new home."

"I can do that," she replied with a weak smile.

"Well, now that I know that you are all right, we can head home." Elaine stood up and kissed Disaya on her cheek. "Take care of my grandbaby, girlfriend, and call me if you need me," she said before kissing Indie and leaving the room.

"I've got a surprise for you," Indie said as he got up and walked to the door. The doctor took her blood pressure as Indie left the room for a couple minutes.

When Indie walked back in, Mona was following him. She was in a wheelchair, and her movements were stiff, but she was still a sight for sore eyes.

"Hey, Mommy," Mona said as she reached up to hold her hand. "I hear I'm going to be an auntie."

Disaya started to cry. "I'll give y'all some privacy," Indie said as he walked out into the hallway.

"Why are you crying, girl? All of your dreams came true. Your Prada Plan worked. You have a good man that is paid," Mona stated. "And you are having this nigga baby. That's child support like a mu'fucka even if y'all don't stay together."

"Mo, something happened. I'm not gon' be able to keep this man," YaYa said.

The doctor left the room, and then Disaya continued. She told Mona exactly what happened with Leah and Nanzi. Mona sat there in shock as she listened to her friend's story.

"I have to tell him," Disaya said as she cried. "I know that he is gon' leave me, but he deserves to know. He deserves better than me. I'm nothing but a girl from the hood, and that ain't what he wants. I've made a lot of bad choices, and now I've got to live with them."

"You can't tell him, YaYa. You better not tell him. You deserve everything that you have now. Yo, forget about Leah. You didn't kill his brother, she did. That bitch is psycho, and you are lucky that you cut her off when you did. Don't tell him, Disaya. Just be happy with him. Start over today, don't think about yesterday. I wish I could start over," Mona said as she thought about the deadly disease plaguing her body.

"How are you feeling?" YaYa asked.

"I have good and bad days. Everybody here is real nice. I'm seeing a therapist, trying to deal with all of this. I just wish I had been smarter, you know. I had sex with so many men after you left Elite, and I never once thought to make them wear a condom. I was popping ecstasy like it was candy, YaYa. I just lost control of my own hustle, you know. I was stupid and blinded by the money. I didn't love myself enough to see that I was hurting myself. See, YaYa, I'm just like you, a ghetto bitch from the neighborhood. I could have chosen to do something different with my life, but I didn't. I took the easy route. I chose to be promiscuous, and now I'm living with the consequences. I'm dying, YaYa. So, see, I'm not just telling you to live it up just for you. I have to live through you because that's the only way that I can live. I want you to get married, have a bunch of big-head kids . . . and you know they gon' have some big-ass heads because Indie fine but he got a dome."

Disaya wiped the tears from her face as she laughed.

"For real, girl, do all of the things that I can't do, YaYa. You deserve this life. Don't sell yourself short anymore. Don't ever let Indie find out about his brother, because if you do, he will never forgive you."

Disaya nodded and said, "I love you, Mo."

"I love you too, girl. Now get some rest so that your man can take you home."

It had been weeks, and Disaya still hadn't tried to contact Leah. Leah was heated at Disaya. She couldn't believe that she had played her the way that she did. *That bitch chose that hustling backwards-ass nigga over me*, she thought as she sealed the large envelope that she had in her hand. *As many times as I licked her pussy, she had the nerve to give it to his ass. She think he love her. I bet you he won't love her after I'm through with her ass.*

Thinking about Disaya had Leah going crazy. She was furious. She had always gotten exactly what she wanted, from whomever she wanted. Rejection wasn't something that she was used to. Disaya had dropped Leah like a bad habit and that pissed her off.

That bitch thinks she's better than me. She should've never let me taste the pussy if she wasn't gon' let me have it to myself.

Leah stepped outside of her house and walked up the street. She turned many heads as she strutted up the block. On the outside she looked like the perfect woman, but on the inside she wasn't all there. She dropped her package in the mail and smiled as she thought about what she was about to do. *Karma's a bitch!*

Indie walked to the outside to the mailbox and retrieved the contents from it. He was shirtless and wore baggy sweatpants, causing the young girls on the block to gossip about his perfect physique. He walked back into the house as he flipped through the stacks of bills and opened up the Black Expressions package that Disaya had ordered.

Her doctor had recommended that she begin to read to keep her stress level low, so Disaya joined several book clubs like Coast2coast online readers and Black Expressions. She was into the street-fiction authors, and Indie didn't tell her, but he was feeling the novels that she ordered. He pulled out two books, *Diary of a Street Diva* and *Supreme Clientele* by Ashley and JaQuavis. "Hell yeah, I can rock with these," Indie said as he put them on the countertop. He had read their first joint, *Dirty Money*, and knew that they would bring the streets to life through their writing.

He continued to flip, until he came across a yellow package. He opened it up and pulled out a VCR tape. *What the hell is this?* he thought as he made his way to the basement and popped it

into the player. He sat down in his leather La-Z-Boy and grabbed
the remote to press play. His heart raced when he saw his brother's
face pop up on the screen.

"I'm about to fuck tonight," Nanzi sang into the camera as he
filmed himself. "Fuck is this?" Indie stated as he sat up and leaned
his elbows on his knees. He recognized his brother's bedroom.
His brow creased in confusion as he saw Disaya appear on the
tape.

"Dance for me, ma," his brother told her.

Indie's blood boiled as he watched her shake her ass for Nanzi.
He clenched his fist and gritted his teeth as he watched her run
off the camera's screen. He could hear his heartbeat in his ears as
he waited to see what was going to happen next.

Minutes later he saw Disaya's ass cheeks appear back on the
screen. He noticed the butterfly that was tattooed on her rear. His
heart broke as he watched her get on top of Nanzi and ride him
slowly. He lowered his head and closed his eyes as he heard the
moans of his future wife. He took deep breaths. *Calm down*, he
told himself. His heart ached beyond recognition as he noticed
the pleasurable look on his brother's face. He couldn't see YaYa's
face, so he didn't know if she was enjoying it or not, but it hurt
him all the same.

He squinted as he saw Disaya begin to reach for something.
When she pulled out a gun and put the barrel to Nanzi's head,
Indie's anger turned to blind rage.

"No!" he yelled when he saw the blood splatter on the tape as
Disaya pulled the trigger. "Aghh!" he screamed in pain. He didn't
want to believe what he had just seen. "Aghh!" he cried as he fell
to the floor and rocked back and forth as he hit himself in the
chest, trying to stop his heart from hurting. He had loved YaYa
with all of his heart. He trusted her and she had betrayed him.
"Aghh!" he cried like a baby because he thought that Disaya's
love for him had been real. He knew that she was a ghetto girl
when he had met her, but he looked past all the negatives he saw

in her and brought out the positive that he knew lived inside of her. Now he didn't know if she had been worth the time and energy. He felt as if he would die as he held his heart.

"Baby!" Disaya called out as she walked through the Harlem brownstone.

The house had an old Harlem Renaissance style, and the deep shades of brown, orange, and cream complemented her style perfectly. She had always dreamed of owning something just like it, and her dreams became a reality when she received the keys to it the day that Indie proposed to her. It had been completely renovated, and the home was exactly what she wanted it to be. Disaya was completely in love with her home and the man that she shared it with.

"Indie, baby, are you home?" she called out as she walked from room to room, unloading the many bags that she had purchased from her shopping trip earlier that day.

"Yo, I'm downstairs . . . come here for a minute, ma. I got to holla at you about something," he yelled from the basement.

Disaya took off her Baby Phat thigh-high boots and eased herself out of her jeans. She hated wearing clothes, and when she was in her own home she seldom wore them. Her turquoise Victoria's Secret thong was swallowed by her voluptuous behind as she switched her hips, a habit that she did even when she didn't have an audience.

"Here I come," she yelled back. She walked over to the refrigerator and grabbed a bottle of water for herself and a Smirnoff for Indie. She also grabbed the Blockbuster tapes that she had gotten on her way home and then made her way to the fully furnished basement.

She smiled as she descended the steps. "I picked up some movies on my way home. . . . I've been shopping all day. I just want to sit back with you and chill," she explained. She approached him and kissed him lightly on the lips as she handed him the drink. She then walked over to the big screen and bent over seductively. She looked back at Indie as he stood and sipped at the Smirnoff.

Indie eyed the butterfly on her ass as she loaded the DVD into the player. Disaya stood up, and before she could even turn around, she felt the sting of the glass break against her face as Indie slammed his Smirnoff bottle into her head with full force.

"Aghh!" she cried out as her hands went up to protect her face. Blood seeped through her fingers and onto the white carpet.

"You fucking sheisty ho," Indie yelled as he snatched her by the hair and pulled her back to her feet.

"Indie, stop it . . . baby, you're hurting me," she screamed loudly as she clawed at his strong hands that were now wrapped around her delicate neck.

He held her away from his body with one arm and pointed his finger in her face with the other. "You dirty-ass bitch! I treat you good. I took your stanking ass out of the projects, and you try to pull some okey-doke type shit on me!"

"What are you talking about?" Disaya asked in tears as she struggled to breathe.

"Don't fucking sit in my face and lie!" he yelled as he slammed her against the wall repeatedly. Tears built up in his eyes, and his stomach felt hollow from her deception. He looked at the engagement ring that he had given her and snatched it roughly from her finger, almost breaking it.

"Indie, no!" she cried as he took the most important thing in the world from her. "Baby, I don't know what you heard, but I haven't lied to you. I wouldn't lie to you. I've kept it real with you since the beginning. Baby, I love you."

She was pleading with him to believe her, and her eyes seemed sincere. He wanted to pull her into his arms and tell her that he could forgive her, that he could look past her disloyalty, but he knew that he couldn't. He had been a major player in the drug game for years, and he'd promised himself that he would never let a bitch knock him off his square, and this included her.

"YaYa, you could have had anything. I would've given you the world," he whispered as the pain of her actions set in.

"Baby, I didn't do anything," she cried.

Indie's facial expression changed, and he loosened his grip on her neck. "YaYa," he said, "I'm gon' ask you a question. I'm only gon' ask you this one time. I want you to think real hard before you answer me, okay, baby?"

Disaya tried to think of what she could have done to deserve this treatment from him.

"Okay," she whispered in reply.

"Have you ever done anything to hurt me? Have you ever lied to me?"

"I swear to God on our unborn child I haven't," she said convincingly as she touched her stomach.

Her words reminded Indie of the seed that she carried inside of her. They had just found out that she was pregnant. He remembered when she first told him, he had been the happiest man in the world. He had never felt more love for a person than he did that day, but now all of his love turned to hate as he stared at Disaya in disgust.

He closed his eyes and saw his brother lying in his casket, and rage overcame him. Before he could think about his actions, he raised his foot and kicked her with all his might. His foot collided with her stomach, and she dropped to her knees in excruciation.

"Aghh!" she screamed in agony. *God, please let my baby be okay*, she thought. It was the first thing that crossed her mind. She was in disbelief. She would never have imagined that Indie would try to hurt her. She definitely wouldn't have thought he would do anything to hurt their child.

"Bitch, shut up! All this time, it was you. You sat back and watched me go through that shit, and all along you were behind it."

"I didn't do shit!" she screamed. She held her stomach as she began to spit up blood.

"Oh, you didn't do shit, huh?" he asked as he grabbed her roughly and pulled her over to the wooden dinette set that occupied space in her basement. He sat her down forcefully and yelled, "Well, how do you explain this?" He stormed over to the entertainment center and pressed play on the VHS player.

As soon as the tape began to play, tears filled her eyes. *Oh my God! Where did he get this from?* she thought to herself as she watched in horror.

"Explain it, YaYa," he repeated as he watched her have sex with his brother.

She was at a loss for words. She couldn't explain herself because in her heart she knew that there was no talking her way out of the situation. He had discovered the one thing that she had tried so hard to hide from him. She closed her eyes as the hot tears steamed her face.

"Uh-uh. Bitch, don't close your eyes. Watch it. I've already seen it from beginning to end. I've been watching the shit over and over again for five hours, hoping that my eyes were playing tricks on me. You fucked my brother and then killed him."

Disaya's eyes got big as she shook her head. "No, I didn't. That's not me, Indie," she pleaded as she looked at the film. From the back there really was no distinguishing Leah from Disaya. With the identical hairstyles and the same tattoo on their asses, no one would be able to distinguish them from behind.

"Bitch, you still gon' lie to me, and I have your stupid ass on tape? I guess it's true what they say. You can take the girl out the ghetto, but you can't take the ghetto out of the girl," Indie said in disgust. "I should've left your ass in the gutter where I found you."

"It's not me," she whispered as she closed her eyes. Disaya couldn't bring herself to open her eyes, but was forced to when she felt Indie's fist collide with her face.

She knew that the video only got worse, but she opened her eyes and watched it anyway to avoid him striking her again.

"I want you to see this, so you'll know exactly why you are going to die," he whispered as his heart broke into two as he watched Disaya ride his brother's dick on camera.

I wish I could go back. I should have told him myself. I could have explained to him how it really went down, she told herself as her mind wandered back to when it all began. *I should have just told him.*

Indie went into his waistline and pulled out his chrome 9 mm. He cocked the gun and pointed the pistol at her head as he closed his eyes.

"Indie, please listen to me!" she screamed.

"Shut up!"

"No, baby, listen!" she cried. "I love you. You are right. I lied to you about some things. I kept a lot of shit from you because I was afraid that you would leave me if you knew the truth. That tape is not what it looks like. It doesn't show the truth. That is not me on that tape. Yes, I was there when Nanzi was killed, but I didn't know that it was going to happen. I had nothing to do with it."

"The tape don't lie, Disaya," he said in a low whisper. He still had the gun pointed toward her head.

"Indie, you know me," she begged.

"I thought I did," he said as he pulled the trigger.

Chapter 14

Disaya didn't feel the bullet hit her because Indie turned the gun at the last minute, causing the bullet to become lodged in the bookshelf behind her. He couldn't bring himself to kill her. He hated her to the bottom of his soul, but the look in her eyes stopped him from taking her life. "If you want to keep your life, don't try to contact me," Indie said as he walked up the stairs and out of the house.

"Indie!" she cried to him. "It wasn't me!" she cried out loud. She felt blood leaking from her womb, and she feared for the life of her child. Her baby was all that she had left of Indie, and she wanted desperately to hold onto his seed. She hurt so badly that she couldn't stand up straight.

When she heard footsteps come down the stairs, she hoped that Indie had come back for her.

"Indie?"

"No, YaYa, it's not Indie," Leah replied in a sinister tone. "Oh, look at you, YaYa. You chose this nigga. I've been watching you for weeks. Day in and day out the two of you have been baby shopping, going to doctor's appointments. I bet you thought your life was perfect, huh?" Leah peered closer at Disaya and noticed the slight bulge in her stomach. She bent down and touched the side of Disaya's face. She snickered at the sight of Disaya in pain. "You chose a nigga that would beat you like a dog while you carry his child. He ain't so fucking perfect now, is he? Life with him isn't as grand as you thought it would be, huh, bitch?"

"Bitch! You fucking set me up," Disaya screamed as she snatched her face away from Leah's hand.

"You set yourself up, YaYa. We could've been happy together. At first I came up with this whole plan so that I could get Indie out of your life. I contacted his brother and set up the hookup. I got the same tattoo as you and styled my hair so that I'd look just like you. I made sure that the camera never caught my face. I knew that Indie would never be able to forgive you for killing his brother," Leah said as she stood with her hands on her hips. She looked down and shook her head in disgust at YaYa.

"I didn't kill him, you did," YaYa protested as she held herself in pain.

"But it looks like you did," Leah replied. "That's really all that matters, YaYa. At first I did this to get him out of the way so that I could be with you. But you played me, bitch! You tried to drop me! You fucking slut, you only think about yourself. You made love to me when you wanted to and then acted like it meant nothing."

"Made love to you? Bitch, it was sex! I got paid to fuck with you, Leah. It didn't mean anything. I did it for the money!"

"Whatever, bitch," she said as she pulled a gun from her purse. "You remember this?" It was the same gun that she had used to kill Nanzi with.

Disaya's life flashed before her eyes as Leah pointed the gun at her. Indie's face popped into her thoughts, and the thought of losing her child caused her to beg for her life. "Leah, please. I'm pregnant. I'm sorry, I'll be with you. Just please get me to a hospital."

Leah laughed at her as she put the gun to Disaya's temple.

"Just fucking do it, Leah! What are you waiting for?" Disaya yelled as she closed her eyes and waited for the bullet to enter her dome.

"Bitch, please, I'm not gon' kill you. I'm going to hit your ass where it hurts. Indie is through with you and he's hurting right now. I'll give him the time that he needs to grieve, and when he's vulnerable we'll meet by chance. I know exactly what he wants in a woman. I learned that from you, so it will be easy to get him to fall in love with me. You told me everything, YaYa. I know how he likes to be fucked, what he likes to eat, how he likes to call you *ma*. Didn't your mama ever tell you not to tell your girls about your man? I'm going to take everything you ever had or wanted and make it mine, bitch. You'll never get out the hood. That little Prada Plan of yours . . . backfired. Indie was your only ticket out, and I made sure he'd never want to fuck with you again. I wonder what the police would say if I sent them a copy of that tape?" Leah wondered out loud.

"Leah, please, what do you want?" Disaya yelled as she placed her hands between her legs to ease some of the pressure building in her womb. The blood that painted her fingertips made her frantic, as she thought about the tiny life that was leaving her body.

"I wanted you," Leah said, her facial expression changing from cold to sincere in the blink of an eye.

This bitch is insane, YaYa thought as she noticed the glazed-over look in Leah's eyes. *God, please help me.* Disaya had never been a woman of faith before, but a part of her knew that only a higher power could save her at that moment. A thunderbolt of pain rushed through her abdomen, causing her to cry out.

"Leah, please, I didn't mean to hurt you. I was in it for the money," she whispered.

"Fuck you," Leah replied calmly as she walked over and grabbed Disaya by her hair.

Disaya could feel her hair snapping strand by strand, and her scalp felt as if it was on fire.

"Now, where is the money?"

"What money? I don't have any money," Disaya whispered.

"Wrong answer," Leah replied as she brought the steel handle of the gun down across Disaya's nose twice, splitting it wide open.

Disaya reached for her face as blood spewed through her fingers.

"Where is the money I gave you? If you want that bastard-ass baby of yours to make it, you better tell me," Leah threatened as she aimed the pistol at Disaya's stomach.

"It's in the safe," YaYa admitted as she doubled over and held her stomach tightly, curling up into a fetal position from the excruciation.

She tried to calm herself. Each time she cried she could feel blood gush between her legs, and she knew that her child's life was hanging on by a thread. She felt between her thighs, and the amount of blood that painted her fingers caused her to breathe erratically and panic began to cloud her judgment. Now was not the time to be proud or play tough. Yes, she was a bad bitch, but she would easily become submissive and cooperative to save the life inside of her.

"It's underneath the floorboards in the laundry room. Now please, Leah . . . I'm begging you." Disaya's pride had gone out of the window. She was willing to do anything to salvage the life growing inside of her womb.

"What's the combination?" Leah asked.

"Zero, eight, fourteen! Now get me some help. This isn't a fucking game. This is my life you are playing with!" Disaya screamed.

She watched as Leah walked into the laundry area and heard the click of the large industrial safe as Leah went inside to claim the riches. Leah emerged with a bagful of money and a satisfied grin on her face.

"I gave you your shit. That's all the money that I took from you and more," Disaya pleaded as she reached between her legs to relieve some of the mounting pressure. There was blood everywhere. "I'm losing my baby . . ." she whispered deliriously as she closed her eyes.

"Good. Next time you will think twice before crossing a bitch like me," Leah said coldly before turning to leave.

Disaya's vision became blurry as she watched Leah climb up the stairs. She felt a hatred for Leah that she didn't know existed.

"Aghhhh!" she screamed, trying to release some of the pain that she was feeling. Her body, mind, and heart were giving up on her, but she refused to give up. She needed help.

She crawled up the basement steps one by one and felt excruciating pain with each motion she made. She gasped when she saw the trail of blood that she was leaving behind as she inched forward.

Disaya dragged her body across the hardwood floor and finally made it to the kitchen. She frantically reached for her purse, spilling the contents all over the floor. She grabbed her cell phone. *This bitch thinks it over. This shit has just begun*, she thought hatefully. *If I lose this baby, I'm going to kill her*. Her fingers dialed 9-1-1, but before any words could leave her mouth, she passed out on the cold, hard floor. Indie's face was the last image that flashed through her mind before her entire world went blank.

The Future

She must learn from past mistakes and forget about the things she cannot change, while she attempts to right all the wrongs in her life.

Chapter 15

Indie couldn't stop the feeling that overwhelmed his chest. "The fuck was I thinking?" he asked himself aloud as he slammed his hand onto his steering wheel as he drove. He kept seeing the image of Disaya pulling the trigger and releasing the bullet that ended his brother's life. The scene kept playing over and over in his head, but he also couldn't shake the visual of Disaya lying on the floor, gripping her pregnant stomach as she bled between her legs. He kept telling himself that his actions were reasonable and that he had a right to hate YaYa, but deep down inside he felt guilty for allowing his rage to control him, causing him to lay hands on her. Inside his head he could see her smiling face. He could visualize the precious pregnant bulge of her stomach.

Guilt ate at him like a deadly disease, as he reflected on his actions. He had undoubtedly killed the baby she was carrying. His baby. His blind rage had made him do something that he swore he would never do—hit a woman. *How could I?* he asked himself. He answered his own question with a concise and quick answer: *Because she crossed you.*

He shook his remorse away as he thought about Disaya's betrayal. "The bitch is lucky *she's* still breathing," he muttered as he crossed the George Washington Bridge and headed into New Jersey.

The ride to his parents' house was unusually long. His thoughts filled the interior of his car, and his heart ached with an unstoppable pain. *I loved her. I chose her out of all the women that I could have had. I picked her, and she's the bitch who killed my brother,* he thought bitterly.

Indie could not believe that his judgment had been so off. Indie let his guard down when it came to Disaya. He had trusted her and would have given his life, if it meant that she could live. She had been his heart, and even though he knew that she was flawed from jump, he still gave her a chance because he thought that she was worth it. No one in his life had ever let him down to the magnitude that she had. She had committed the ultimate sin against him.

If Indie had not seen it with his own eyes, he would have never believed that Disaya could do something so horrible. She was coldhearted and untrustworthy. The woman he had loved and had deemed worthy of having his child was a phony with larceny in her heart.

Indie knew all of these things, yet he still could not stop the aching in his heart from losing a love like the one he had for Disaya. Finding out the truth about Nanzi's death brought back all of the emotions that he had thought were buried the day of the funeral. Now, knowing that he had been sleeping with the enemy, he felt as if he had been disloyal to his own family.

Indie pulled into his parents' driveway and sat silently inside of the car. He wasn't ready to go inside. He closed his eyes, and behind his lids was where Disaya dwelled. He could see every detail of her face in his mind. Her smile, her eyes, her lips . . . it was all embedded into his brain like a mental tattoo. He knew that it would be a long time before he would be able to get her out of his system. Everything about her was addictive to him. The sway of her hips, the infectious tone of her laughter, the gentleness of her caress. He would have to slowly wean himself off of her. Like a junkie to heroin, Indie had been addicted to his love for Disaya. It would not be easy, but he had to let go. If not, the results would prove deadly . . . for her.

Even looking up at the colonial house in front of him reminded him of her. The last time he had been to his parents' home was when he had first introduced Disaya to them, and he felt like he would never be able to escape her memory. *I've got to get the fuck out of here*, he thought as he stepped out of the car. He approached the house and opened it with his own key. The smell of soul food permeated the air as he made his way toward the kitchen.

The further he walked inside of the house, the more his heart tugged at him. Pictures of Nanzi lined the wall and Indie felt weak. He paused as he took in his brother's presence. He was deeply wounded, and because of Disaya he would never see Nanzi's face again. He could feel the pressure accumulating behind his eyes as he struggled to keep the floodgates up so that his emotions would not spill out.

He could hear his mother humming softly, and he walked silently toward her. He paused when he got to the kitchen entry-way. She was so busy cooking that she didn't even hear her son standing behind her.

"Ma?" he called out, his voice hardly recognizable.

Startled, Elaine dropped her dish towel and turned to face her son. When she saw the expression on his face, she rushed to his side. "Indie? What's wrong? What happened?" she asked.

Indie, stricken with rage and crippled with guilt, could only embrace his mother as he allowed himself to be weak in front of the one woman who wouldn't judge him for it. He knew that in his mother's arms he could find comfort and she would not look down at him or hold him to society's viewpoint that men should not cry. He needed to cry. He couldn't stop himself from weeping, but he did not want to because he was with the woman who loved him unconditionally. She would not look down on him or take advantage of his weakness. His arms wrapped tightly around her and he cried onto her shoulder.

"Indie, talk to me, baby. What's wrong? Is it YaYa? Did something happen to her and the baby?" she asked out of concern.

"Yeah, something happened, Ma," he said as he pulled back from her embrace. He stood upright and held the bridge of his nose as he regained his composure. "If I tell you what happened you might look at me differently." He turned to walk away.

"What about the baby, Indie? Is my grandbaby okay? I can see you are not ready to talk about it, but at least tell me that much. Where is YaYa?" she inquired.

"There isn't going to be a grandbaby, and I don't even know who the fuck YaYa is anymore," he said, malice lacing every word that he spoke. Before he walked away he added, "I'm leaving town in a couple days. I need to get away and clear my head."

"Running away from your problems won't fix them, Indie," Elaine said.

"This problem can't be fixed. I'm not running . . . just walking away from a bad situation before anyone else gets hurt."

"Well, what about the woman and child you are leaving behind, Indie? What is that girl going to do? You can't just run away from YaYa," Elaine stated.

"You wouldn't be defending her if you knew what I knew! This ain't some bullshit-ass fight that we're having. This is my life! You might as well forget about Disaya. . . . I wish I could," he yelled.

"Boy, you better lower your tone when you're addressing me," Elaine warned, her finger held out and one hand planted on her hip. "Now, you're right. I don't know what's going on, and obviously you don't want to tell me—"

"It's better for everybody if you don't know," he interrupted.

"Well, that's neither here nor there. I'm just trying to give you some good ol' motherly advice. You love this girl. Even a blind man can see that, Indie. You need to ask yourself, is what she did really that bad? We all do things in life that we regret. We all have skeletons tucked away in a closet. Is what she did so unfor-givable that you are willing to punish yourself? Because the hurt that you're feeling in your heart ain't gon' get much easier. It'll always be with you as long as she ain't."

"I'm leaving tomorrow," Indie concluded.

"Why, Indie? No matter how far you run, your problems with YaYa aren't going to go away. Where are you going to go?" Elaine asked.

"Anywhere but here. I can't stay here, Ma. I don't know what I might do to her if I stay. I've got to go." Indie resisted the urge to drive back to Manhattan and finish the business he had started with Disaya.

Elaine put her hand on her forehead as she closed her eyes and shook the tears away. She had never seen Indie this troubled and knew that she had to support him, no matter what. It was her job as a mother to be there for him even if she thought he was mak-ing a bad decision. "Okay, Indie. I understand, but at least go somewhere that is close to family. I just lost one son. I'm not try-ing to lose another. Now, I don't know what's going on, but do me a favor and go visit your grandma for a while. If you decide to stay, that's fine, but at least you will be near your family. Do that for me, okay?"

"Yeah, okay. If it'll make you feel better, I'll go to Houston," Indie stated. It didn't really matter where he went, as long as it put space between himself and Disaya. He kissed his mother on her cheek and then walked out of the room.

Elaine could see the distress in her son's face, and she had to force herself to bite her tongue just to keep from prying, but silently she wondered what could have occurred to make Indie so volatile. She could look in her son's eyes and see that his heart was broken. She only hoped and prayed that one day it would be mended.

With nothing but the clothes on his back and a trunkful of money, Indie regretfully left New York City. There wasn't enough distance on this earth that he could put between himself and Disaya, but he chose the next best thing and decided to relocate back to his Southern roots of Houston, Texas. He was born there, and it was where his grandmother still resided. He hoped that the pleasant memories of his childhood would drown out the horrid ones of his present life.

He knew that it would not be hard to set up shop in Houston. Being from New Yitty had its perks, as far as the dope game was concerned. He copped his work from a chick named Zya from Harlem, and she supplied him with the "fish scales." He had the best dope that money could buy. With a healthy East Coast connection, he was certain that, once the country boys got a taste of his product, it would be easy to take over and solidify a new spot at the top of the game. His focus would be on getting money so that he could forget about his past demons and hopefully relieve himself of some of the agony he felt over losing his only brother.

The drive was long, but gave him enough time to think and strategize on how he would introduce himself to Houston's drug trade and establish his own territory. He was only one man, so he would first have to acquire a team. He didn't want too many people around him. He would follow the same path that had led him to undetected success in New York, which meant only having a few people underneath him.

Indie didn't view himself as a hustler because hustlers were stupid. They stayed in the game past their prime and dealt with any and everybody who had the money to cop from them. Indie saw himself as a businessman. He was going to Texas to tap into an unclaimed market and would only deal with a select few. When the market was dry and he was at the top, he would make his exit and legitimize his money. He didn't want to ride the wave until it crashed on the shore. He would make sure that he got out before he showed up on the feds' radar. The streets were like his bottom bitch. He planned to pimp them into submission, but wanted to leave them alone before they grew tired and turned on him.

It was close to midnight when he arrived. and he could tell

from the darkened windows that his grandmother was asleep. The still night of the country atmosphere was foreign to him. He had never been able to see the stars in the city, and as he swatted at a mosquito, he knew his new surroundings would take some getting used to.

Indie knocked on the door and leaned against the frame as he waited for someone to answer.

"Who is it?"

He heard his grandmother's frail voice. "It's me, Nammy," he answered, calling her by the nickname that he had given her when he was just a baby.

"There's only one boy out here calling me Nammy. You were too dumb to say *Granny* and it just stuck with you all these years," she said lovingly as she opened the door and ushered him inside.

Indie chuckled and kissed his grandmother's cheek. She was ninety-one years old, but a living example that the saying, black don't crack, was true. "How are you, Nammy?" he asked.

"How are you, baby? When your mother called and told me you were coming, I knew something was wrong. You ain't never been keen to these parts, so what you running from? You in some kind of trouble?" she asked. Her gray hair was more like silver, and her light skin was as soft as silk.

"Nah, Nammy, I wouldn't bring any trouble to your doorstep. I contacted a realtor before I left New York, so it shouldn't be long before I cop my own spot. I just need a new environment," Indie replied.

"Well, you know you are always welcome in my home. We will talk more tomorrow. I'm going back to bed. This old woman has to get her beauty rest. I've already put fresh sheets on the bed in the guest room. There's a spare house key underneath the plant on the front porch. Make yourself at home, baby."

Indie nodded as he watched his grandmother walk up the stairs in her home. He heard the door close as she retired for the night.

After the twenty-six-hour drive, Indie was physically and mentally spent. He knew that his emotions were unstable. He had always prided himself on being in control and never allowing anything or anyone to dictate his happiness, but Disaya had changed that. By giving her the key to his heart, he had also given her access to his mental state. It was something that he had thought he could trust her with, but now he was left confused and enraged. The spectrum of feelings that were rushing through him would drive any man crazy, and he was having a hard time keeping his composure. He wanted revenge. He wanted to rewind the clock and be there for his brother. A part of him wished he had never met Disaya, but there was still a part that wished he could have changed her somehow and kept her in his life. The tiny piece of him that still loved her was what allowed him to let her live, but he knew that he would never be able to forgive her for what she had taken from him. Indie hated her for what she had done, and it was something that he would never be able to forget. The image of Nanzi's final moments would forever haunt him.

Indie collapsed onto the couch and released some of the stress that he was feeling with a long sigh. He leaned back as he tried to shake Disaya from his thoughts. Indie knew that he didn't have time to dwell on his past. He had to focus on his hustle . . . his business and find his niche in Houston's drug trade. He had one hundred and fifty thousand dollars to his name, but he knew that he could easily flip that four times over. All he had to do was find his way into the game.

Chapter 16

I ndie awoke the next morning to the smell of a fresh country breakfast. His lean, muscular frame was tense as he arose and made his way downstairs. As he entered the kitchen he noticed his grandmother standing near the counter with a needle in her arm.

"Everything all right?" he asked, startling her. She jumped slightly and fumbled to put the needle away, but Indie approached her and gently took the contents from her hands. He read the label and discovered it was insulin that she had just taken. "You've got to eat better than this, Nammy," Indie stated sternly. "You have diabetes. You can't eat the same way you used to."

His grandmother rolled her eyes at him. "Boy, sit down and eat this breakfast. These diabetes ain't gon' stop me from eating how I want to. The Lord is gon' take me when He wants to anyway. You got to learn to put it in God's hands, baby. He'll fix it all, if you have faith," she lectured.

Indie knew that there wasn't any point in arguing with his grandmother, so he left the subject alone and sat down. Just being in her presence was refreshing, and for the first time since his discovery of Disaya's deception, he found himself breathing easy.

"So, you ready to tell me what brought you all the way down here?" she asked as she sipped her coffee. "Your mother already told me about some girl you left."

Indie sighed and placed his fork on his plate. He was reluctant to have this conversation with his grandmother because he didn't want his family to know what Disaya had done.

"It's complicated, Nammy," Indie replied vaguely.

"There ain't no such thing as a complicated situation, just complicated people. Now there ain't much I haven't seen or heard in my ninety-one years, so quit dancing around my question and tell me what happened between you and this girl. Your mother says that you love the girl."

Indie sighed but knew that he didn't have a choice but to tell her something. "I used to love her," he admitted. "But you can't love someone you never really knew. She wasn't who I thought she was."

"A man doesn't just desert his responsibilities. It doesn't matter what she did, Indie," she replied.

"I don't want to talk about this right now," he stated. He kissed his grandmother's cheek and then walked out of the room. "I'm going to get dressed. I have to go out for a while. I won't be out late."

Indie headed toward South Park. It was the neighborhood that he had grown up in before he had moved away to New York, and he was well aware of how lucrative the blocks around that way could be. The evidence of a dilapidated system could be seen as soon as he turned onto MLK Boulevard. It was funny how every street in America named after the esteemed black leader was in the middle of a ghetto that was forgotten by society.

The Southern heat allowed all of the corner boys and ghetto girls to drape the concrete jungle like decorations on a Christmas tree. He parked his luxury vehicle around the corner, but when he stepped out of the car, his appearance was that of a wino. He wore dirty clothes and had splattered grime all over his face. To onlookers he appeared to be one of the many bums that cluttered their city's streets. But everything Indie did was strategic. By appearing to be homeless, he blended in without being noticed. He wasn't a threat to the local d-boys so they would be careless around him, allowing him to hear and see the things that went down among them.

Indie passed a group of young hustlers, wobbling drunkenly past them. He stumbled into one of them, to make his performance more real, even allowing one of them to push him down. He sat down on the concrete a few feet away from the crew and observed the way that the block worked. *These hustlin' backwards-ass mu'fuckas*, he thought as he noticed the carelessness in the drug operation. *Don't nobody do hand-over-fist sales no more? What the fuck is this, the eighties?*

Indie had to smirk to himself as he lifted the beer bottle, which had been drained and refilled with water, to his lips. He had to admit that although the method to their madness was different, the dope boys were definitely making money. There were fiends everywhere, just waiting to be served. He looked on as he watched a group of young hustlers patrol the block. They each played their roles. One re-up kid, one lookout, one seller, and an array of dudes to crowd the spot just because; inadvertently making the block hot.

The first thing Indie planned on doing once he took over was clean up their dirty habits. The extra niggas that were hanging around would be the same niggas who got caught up and tried to snitch their way out of trouble. He could tell that his presence was unknown, because the boys were too comfortable around him.

A white man pulled up on the block driving a Honda Accord, and the crowd of boisterous trap boys grew silent. Pondering eyes swept over the white man's car, and Indie watched as the group of men shifted nervously as they tried to figure him out. Inquiring minds wanted to know who the man was, but fear-filled hearts stopped anyone from asking any questions. Indie was curious to see how they would react to the situation. Depending on how they handled it, he would decide whether he could use them on his own team when the time came.

"Who the fuck is this Forrest Gump mu'fucka sitting on my block?! I know this mu'fucka better crank up that cheap-ass Honda and roll the fuck out before he have some trouble! I got something for his ass! Niggas lurking like they the feds!" one of the dope boys called out obnoxiously.

Indie heard the comment, and shook his head. *He's too loud. Loud niggas talk so much that they forget to do what they say they gon' do. If he was really prepared to do what it takes to move duke off his block, then the man would be gone already,* Indie thought. *That's what's wrong with the game now. Too many niggas wanna be Gotti.* Turned out that the white boy was just trying to score some rocks, and once the transaction was handled, everything went back to normal.

Indie watched every single transaction, he listened to every redundant conversation, and was observant of all the movement that was happening within his range of sight. He knew that he had to be perceptive in order to stay ahead of the game. He kept one hand on his .357 pistol, just in case anyone wanted to jump stupid. Stupid niggas did stupid things, and he would never be the hustler that was caught slipping. With his eyes and ears to the streets, he was hungry. Not because he necessarily needed the money, but because he wanted the power and the distraction that came with the game. Getting money was the only way he knew to keep his mind off of Disaya, and he embraced the streets, to welcome the mental interruption.

"Look at this ol' bummy-ass nigga!"

Indie turned his attention back to the loudmouth hustler as he clowned another young man who was coming up the street. It was obvious that the boy didn't have much. His appearance was disheveled, almost raggedy. He looked like a bum nigga without a purpose, but the youth in his face revealed that, whatever his circumstance was, it wasn't his fault. The humidity from the Texas heat had caused wet spots of sweat to form a ring around his dingy white T-shirt. The boy's hand-me-down kicks were begging to be thrown away. Even his jeans were dirty and worn.

"Man, Trey, why you always got jokes? I'm just trying to make it out here. When you gon' put your boy on?" the kid asked.

"I already told you, I can't use you right now. Mekhi ain't putting no more niggas on. I told you I'll pay you a little something to run some errands and shit for me," Loudmouth replied arrogantly. He didn't even show the boy enough respect to look him in the eyes.

"I'm just looking for work, fam. On some real shit. I need to be out here."

"A'ight, I got some work for you, little nigga," the hustler stated.

Indie watched the entire time and could see the hope filling in the young dude's eyes.

"Word? What is it? Whatever it is, I'm down," he stated eagerly.

"I want you to take care of my dogs," the hustler stated as he looked up and down the block while standing with his hands tucked securely in his pockets.

"Your dogs? Man, you got like six or seven! I ain't feeling that, yo', for real," the little dude stated.

"Yo, I ain't trying to hear all that shit, man. You trying to get this money or not? I see your mama out here selling her ass for rocks. I know you got your little sis at the crib to take care of. Your dirty ass ain't seen no running water in who knows how long. Now you can front on this money if you want to, or you can swallow your pride and fuck with these dogs. I don't like to get my hands too dirty. You can clean up after 'em. They shit all over the fucking place. I'll give you a couple hundred dollars to make sure they're straight."

The other hustlers around the block chuckled a bit at the situation. It was a job that nobody really wanted to do. It was a slum job; a way for the hustler to son the little dude, and a reason for him to become the flunky of everyone on the block who was above him.

Indie could see that the little hustler was placed between a rock and a hard place. Anybody could see that dude was embarrassed, but he obviously needed the cash because he relented.

"A'ight. What I got to do?"

"What you doing right now?" the hustler asked.

"Shit. Why, what's good?" the little dude asked.

"I need you to walk my dogs," the hustler replied. He motioned for one of his workers to open a gate and six ferocious pit bulls came out barking.

The little dude's eyes grew big. "W—where the leashes?" he asked, stuttering nervously.

The hustler ignored the dude and then snapped his fingers to get his dogs' attention. They were well trained and focused on their owner. "Pschh, pschh," he antagonized them with his teeth clamped tightly. "Get 'em!" he stated harshly and pointed at the little dude.

The dogs attacked on command, and the dude took flight, running like Flo Jo down the streets of Houston. Fits of laughter broke out throughout the group of unintelligent thugs.

Loudmouth called, "When you come back, I'll have your money, fam. Make sure they get a good workout in!"

Indie shook his head as he watched the hustlers make a fool of the young dude. He looked to be around seventeen or eighteen and didn't deserve the treatment he had received. He knew the streets. Embarrassment was a way to let a mu'fucka know that you were boss, but it was also a sure way to make unforeseen enemies. He had seen enough for today. He stood up and hobbled drunkenly back up the block and around the corner. He never created suspicion and was gone as quickly as he came, but he would be back tomorrow and the day after that, to make sure he knew what he was getting himself into.

Chapter 17

When Disaya finally opened her eyes, her head felt as if it would explode. The pounding migraine that plagued her brain made it hard for her eyes to adjust to the darkened room. She was drowsy from the medications that the doctor had given her, and even lifting her head off the bed seemed to be a huge task. Disoriented and in tremendous pain, it took her a while to gather her bearings. Her entire body felt as if it had been abused; there was no part of her that didn't ache, including her heart.

"My baby," she whispered frantically as she reached down and rubbed her stomach. Remembering the kick to her abdomen, she panicked. She was only six weeks and couldn't tell if her pregnancy had survived or not. The tenderness of her womb made her think the worst, and she began to panic. *There was so much blood*, she thought as she closed her eyes in an attempt to keep her tears at bay. *God, please tell me my baby is okay.*

Her fingers searched the bed for the call button, and when she finally located it, she pressed it anxiously to signal that she needed help. Seconds felt like hours as she waited for someone to come, and she was overwhelmed by the thought of losing the only thing that she had to live for. She pulled herself up, her weak limbs barely allowing her to move. When her bare feet hit the cold tile floor of the hospital, her knees almost buckled. Her legs were unstable, and as much as she wanted to, she couldn't will her legs to move. She didn't have enough energy and as she felt herself become faint, she reached for the call button and pressed it repeatedly, until finally someone came to her aid.

"What are you doing?" the doctor asked as she rushed to Disaya's side and helped her back into the bed. "You're supposed to be resting."

"Did I lose my baby?" YaYa asked. The tone of her voice was weak, and the tears that inhabited her eyes were unrelenting as they fell down her cheeks.

"That will be completely up to you," the doctor replied. "You have a strong child growing inside of you. Your baby survived the attack, but you are now what we consider a high-risk pregnancy. Your body attempted to miscarry your pregnancy, but we have regulated the bleeding, and we expect it to stop completely within the next day or so. However, even the slightest exertion of energy could cause you to miscarry. I'm suggesting bed rest until this baby is delivered, and we are prescribing special prenatal vitamins that will ensure healthy fetal development. More than likely you will go into labor prematurely, but if we can get you to even six or seven months, then your baby at least has a fighting chance. Do you understand everything that I'm telling you?"

Disaya closed her eyes. Her heart ached at the fact that she might deliver a premature baby, but she was still grateful. She nodded her head. "Yes, I understand."

"Do you have someone at home that will be able to help you out for the next couple of months?" the doctor asked.

"Yes, I'll be fine," YaYa lied. She had no one. She couldn't depend on anyone but herself, but she would find a way to manage. She didn't have a choice.

"The police may want to ask you some questions when you are

up to it," the doctor informed her. "My name is Dr. Marcellis. If you need anything or have any questions, just press your call button and a nurse will assist you."

"When can I go home?"

"Tomorrow. We're going to keep you one more night for observations."

The next day Mona rolled Disaya out of the hospital in a wheelchair. Disaya was unusually quiet. The swelling of her bruises made her face seem twice its normal size, and the silent tears that etched their signature on her cheeks revealed the misery that she was experiencing. The silence was uncomfortable, and Mona did not know what to say to comfort her friend. They had known each other a long time, and Mona had never seen Disaya in such disarray.

Disaya had always been the smart friend. She was the strategic one, the one that all the men wanted, and all the bitches hated. She was the leader, but in the blink of an eye, life had dealt her a losing hand that had cost her all of her riches. Disaya had gambled with her life and had lost the one man who had truly loved her.

"Do you want to stay at my crib for a while?" Mona asked as she drove toward her own apartment.

"No, just take me home, Mo," Disaya replied absentmindedly as she stared out of her passenger-side window.

"YaYa, you don't have to go back there," Mona whispered as she gripped Disaya's hand.

Disaya didn't respond, and Mona reluctantly turned the car around and headed toward Manhattan.

When they pulled up to her home, a lump formed in Disaya's throat, and her breathing became erratic as she stared up at her brownstone. She slowly made her way out of the car, and with the help of Mona she climbed her front steps one by one. Mona opened the front door as Disaya stood weakly on the threshold.

When she entered the house Indie's scent invaded her nostrils, and the thought of him quickly clouded her brain. "He's really gone," she whispered.

Her voice was unrecognizable. It was almost childlike. She sounded like a little girl who had lost her parent in a congested crowd. She had lost her love . . . her king . . . her world. Indie was her life. The pain was crippling, and YaYa knew she had no one to blame but herself.

Mona guided her up the stairs and into her bedroom, where she removed Disaya's hospital-issued clothing. Mona's eyes watered when she noticed the black-and-blue marks all over Disaya's body. She had to admit that Indie had fucked her girl up, but she could not say that she blamed him, though. Disaya had been playing with fire by fucking with Leah; they both had danced with the devil by choosing to sell their body for money.

Mona only hoped and prayed that Disaya's baby made it through the ordeal.

Mona slipped a silk gown over Disaya's head and fluffed her pillows before tucking her into bed. She grabbed the Tylenol that the doctor had prescribed and gave Disaya two pills.

"I can't believe this is happening to me," Disaya cried helplessly as she curled up beneath the covers.

Mona sat on the edge of the bed and rubbed Disaya's head softly. "I know, girl," she comforted as she thought of her own fate. "I know. Everything will be okay. I promise it will get better."

Disaya cried so hard that her eyes strained to produce more tears. Her chest heaved up and down. The more she tried to contain her pain and stifle her heartache, the more it hurt. Within half an hour she had cried herself to sleep. The mixture of exhaustion and medication put her in a temporary state of peace.

Mona arose and went into the basement to clean up the mess that had been made. There was a dried-blood trail leading from the kitchen all the way down the steps, and the overturned furniture signaled that there had been a struggle. Her stomach churned at the gruesome sight, and she shook away her own tears. She had to be strong for her girl. Disaya had always been in Mona's corner, and now it was time for her to step up and take the lead to return the favor.

She went into Disaya's cleaning closet, pulled out some supplies, and filled a bucket with bleach and water. She sighed as she looked at the mess before her. She couldn't believe that the wind had blown their lives in the direction that it had. She remembered when they were two little girls coming up together, trying to raise themselves in a fucked-up world. Now they were grown women; one carried an infectious and deadly disease while the other carried a baby who was struggling to be born into a fucked-up world.

As she got on her knees and began to scrub the bloodstained carpet, she silently prayed that God would spare her friend the pain of losing a child. Although they had each chosen their lifestyles, neither had ever thought about the impact that their irresponsible actions would have on their futures. Mona regretted the day that she had ever stepped foot inside Elite. It was where all of their problems began. She couldn't help but wonder how they both had ended up this way.

She wanted to blame it on their childhoods. Both came from broken homes. Thrown into the system at such a young age was devastating to their upbringing. Their entire perspective on life was changed the moment that they were forced away from their homes. All little girls need direction, but in a system where no one cares about abandoned children, they were left to find their own way in life. Misguided, unloved, and vulnerable to human deception, they both sought happiness in the wrong way.

They never had anything, so sacrificing their bodies and disrespecting their womanhood seemed like a small thing to give up as long as they were getting paid. Opening their legs to anyone who could afford it, they never realized that they were inviting disease and heartbreak. They completely destroyed their own self-worth. Two young women who could have been anything in life had been reduced to tricks and whores.

Mona wanted to blame Ronnie B, but deep inside she knew that the only person that was to blame was herself. It didn't matter to her that she never had a mother. She had never been able to depend on anyone in her life. Self was all she knew, so she felt stupid for allowing herself to be manipulated. Now because of her shallow viewpoint and thirst for money, she was being judged by God in the worst way possible. He was killing her slowly, with a disease that society outcast you for. She was HIV positive.

Filled with a lot of regrets and little hope, she did not know where her life would lead her. It seemed that her time was about to expire, but before she left this earth she was determined to help Disaya put her life back in order. She wasn't going to let YaYa throw her life away, just because it was not perfect. Fuck a nigga, fuck a dollar; Disaya didn't need either.

YaYa had all that she needed in the world growing inside of her. It was what had been missing in their lives from the very beginning. YaYa was harvesting love; a baby that was made between two people who loved each other at one point, regardless of how they felt now. Disaya's baby would never stop loving her, and Mona was envious and proud all at the same time. After all of the bullshit they had allowed themselves to endure . . . Disaya had found the one thing they both desperately needed. Love.

Chapter 18

Indie looked at his Movado watch as he leaned against his car and stared up and down the block. This time he wore his normal clothing. He had watched little man for a week and knew every single move that he made. He waited patiently for the kid to come strolling up the block, and like clockwork, a few minutes later he appeared. *I'm going to have to teach him not to be so predictable. If I was a nigga lurking to get him, he would've been got,* Indie thought as he mentally noted the flaw. The kid walked slowly as the pit bull on the chain jerked violently forward. Indie smirked because it looked like the dog was walking the kid instead of the other way around.

The average eye would have overlooked the young'un. They would have taken advantage of him, as the local hustlers in Houston had already proved, but Indie understood the kid. He had done his research and found out that the boy was the eldest of two children. His mother was badly addicted to crack cocaine, which left her son Chealsey and younger daughter Trina to fend for themselves. Indie knew that he needed to be put on. He was merely a boy trying to become a man and take care of his family. Indie saw hunger in the kid and immediately decided to put him on.

The type of hunger he had wasn't something that could be acquired. It was an innate instinct that came from living without. The fact that he had been disrespected by the locals for so long only added icing to the cake. Indie knew that the kid had no loyalty to the street hustlers he knew because they had disrespected him for so long and kept him starving. Indie was about to feed the little nigga, and because of that he knew that he would have his psychological loyalty for life. Even if he was tempted to betray Indie, the kid never would, because Indie would be the first one to give him a chance to eat.

"Yo, Chase, let me holla at you for a minute, fam," Indie stated as the boy walked by.

The kid stopped and eyed Indie suspiciously. He looked behind him to make sure Indie was talking to him.

"Chase? You got the wrong nigga, homie. That ain't my name," the boy responded as he resumed his chore of dog walking.

"Chase, you want to make money, or you want to keep walking those stanking-ass dogs?" Indie asked bluntly.

"Look, fam, my name ain't Chase," the dude stated.

"I know your name *Chealsey*. You live in the Southland Projects with your baby sister Trina and your mother Ava, who is badly addicted to drugs. You wear the same clothes because there is no money to get you anything new. You steal packs of bullshit noodles from the corner store because there is nothing for you and your sister to eat at home. I'm trying to help you eat, fam," Indie stated seriously as he stared intently at the young soldier in front of him. "Your name is Chealsey. I know your name, fam, but from the looks of things, niggas out here don't respect Chealsey. You fuck with me, I'ma help you get respect, but I can't fuck with Chealsey. Chealsey walks other niggas' dogs. Chealsey run errands. Chase is the nigga you gon' become if you let me teach you the game."

"Chase?" the boy repeated as he shook his head from side to side.

"Them cats you working for have chased you off the block, reducing you to their flunky. Now it's your turn to chase a nigga off the block. You trying to eat or not, Chase?" Indie stated.

"Man, you talking that fed shit. I don't know what you talking about," Chase replied. He was weary of Indie. He had never seen him around, and his obvious East Coast accent let Chase know that he was an out-of-towner. Indie knew things about him that he had tried his hardest to hide from everyone. The only people he knew who could find out that much information on someone were the feds. *He could be them black and blue boys. I ain't never seen him before. He's probably an undercover narco or something.*

Indie frowned and shook his head. "Nigga, I ain't a fucking cop." He hit the release button on his key chain, and his trunk popped open slightly. He stepped over to the rear of the car, his natural swagger commanding attention. "Let me show you something," Indie stated, his tone showing his authority and not giving Chase the option to say no. He could see that he was going to have to spell it out for Chase in order for him to really understand what he was offering.

Chase tied the leash around a fire hydrant, and the dog began to bark furiously. He reluctantly stepped toward Indie.

Indie lifted the trunk then pressed his key chain a second time. The floor of the trunk slid up and revealed a compartment below where ten bricks sat sparkling inside.

The off-white twinkle of the neatly wrapped packages of cocaine made Chase's eyes widen in surprise. Everything that he had been trying to achieve was sitting in front of him. He could see his struggling past dwindling in his mental rearview. He was seventeen in biological years, but mentally he felt the exhaustion of an old man. His entire life had been about surviving.

As far back as he could remember his mother had never been the type of parent that he needed her to be. In his younger, more naive years he even remembered his mother sending him to the local d-boys to retrieve vials of crack cocaine. In the morning instead of awaking to the smell of bacon and eggs, he awoke to the pungent stench of baking soda and coke. He had learned that in life there were simply two types of people: the haves and the have-nots. He was sick and tired of being the latter.

"I'm putting a plate in front of your face. What you decide today can change your life tomorrow. Now I'm going to ask you one more time. You eating or what?" Indie asked.

"Chase, huh?" Chase responded as a smile spread across his face. He extended his hand and embraced Indie, knowing that he had just been given the chance he had waited so long for.

"Chase, my nigga," Indie affirmed, pleased with Chase's acceptance. "Chealsey was the boy . . . I'ma teach you how to become the man."

The pit bull barked angrily as he lunged at Indie. Indie pulled a pistol from his waistline and handed it over to Chase. "It's time for you to send a message. Send them niggas that shits back in a box."

Chase took the gun, adrenaline pumping because he had never actually held a piece of steel before. He aimed it at the pit, turning his hand sideways.

Indie shook his head and scoffed as he shook his head and asked, "What the fuck are you doing? Straighten out ya' hand, fam." Indie turned Chase's hand until the young boy was holding the pistol straight. "That sideways shit is for niggas that don't really bust they guns. They're trying to look cool. When you pull your gun be ready to pop off. Keep your hand straight and steady, so your aim will be on. That sideways shit will get you slugged first."

Chase nodded his head, absorbing the knowledge that Indie was dishing out, then he pulled the trigger. The bullet was symbolic. It was the death of his hard-knock life, and as he got into the car with Indie, he breathed in new life as a new man . . . Chase.

"All that shit you see in the movies about being a gangster will get you locked up," Indie explained as he sat across from Chase, schooling him on the rules of the game. "The real hustlers that are getting money are the ones who move silently, nah mean?

You've never even heard of the real men who run these cartels. Nicky Barnes, you heard of him?"

"Yeah, that's dude who used to get it in New York back in the day . . . who haven't heard of him," Chase replied.

"What about Rich Porter and 'em?" Indie grilled.

"Yeah, the Harlem cats, right?"

Indie nodded and smirked. "Ok, okay, I see you know a little bit of something. What about Rayful Edmond?"

"D.C.," Chase concluded with ease.

"Well, let me tell you something about them niggas. They're not real gangsters. They're the faces that the real hustlers put out there to distract the feds. They are expendable. The real boss is the man behind the hood man, you feel me? They are the faces that never get caught up in court cases, and if they do, the judge and everybody in the judicial system are paid off before the trial even begins. Those are the real hustlers, the real gangsters. Everybody else is just the fall guys. You ever heard of Khadafi from the Midwest, Toni from Jersey, or the Cartel in Miami?" he asked.

"Nah, I ain't never heard of them," Chase admitted.

"Exactly, because those are the real hustlers. They are the invisible hand that pushes the buttons. I got money in the Yitty for five years without as so much as a traffic ticket. That's what I want to build here, an empire that flies under the radar."

Chase simply nodded his head as he tried to absorb Indie's every word. They had been going over techniques of the street for over two months, and he listened attentively, never growing bored.

"You can't have any emotion when you're out there." Indie's thoughts went to Disaya right after he said it. It was true, emotions were a weakness. They were threatening to cripple him at that very moment, so he continued without interruption. "If a nigga don't have your money on time, make him get it. If you have to ask more than once, kill him. We are not in the business of making fools out of niggas. Embarrassing grown men can be deadly. They'll feel a certain way about it, and you will make an enemy out of him. So don't play the showboating games with these niggas. If they don't have your paper, it's curtains. Be feared, but respect and recognize any man that you feel is on your level. All of them cats on your old block who clowned you and didn't show you love before . . . get rid of 'em. Out the gate, niggas have to take you seriously. They got to know you mean business," Indie preached.

Indie looked around the dilapidated project apartment. He knew that he would have to get Chase and his baby sister out of that environment because, once Chase started making money, he would be susceptible to robbery in the middle of the ghetto. "You know how to cook coke?" Indie asked.

"Yeah, I've seen it done," Chase responded.

"Seeing and doing is two different things, baby, two different things," he repeated as he stood and pulled an ounce of out of his baggy jean pockets. He put it on the table. "The objective is to bring twenty-eight back without losing any. I need you to learn how to cook it because you are going to teach the bitches we recruit how to bring it back." He stood and walked over to the stove.

Indie grabbed the box of baking soda out of the back of the refrigerator, a glass container, and a pot, then began his routine. It was something he had not done in years because he had hired people to do his dirty work, but cooking coke is like riding a bike; once you learn how to do it . . . you never forget. He had it down to a science, and he noticed how good of a student Chase really was. He blended a batch of cocaine over the stove like a skilled chemist.

"What about Khi-P?" Chase asked. "He's known for beasting with niggas over his blocks. He comes blazing first, asking questions later."

Indie scoffed. "Khi-P?"

"Mekhi, he's like king around here," Chase revealed.

"The king, huh?" Indie patronized. "He doesn't want it with

me," he assured. "Especially not right now. I'm in the mood to murk a mu'fucka. If he got beef, I'll handle it. You don't need to worry about that. Now tell me everything you know about his operation."

"Khi-P is the man in Houston. He runs every trap house in town. Niggas ain't gon' be trying to go against the grain. Khi don't take lightly to traitors. He gonna feel real disrespected if we start selling on his blocks," Chase said.

"What he pushing?" Indie asked. "You know who he cops his work from?"

"This Mexican cat named Lupé, he's running it straight here from Mexico."

Indie wasn't worried about Mekhi's organization, because Indie had better dope. His shit was straight off the boat from Cuba. He had pure coca that had never been stepped on, and he didn't plan on doing it for the stretch. He knew that he needed to keep the potency so that he could steal his competition's customers. It was a known fact that any dope coming from Mexico was not of the same quality in comparison to that from Cuba or Colombia.

He had watched Khi-P's blocks for weeks, and their sloppy habits would be his downfall. He was ready for war, or whatever else it may take in order for him to gain control in Houston. He had his first loyal worker in Chase and was confident that, once he was done schooling him, he would be a killer and a hustler in his own right.

Indie was lost in his thought when Chase's mother came in. She was obviously blasted on her latest fix, and her eyes were dilated. She was filthy, her hair matted, and her once womanly shape was nonexistent. She looked like the living dead and made Chase instantly embarrassed.

"Hey, baby," she said as she looked around the kitchen. "What you cooking in here that smell so good?" she asked. "Let Mama taste."

Chase was beyond the point of anger. He had seen his mother do unspeakable acts just to score the very thing he was about to commit to sell to someone else's mother, but that was the way things were. Chase wasn't the one strong enough to break the cycle. He wasn't trying to be a martyr, just to make enough money to take care of his sister.

"Let me finish up in here, Ma. It'll be here for you when my company leave," he stated. "All I got is a twinky for you, though, and shit over here ain't free. You got some money?"

"Yeah, baby, Mama got money right here," she said as she went inside her bra and pulled out some crumpled ones.

"I'll take care of you in a few. Go in the back," Chase instructed.

Indie did not show his shock, but instead respected Chase's hustle. He knew then and there that he had not made a mistake in choosing Chase. If he had the heart to sell crack to his own mother, there was no limit to what he was capable of doing. The sight broke his already broken spirit, but he knew that the situation was not uncommon in households with drug-addicted parents.

Indie reached in his pants pockets and pulled out a honey-bun-sized knot of money. He peeled off a sufficient amount and put it in Chase's hands. "Tomorrow go and grab you and your sis an apartment somewhere low-key. Make sure it's in a better area too, but not too good where you will have white people peeking out they blinds trying to see how you living," Indie instructed.

Chase took the money. He was hesitant because no one had ever given him anything without wanting anything in return. He felt like less of a man for accepting it, but the hunger pains in his stomach and the roaches scattering across the floor told him to be smart. He slapped hands with Indie and nodded. "Thanks, fam. I'ma pay you back every dollar. I swear on everything. I got you," he promised, endearing himself to Indie, sincerely grateful for the loan.

"Fuck all that. That's just the tip of the iceberg. Don't worry about it. Repay me with your loyalty."

"No doubt, fam, you got that," Chase replied.

Indie departed and made his way back to his grandmother's.

He was excited about beginning a new life, starting a new hustle
in a new city, yet old memories plagued his heart at every moment of every day.

He picked up his iPhone and thumbed through the contacts
until he reached Disaya's name. Her smile called out to him, urging him to pick up the phone. He really just wanted to know how
she was. It had been two months since he had abandoned her,
and every day he tried to find a way to forgive her. He couldn't
and knew that he never would. In fact, the line between his love
and hate for her was so thin that he did not know where one
ended and the other began.

As he pulled onto the dirt road that led to his grandmother's,
he cursed silently as the tiny rocks bounced off of his car. He
threw his phone in his passenger seat and maneuvered slowly
through the thick country darkness until he arrived.

As soon as he pulled into the driveway he saw his grandmother
peeking through the curtains. It did not matter how late he came
home, she always waited up for him. Indie smiled at her concern
and walked into the house. His heart was full of burdens, and his
head clouded with thoughts of Disaya.

"Hi, Nammy," Indie greeted as he leaned down to kiss her
cheek.

"What's weighing down your soul, Indie?" she asked, her wisdom making her aware of his disposition.

Indie was astonished that she knew him so well, but still he denied it. "There's nothing wrong, Nammy. Just get some rest. I'll
see you in the morning."

Indie ascended the steps and retired to his temporary bedroom.
He lay back on his bedspread, his hands tucked behind his head.
He inhaled deeply then exhaled slowly as he wondered how
much longer he would be haunted by visions of Disaya and the
child he most surely had murdered in an act of rage. He did not
doubt that she was hurt by his actions, but fuck it, he was hurt by
her actions, and she had proved that she was the more deceptive
of the two.

Chapter 19

Every day Indie schooled Chase on a new aspect of the trade of the streets. He was in no hurry to get in the game. He didn't want to rush it. He would know when the time was right. In the meantime, he trained his first soldier as if he were preparing to go to war against a thousand armies. Indie had to mentally reshape Chase. He had to teach him to fear no one, while at the same time making everyone fear him.

Chase became a killer. He wasn't meant to be a right-hand man, so Indie didn't train him as such. He was teaching him how to become a goon. A goon is the one who goes in to murk a mu'fucka when there's an issue. He's the nigga that'll bag your bitch in front of your face and dare you to say a word. He's the one that will talk shit to a giant because he knows he has the artillery to back it up. To be prepared to die as long as you take a nigga with you was what Indie instilled in Chase's head. It was his motto. Chase was the muscle, and his aggression toward the world as a result of his upbringing fueled the fire that allowed him to be so ruthless.

The difference between Chase and the average was that he was smart. He analyzed everything and was valued by Indie as an asset to the team.

Indie made sure that Chase had a marksman's aim and was knowledgeable in every aspect of the game. He made Chase practice shooting at both still and moving targets. He made him pull triggers for hours, until the instinct to jump at the sound of the blast disappeared. That split second when the bullet erupts from the chamber and the shot deafens your ears could get you killed if you froze.

Chase used to freeze, until he met Indie . . . now Chase didn't freeze. He barely even heard the bang, because he became so used to the sound. He learned how to cook the coke and quickly mastered it, passing his skills on to his little sister. She in turn recruited four of her best friends and taught them the game.

At first Indie was against having teenage girls cook up his product, but once he thought about the logic, he agreed. Trina and her friends were only fifteen years old and in their second year of high school. If anything ever went down with the cops, they could not be charged as adults, and juvenile sentences carried little to no time at all. It was genius, actually. They would be taken to juvenile court and have their records expunged at the age of eighteen.

Indie kept their pockets laced and paid each one of them five hundred dollars a week for their services. To teenage girls they were in heaven, so the arrangement worked out nicely and stayed low-key, since everything took place in an apartment that Indie had leased under an assumed name.

Even Chase's gear had changed. Because of the fifteen-hundred dollars Indie paid him each week, Chase was able to get fresh, and because he had never had anything, he quickly adopted a fetish for clothes and shoes. Indie became his mentor, and it was something that Indie did not take lightly. He knew what it felt like to be disappointed by someone you loved. The love of his life had hardened him and cut him so deeply that he was sure he would never trust another again. He didn't want to be that disappointment to Chase, so he embraced their close friendship and tried to show Chase all that he knew in and out of the streets.

Indie did not want to be the one responsible for turning another black man on to the street life. It was simply a means to an end. He still had plans of getting out of the game, but right now he needed it. He needed it like he needed air. He was trying to shift his focus and forget all that he had left behind, but in doing so he was compromising everything that he stood for.

He had wanted to make an honest woman out of YaYa. He wanted to make her his wife and for her to bear his children . . . his child; the child he had brought harm to. A part of him didn't want to contact Disaya, not because of what she had done, but because of what he had done. His rage was uncharacteristic. He never wanted to feel that much pain and anger again, which was the true reason he had chosen to move so far away. Her betrayal led to his emotional anguish. He felt like a child who had been let down on Christmas by his mother. His love for YaYa had been just that great. It had transcended the typical format of woman-man, girlfriend-boyfriend. She had been his nigga, his friend; she was the one person he rocked with when the rest of the world didn't understand him. She was the yin to his yang, the Bonnie to his Clyde, and the purpose to his life. She used to be his rib, and without her he was suffering, but he knew that if he stayed with her, she would suffer for what she had done to his brother. He had to leave.

He still felt obligated to her for some strange reason, and because of it, each month he sent her five thousand dollars to make sure that she was maintaining. He never put his name or a return address on the envelope, but he sent it all the same, even though it was only to soothe his own conscience.

Indie promised himself that he would never betray the trust of another, which was why he was careful in the way he dealt with Chase. Chase was eager to learn and looking for someone to mold him. Indie took that responsibility seriously, and once he made enough money to exit the streets for good, he planned to take Chase with him if he proved worthy.

Chase sat shotgun with Indie as he maneuvered through the

city streets, their destination: Mekhi's most profitable trap house. Chase hadn't been around since he had linked up with Indie, and the hood fellas around the way had not seen him since he had begun working for Indie. He wasn't the same man that he used to be, and the hood was about to witness his transformation.

Indie pulled up to the same curb where he had discovered Chase. "You ready?" Indie asked. He wanted to be sure that Chase was built for what was about to happen, because after today there would be no turning back. It was all or nothing.

"Yeah, I'm good, fam," Chase responded. He got out of the car, grabbed the large box out of the trunk of Indie's car and approached the hustlers posted against the brick apartment building.

"Yo, Chealsey, nigga. Where the fuck you been? Nigga, you've been missing with my fucking dog for weeks, and you ain't been by to take care of the other ones either, mu'fucka! Where the fuck you been?" The hustler who Indie had labeled Loudmouth popped off as soon as he noticed Chase crossing the street. "Nigga, I'ma smack fire from your simple ass if you ain't got my fucking dog," he threatened.

Chase kept his cool, letting the insults bounce off of him. "I got your dog, family," Chase mumbled with casual nonchalance as he handed the dude the box.

"Fuck is this?" Loudmouth sneered as he opened the lid. When he saw the contents, he dropped it instantly, and his once prized dog's head rolled onto the sidewalk.

Chase had saved the badly rotten dog's head in a deep freezer entirely for this moment.

Loudmouth's bewildered eyes raised just in time to see Chase come out of his waistline with a snub-nosed pistol.

"I got your dog, mu'fucka," he repeated sarcastically as he filled his victim up with lead. He didn't stop shooting until his chamber was empty. Each hollow was like get-back for all of the insults, all of the degradation, and all of the disrespect that the hustler had showed him over the years.

The gunshots triggered pandemonium on the block as bystanders fled for cover, purposely not looking at the scene. The less seen, the less could be told, and nobody wanted to be a snitch, so everyone worried about their own safety and minded their business.

A few of the other hustlers were halted by Chase's pistols as he pulled a second identical gun from his waistline and cockily aimed it their way.

"Y'all niggas want to die, or y'all niggas want to get this money? Those are your only choices, choose one," Chase stated.

"Chealsey, man, we don't want no trouble," one of the hustlers spoke up humbly.

Hearing the dude call him by the name that people had deemed him weak under enraged him. He knew that he had to make an example. He approached dude and put the pistol directly against the guy's forehead. "Let me say this once so everybody can hear it. Chealsey is the nigga y'all *use* to chump. Chase is this new nigga that's putting the flame under your ass. Don't let the wrong name fall out of your mouth again. A'ight, shawty?"

"Y—yeah, Chase. My fault, man, I ain't know. Chill out baby, it's all love," the dude begged.

Chase removed the pistol and kept it aimed, then continued. "Now, I don't have no personal beef with y'all niggas, but this block right here don't belong to Khi-P no more." His voice was authority-filled and unafraid as he spoke down to the hustlers, letting them know that if they valued their lives it would be best to cooperate. "Y'all see that nigga sitting over there in the lac? That's boss. These here are his blocks now. Now you can continue to get money on this block, but you pushing our product now, understand?"

The hustlers were silent as they eyed one another, yet they nodded uneasily in agreement. They felt like they were stuck in a lose-lose situation because they feared their boss Khi-P just as much as they feared the gun being waved in their faces at the moment.

Chase noticed the hustler he had held at gunpoint was eyeing him with the screw face. He walked up to him and extended his open hand to show dude that there were no hard feelings. The dude reluctantly opened up his core for a handshake and embrace, and unexpectedly Chase slumped him against the brick wall.

Never embarrass a nigga. He'll feel a kinda way about it, and you'll make unknown enemies. Indie's words echoed in his head. He had just gotten rid of one less nigga with larceny in his heart. He continued his shakedown as if nothing happened.

"Y'all can get twenty points off each package. It's not a negotiation. You work for Indie, or you don't work these blocks," Chase said. "I'ma be around these parts every day. If I see anybody pushing any other product besides ours then I'ma leave you stinking like ya mans and 'em down there." Chase hopped in Indie's awaiting car, and before he rolled away Indie threw up a peace sign.

"You did good, fam," Indie stated.

"No doubt, baby. I learned from the best," Chase answered. His adrenaline pumped furiously. He had never felt so much power in his life. There was no remorse for his actions. He knew that he was a killer. Murder was too easy for him to commit.

Chapter 20

YaYa looked at the cashier's check that was in her hand. It was made out for five thousand dollars. They had been coming once a month ever since she'd gotten home from the hospital. The checks were never accompanied by a note, but Disaya knew who they were from. The fact that Indie cared enough to send her money gave her hope that maybe one day he would forgive her and come back. She was grateful for his financial assistance because without it she would have been out on her ass.

She touched her baby bump and rubbed it gently. "Just hang on, little diva," Disaya whispered sadly as she brushed a tear away. "Stay in there for a couple more months. Mommy needs you. You're all I have left."

YaYa was almost five months along, but her pregnancy was not an easy one. The bleeding had never stopped, and although it scared her, all of her doctors told her that everything was progressing and that her baby was okay for the time being. She had been through seventy-three long and miserable days without her man.

Two and a half months had passed since Indie had left her, and he hadn't tried to contact her at all. She wanted to give him his space, but at the same time she needed him to be there. There were days when the loneliness consumed her and she thought that she would go crazy without him.

Every day she wanted to pick up the phone and dial his number, but something always stopped her. What could she say to him? How could she justify her actions when even she herself knew that she did not deserve to be with a man as good as him? She needed him in her life, but having his child was an adequate substitute, and the thought of being a mother was starting to feel natural for her.

Her upcoming motherhood filled a void in her life. She had once sought fulfillment in material possessions, but because of Indie, she knew that she was worth so much more. She hoped that Indie would be able to share in her newfound joy. She wanted him to see that he had changed her for the better, but realistically she knew that he might never forgive her, and was never coming back to her. Leah had made sure of it, and the taste of revenge was still fresh on her tongue.

Hate was the only word to describe how Disaya felt about Leah. She had ruined Disaya's life by taking away the one man who had ever loved her for more than the expensive orgasms that she provided.

In fact, if Disaya ever saw Leah again, she knew that she wouldn't be able to hold back. She couldn't be responsible for her actions if they ever crossed paths, but in her current state, there really was nothing that she could do. Bedridden and in fragile condition, her main priority was to keep her baby safe. She would figure everything else out after she gave birth.

Disaya heard a knock at the door and tucked the check underneath her pillow.

"Bitch, what are you knocking for?" Disaya called out.

Mona walked into the room. Her appearance was changing by the day. Her hair had grown thin, and she seemed to be tired all the time. The dark and sunken circles beneath Mona's eyes made her look sickly, and YaYa instantly knew that Mona had not been taking her medications. Mona had been battling depression ever since she had come to live with YaYa, and it seemed that she was in denial regarding her HIV-positive status. She refused to take any prescription that the doctors gave her, and because of it she stayed in poor health.

Mona walked to Disaya's bedside and replied, "I'm not gon' be too many more of your bitches. You're lucky you're pregnant and I can't beat your ass right now."

"Yeah, whatever . . . bitch," YaYa responded with a smile. "How are you feeling, Mo?"

"Useless," Mona replied.

"You're not useless, Mona. I need you," Disaya stated sincerely. She rubbed her growing belly and took Mona's hand. "We need you, Mo. We're all we've got . . . don't give up."

When Mona didn't respond, YaYa decided to change the subject. "Did you bring my food?" Disaya asked with a wave of her hand.

"Yep, take this stanking-ass shit. I don't know any black people who actually eat anchovies on their pizza," Mona said playfully as she sat the cardboard box on the side of the bed. "How are *you* feeling today?"

"I'm okay. I'm just tired of being in this damn bed. I need to get out of here. I need some sun or something. I feel like I'm hiding out in this house," Disaya complained. "I remember when Indie first bought this place for me. It was my dream house. I haven't even been here a full year, and my household is already in shambles, Mo. I just can't help but think that all of this is my fault."

"You need to shut that shit up," Mona stated harshly. "I'm tired of hearing that, for real, YaYa."

"What?" YaYa responded in confusion.

"All that 'woe is me' shit you talking . . . you've got to stop blaming yourself for what happened. You didn't do this. Yeah, you played a part in Nanzi's death, but you ain't the bitch who pulled the trigger. Leah gon' get hers in time, but right now she should be the least of your worries. You need to think about my lil' niece that you're carrying in your stomach. Stay focused on her . . . on keeping her healthy. Fuck everybody else right now."

"That's easy to say, Mona. You're not in my shoes; you don't know how I feel. I don't want this life if I can't have Indie in it," Disaya whispered as she felt herself becoming emotional all over again.

"I'd rather be in your shoes, YaYa," Mona answered with a tear-streaked face. "You have everything to live for, and more importantly, you have the option to live. I'm not trying to hear that bullshit you're talking. You need to be thanking Leah. Yeah, she took your man from your life, but because of her you left Elite. I stayed, and look where it got me."

Disaya was speechless. She was so busy feeling sorry for herself that she had forgotten that Mona was fighting a battle much tougher than her own. She was being selfish, while her best friend was bearing a cross that was too heavy a burden.

The embarrassment written on her face caused Mona to laugh out loud and break the awkward tension that had filled the room.

"What the fuck's so funny?" Disaya yelled.

"How that foot in your mouth taste?" Mona asked.

Disaya threw a pillow at Mona's head and smirked as she folded her arms across her chest.

"Your problems don't seem all that big compared to mine, huh?"

"You're right, Mo. I'm sorry. I'm being a bitch. It's just that I miss him, that's all."

"It's cool, girl. Just count your blessings. You have your health, and you have your daughter. That should be enough," Mona replied seriously.

"When did you become so damn wise?" Disaya asked with a playful smile.

"When your ass became so damn dumb and started letting grimy bitches like Leah throw you off your square," Mona answered. "Now you want to get out of this house or what?"

"I want to, but the bed rest has me rooted," YaYa said sadly.

"We'll be careful. You staying in this house like a hermit can't be healthy. Even if we don't get out of the car, I'll just take you for a ride around the city."

Disaya relented, and she and Mona moved cautiously as they descended the stairs. YaYa held on to Mona with one hand and secured her belly with the other, as she took her time getting to the car. She made sure that her feet didn't hit the pavement too hard. Her doctor had made it very clear that the least bit of stress on her body could cause her to miscarry her baby or deliver extremely early.

At only four and a half months, delivering her baby right now could be deadly for her fetus. She needed to keep her baby inside the womb as long as she possibly could, to ensure the child's survival.

Once she was in the car, she leaned the passenger seat back all the way as the sun absorbed in her skin. It felt so good just being outside of her home. It had begun to feel like a prison and outside was like freedom.

Mona eased into traffic, and for the first time since finding out about her condition, she forgot that she was sick.

"Don't fuck up my car. You know your ass can't drive," YaYa stated seriously, reminding Mona of old times.

"Just ride and quit passenger-seat driving," Mona stated. "YaYa, if I never told you before, I want you to know that you're my girl and I love you. You've been my only family for a long time, and even though I'm fucked-up and dying, you still look at me as me. I love you for that . . . for never passing judgment on me."

Teary-eyed and emotional from her hormones, YaYa laughed and wiped the tears from her eyes. "I love you too, Mo. You're my girl, and I'm not trying to hear that about you dying. Bad bitches don't die, Mo. You'll always be in my life 'cuz, I'll know when I'm fucking up, you will be up there shaking your damn head and cussing me out. You're my sister. I love you. Everyone makes mistakes. God is going to take care of you, Mo."

Mona was crying too by this point. "How do you know, YaYa? What if I'm not meant to go to heaven?"

"You are. Heaven doesn't have an angel like you yet, and although I've already lived to fuck up, my baby—your niece—has not. You're her guardian angel. I'm counting on you to be there for her when I can't be," YaYa said as she gripped Mona's hand tightly. "I'll never forget you and will make sure your niece knows you loved her every day."

"You promise?" Mona asked.

"I promise, Mo," YaYa replied.

It was the most intimate conversation they had ever had with each other, and it tore YaYa to pieces to know that Mona would not always be with her. She cherished the time that she had left with her best friend and honestly didn't know what she would do without her.

Silence filled the interior of the car as they each were trapped in a world within their minds. Their thoughts were on the future. Neither knew what tomorrow might bring, but for one the future looked bleak and the other fulfilling.

Mona took the city streets toward their old block. They had been in the car so long that YaYa's bladder began to bother her.

"Ooh shit, I got to pee . . . pull over, Mo," YaYa said as she began to dance around in her pants.

"Bitch, where are you going to pee at?" Mona asked.

"Right now I don't care where I pee. Just pull over at that station on the corner real fast," YaYa stated.

Mona saw the hoodlum-filled gas station and sighed. She didn't feel like dealing with a crowd today but knew that if she didn't stop, YaYa might not make it to the next restroom, so she pulled over. She parked on the curb and hopped out to help Disaya out of the passenger side.

Disaya moved slowly, and it took her a while to make it into the store.

Mona browsed carelessly through the aisles as she waited for YaYa to handle her business.

YaYa finally emerged from the bathroom.

"Damn, I thought you were having a baby in there," Mona stated.

"Shut up," Disaya sneered. "You ready?"

Mona and YaYa were about to step out of the store but bumped into the last person in the world that they expected to see . . . Bay.

"Bitch, I've been trying to see you for a while now," Bay stated with malice in his tone.

YaYa's eyes met Bay's, and her instincts told her to run. Staring into his eyes was like witnessing her own demise, and fear filled her from the tip of her toes to the top of her pretty little head. YaYa remembered the last words he had said the last time that they had spoken. *"That nasty bitch gave me HIV. Word is bond she's dead when I catch her!"*

"Run, Mo, run," Disaya whispered frantically in Mona's ear.

Fear filled Mona's eyes because word had been put out that Bay had threatened her life. Mona already knew why he wanted her dead. They had been having unprotected sex since she was a young girl, and she had unknowingly passed the virus on to him before she had been diagnosed.

She wished she had time to explain, but when Bay went into his waistline to retrieve a pistol, she went into action. She brought her knee up and kicked him straight in the groin then picked up a wine bottle that was to the left of the door and smashed it across his head.

"Aghh! Bitch!" they heard Bay yell out in pain, but never looked back.

Disaya took off behind Mona, racing back to the car. Disaya could feel each step in her womb.

Bam! Bam! Bam! Bam!

Each time her feet hit the ground, her uterus protested in agony, but she knew she couldn't stop running. "Go! Go! Go!" she yelled when they leaped inside the car.

Mona took the wheel and floored the HEMI engine, not caring who stood in her way.

YaYa felt an extreme gush of wetness between her legs. "Oh my God! Mo, the bleeding . . . it's getting worse, Mo!" she shouted. She turned to look out of the rear window and panicked. "He's following us, Mo! Oh my God! Oww!" she cried out as pain erupted through her midsection. "Mo!"

The distress on YaYa's face spoke volumes, and Mona knew that it was now life or death for Disaya and her baby. Her heavy foot caused the car to go from zero to ninety in seconds, as she tried to get away.

"I know, YaYa, just hold on. Let me shake this mu'fucka! Everything is going to be okay," she said. Mona zoomed through the streets like a NASCAR racer, hitting sharp turns and flying through the city at top speed; but no matter how hard she tried, she could not lose Bay.

Disaya was hysterical and in tremendous pain. "Mona, please hurry!" she yelled. She turned and looked at Bay, who was gaining on them. "Aghh, he's coming, Mo, please go! My baby, Mo, please hurry!"

"I'm trying . . . oh, shit," Mona cursed.

Bay raced in his F-150 to catch up with Mona. He switched lanes, causing oncoming traffic to move out of his way. It was obvious he wasn't going to give up. He had waited for months to get his revenge, and he wasn't about to let Mona get away. He rammed the side of his car into the side of Disaya's Magnum, causing Mona to swerve wildly.

"Aghh! Oh my God! Bay, stop!" YaYa screamed. She was terrified and in tremendous pain. "Stop!"

Mona desperately fought to keep the car on course, but Bay's truck was too big to dodge. He slammed it into them repeatedly, metal meeting metal.

CRUNCH! SCREECH!

Their cars collided repeatedly, sending sparks and car parts flying everywhere, the melody of the impact deafening Disaya's ear. Bay rammed into them over and over, until finally he sent them flying through the air out of control.

Disaya felt the car flip numerous times. She heard the crunch of steel as the concrete threatened to tear the car apart. Everything happened so fast. Fear paralyzed her heart, and glass shattered throughout the car, as the windshield exploded in her face just before her passenger door slammed against a brick wall. Pain seared through her, and blood dripped freely from her face, but the only thing she could worry about was her baby. "Aghh! My baby. Mo, I'm losing my baby," YaYa cried.

Mona seemed to know that she was about to die. A calm settled over her face. She was stuck behind the wheel of a crushed car, yet she didn't scream or cry out in pain. She simply looked at Disaya and said, "I'm so sorry, YaYa. I love you."

It was then that Disaya saw Bay approach Mona's window. The sunlight reflected off the gun in his hand. He stuck the pistol through the broken glass of the driver window. "You dirty bitch," he muttered, blood staining the rim of his white T-shirt, insanity filling his gaze.

Mona closed her eyes, and YaYa screamed, "Noo!"

Her cries fell on deaf ears. Bay pulled the trigger without hesitation, sending mucus and brain matter spraying throughout the car. Half of Mona's face had been taken off, leaving behind a stomach-churning and gruesome sight.

"Oww." Disaya cringed from the pressure in her abdomen.

Bay stood frozen outside of Mona's window. The gun was still gripped in his now shaking hand.

"Bay, please don't do this. Please just help me!" Disaya called out. "I've known you forever . . . please, Bay, don't do this to me. I'm pregnant!" She could see tears in his eyes. He seemed to be in a trance.

He looked into YaYa's eyes and said, "She took my life away from me, ma. She gave me death."

"Aghh!" Disaya's teeth were clenched so tightly that her scream sounded more like a roar. "Get me out of here!"

Bay shook his head as tears fell from his eyes. Living with HIV was worse than dying to him. He looked at the gun in his palm and then turned it on himself. He pulled the trigger before he ever had a chance to change his mind.

Two bullets. That was all it took to the end the lives of two people she had been close to for years. HIV had been enough motivation for Bay, a man who both she and Mona had trusted fully, to commit murder and suicide. HIV was truly a monster, and she had witnessed firsthand what it could do to someone she loved.

Mona's head slumped onto the horn, and Disaya released a scream from the pit of her stomach. It originated from the pain in her soul, as she screamed hysterically for anyone to come rescue her from the bloodbath in front of her. The angst overtook her body, and she was dizzy from the crash. She tried to pull herself from the car, but her legs were trapped, and her white summer dress looked as if it had been tie-dyed in crimson.

A crowd began to form around the gruesome scene.

"Help me, please!" she cried as her eyes scanned Mona's dead body in fear. "Please, somebody help me!"

She could see people in her peripheral looking on, but everyone was too afraid to get involved. She heard the distant wail of sirens, and for the first time in her life she welcomed the idea of authority coming to get her. She knew that they were too late for Mona; she only hoped that they would make it in time to save the baby that was slowly leaking out of her womb against her will.

Chapter 21

Money flowed like fine wine in Houston, and within a month of taking over, Mekhi's blocks were already bringing back a profit. They had received little to no resistance from Khi-P's lieutenants, who merged seamlessly into Indie's operation. It didn't matter to them who they hustled for, as long as they were getting paid. Loyalty and allegiance didn't exist in an age of snitching. It was easy to make Khi-P's workers switch teams. The ones that did protest were disposed of, and Chase did his job with such expertise that the police weren't a factor. No body, no crime, and Chase could make a corpse disappear like he was a skilled magician.

"Your boy Khi-P has been talking real greasy, fam. He's plotting on you for real. Don't sleep on that nigga, Indie. He's been running Houston for the past five years, and now the nigga salty behind our takeover. Word on the street is that he's ready to put that contract on you," Chase warned Indie as they sat in Chase's luxury apartment home, counting the week's take.

"Oh yeah? What else you been hearing around the way?" Indie asked casually, as if the notion of Khi-P being a threat was ridiculous. He didn't want to alarm Chase, but he knew that he would have to take care of Khi-P personally. Indie was well aware that he wasn't bulletproof and that he needed to nip the problem with Mekhi in the bud before it escalated.

"You remember the nigga Trey? The dude that I bodied up that first day on the block?" Chase asked, jogging Indie's memory.

"Loudmouth, yeah, what about him?"

"His older brother got blood in his eyes. He from Tallahassee, and word is he came here to see you. I think they call him Duke," Chase informed. "Other than that, I ain't heard shit. I can handle that. All you got to do is say the word. I know where Khi-P is right now. It's Friday night, and he's known to frequent this gambling joint on the west side. All the hustlers go there like clockwork. It's a truce zone, though, but I can catch 'em slipping on his way out. It'll be done before the sun come up."

"Nah, fam, I can handle Mekhi. Where you say that crap joint at?" Indie asked.

Indie parked his car on the side alley near the hole-in-the-wall bar. It was closed, but Indie knew that the real activity took place inside after hours, when the trap boys came out to play and shoot dice. He emerged from the car. His three-link diamond chain hung from his neck, a single solitary earring was in his left ear, and a matching diamond bracelet adorned his wrist. He was clad in fresh Red Monkey jeans, cool in a white Ralph Lauren polo, and high maintenance in his plaid Polo shoes. With his bitch, a chrome 9 mm, tucked in his waistline, he was confident as he knocked on the bar's door.

"We're closed! Read the sign," a feeble voice yelled from behind the door.

"I'm here for the crap game," Indie replied.

"I don't know what you're talking about, son. You're not saying the right thing," the old man stated.

"Yo', fam, open the door. I know ain't shit free in the world. I don't know the passwords and all that bullshit. I'm just trying to get in the game, nah mean?"

The door cracked open, and before Indie could step inside, a long barrel to a shotgun was pointed out at him. An old black man with gray hair and ruthless eyes stood before him, scanning Indie up and down.

"Whoa . . . old man, hold up," Indie stated. "Like I said, I'm just here for the game. I'm not bringing any malice to your doorstep."

Indie held his hands in front of him and reached inside his baggy pockets. He pulled out a knot of cash and peeled off a couple hundred for the owner. He placed it in his hands, and reluctantly the owner withdrew his weapon.

"The game is down the stairs. Ain't no bullshit going to be tolerated up in this here place. Any beef you got need to be left out there in the alley," the old man warned.

"You have my word," Indie replied as he was led down the steps.

The weed smoke in the basement made Indie feel as if he was walking through a thick morning fog. Indie spotted Khi-P in the exact same moment that Khi-P noticed him. Fury filled their gaze, and Indie smirked as he removed a hundred-dollar bill and got in the game. His perception never wavered as he pretended to concentrate on the crap game in front of him.

He was secure with his twin Berettas on his hip, yet he did not sleep on Mekhi. They didn't call him the King of the South for nothing, so Indie was sure to be on his p's and q's.

Indie flossed hard at the crap game and faded Khi-P every time he touched the dice, raping him of his money and throwing salt in Khi-P's wounds. Popping off at the mouth was commonplace in a dice game, so the spectators talked big shit to Khi-P about the ass-whooping Indie was putting on him.

Indie had always been blessed with the ivory and was known in the Yitty for having great luck when it came to the game, so it was easy for him to bleed Khi-P dry.

No one knew the significance behind the crap game, but Indie and Khi-P were well aware. They played with hundred-dollar bills and pulled them from their pockets effortlessly. They both had a point to prove, a status quo to maintain.

There was only one problem . . . Khi-P couldn't keep up because Indie's pockets were longer.

Once he was done with Mekhi, other dudes tried to challenge Indie and get a chance to take all of the money that Indie had just won from Khi-P, but Indie declined.

"Some other time, I'm up," Indie stated as he collected his cash and hit Khi-P with a head nod. "You got slippery fingers, fam. You got to learn how to hold on to what's yours. I've been taking a lot of shit from you lately," Indie stated smartly with a conceited grin. He could practically see the steam rising out of Mekhi's shirt, who was hot as Indie swaggered up the stairs and out of the shop. He knew exactly what he was doing. He had antagonized Mekhi.

As he walked back down the deserted alley, he counted his money. He was eight stacks up. *Not bad at all for a hood game*, Indie thought. He tucked the bills securely in his pocket and hit the alarm on his car. He climbed inside and was about to start the car, when his passenger door opened and Mekhi sat down with a pretty chrome .357 in his palm.

"Yeah, nigga, you real quiet now, mu'fucka," Khi-P stated viciously. "Show me those hands, shawty."

Indie nodded his head and put his hands on his steering wheel as Khi-P checked his pockets, relieving Indie of the cash that he had just won.

"Who's getting touched now?" Khi-P asked.

"I don't get touched," Indie replied calmly. "You played right into my hands, baby. Turn around, I got something for you."

Khi-P turned his head and became acquainted with the barrel of Chase's .45. He couldn't help but to scoff in disbelief. He had fallen right into a trap.

"Now you've got an option," Indie stated. "We can turn this mu'fucka into a bloodbath, or we can settle this shit like grown men. Either way suits me fine. I'm ready to die. When you're in the game, you have to expect to die, so we can go out guns blazing, if that's how you want to play it, but for some reason I'm

thinking you ain't built like me. You wanna go home to wifey . . .
what's her name—Tamia, right?"

Khi-P's eyes bugged out when he heard Indie mention the
name of his baby mother. That meant that he had gotten close,
and Mekhi didn't want anything to happen to his seed or his girl,
so he lowered his pistol reluctantly.

"What do you want?"

"I want to offer you a proposition," Indie stated.

Chase never wavered, or lowered his weapon.

"Oh yeah, what's that?" Khi-P remarked with sarcasm.

"A partnership," Indie replied. "I respect your hustle, fam. I
don't want to stop you from eating, but as you can see, I have the
ability to. In a matter of months I've taken over every one of your
blocks. Every one of your workers has jumped ship on you so that
they can fuck with me. I know you feeling tight about that shit.
That's why you let your better judgment go out the window when
you followed me out to my whip tonight. Your emotions told you
to get at me, but as you can see, I can't be gotten to. We can beef
out and go to war over streets that we don't own, but that would
be senseless. A war between us would stop cash flow and draw unwanted attention. Nobody would eat."

"So what you saying, shawty?" Khi-P asked.

"Yo, for one, you can kill that shawty shit. I'm not your little
nigga so don't try to *son* me. I peep game, so you can miss me with
that shit, *son*," Indie stated, showing him who was boss. "Now, I
can give you your blocks back, but I want in. I've got a lot of
weight, but I'm not for the day-to-day hassle of running the
block. I'm willing to give you back the streets, if you're willing to
push my dope."

"I got my own *D*. Why would I push yours?" Khi-P asked.

"Because I got the best. I got the fish scales. You heard of supreme
clientele?"

"Nigga, quit bullshitting. You not fucking with that Mafia
shit," Khi-P stated in dismissal. "Every nigga from New York think
he connected."

Indie reached underneath his seat and pulled out a neatly wrapped brick. He tossed it in Khi-P's lap. The sparkle and texture of the cocaine spoke for itself.

"The split is sixty-forty, and my man here is head lieutenant. I want to stay in the know about everything. No exceptions. I keep my ears to the streets, so if I hear something before your mouth tells me, we've got a problem, nah mean?"

"Yeah, I hear you," Khi-P responded. He wanted to resist what was being put in front of him, but he knew that, with a better quality dope, he could flip his money twice as quickly. Khi-P was a hustler from the day he learned to talk, and getting money was what he did best. He had heard about the infamous fish scale product but had never been able to get his hands on it. The clientele for it was exclusive, and Indie was his way in.

"So are you in or out?"

"In. Now can you tell your little nigga to get his pistol out my face," Khi stated in irritation.

Chase removed the gun, and Indie held out his hand to Khi-P, who shook his head in disbelief before shaking it.

"I'ma be in touch," Indie stated.

Khi-P reached for the door handle and prepared to step out of the car.

"Mekhi," Indie said, stopping Khi-P in his tracks.

Mekhi turned around.

Indie extended the brick of cocaine. "Keep it. Consider it a signing bonus."

"You wild, man," Mekhi stated as he tucked the product in his jacket. "Look, I'm throwing a party at Club Mansion on Friday night. Come through. We can kick it and iron out this business."

"Yeah, a'ight, I might see if I can make it. Don't be looking for me, though, I can't make no guarantee," Indie stated. He had every intention of showing up at Mekhi's party, but he wasn't in the habit of letting other niggas trace his footsteps. Niggas didn't need to know how he moved. It was something that he would eventually teach Khi-P, if he proved to be trustworthy.

Chapter 22

Indie and Chase pulled up to Club Mansion in Indie's black convertible CLK 550. The club was packed, and there was a line that circled around the block. Indie had contacted the club owner and paid him to allow Indie to hire the bouncers that night, so although Indie and Chase were not deep in numbers, they were highly protected. There were twenty different bouncers in the club in various sections, and they all had their cannons on them, so if anything went down between Khi-P and Indie, Mekhi would be the one leaving out in a body bag.

Indie wasn't for games, and although Khi-P had agreed to the partnership, Indie didn't fully trust him yet. He didn't want to walk into a setup, so he took extra precautions and paid the ten stacks to hire new bouncers in the club.

He and Chase made their way to the entrance and walked in with ease, without being searched and without paying the cover charge. Indie was dapper in black Fendi shorts and a white V-neck T-shirt that fit his toned upper body. Black Jordans graced his feet, and a black fitted crowned his top. His jewelry set it off as always, and he looked like money as he made his way up to VIP, where they found Khi-P popping bottles of Rosé. He spotted Indie and nodded his head, then approached with his hand out-stretched to show love.

"My man, what's popping, baby?" Mekhi greeted as he pulled Indie in for an embrace.

"Ain't shit, just thought I'd come through to show love," Indie replied as he surveyed his surroundings. He took mental pictures of the other hustlers in the room.

Mekhi noticed the tension. "Nah, baby, I told you I'm in. It's all love. Ain't no bullshit going down in here tonight," Mekhi assured. "By the way, I had my man check out that product. It's A-one. The best shit that's been around these parts for years."

Indie nodded but didn't respond, because Khi-P was telling him something that he had already known.

"I put that shits on the streets, fam, and ran through it in two days. A brick in two days! Nigga, we about to create a movement," Khi-P stated.

A group of women walked in between their circle, purposely interrupting their conversation. All three men focused their attention on the half-naked bodies that had just passed them. Indie had never seen an ass like the ones that they possessed. They were country bumpkins, and they had a different demeanor than the city chicks he was used to, but their beauty couldn't be denied. Their bodies were tight, faces were right, and they had ass for days. He couldn't help but to look.

"Let's get up on some of these hoes, duke. That business shit is a wrap. I'm in, and you don't have to worry about no shady niggas. I dispose of niggas that show me shade," Khi-P stated.

"So do I," Indie replied, implying that Mekhi was expendable. "Any nigga, nah mean?"

"Nigga, we good, that's my word," Mekhi stated. "Now let's kick it and celebrate because we about to take over, baby. Everything's on me! Come pop some bottles with your boy."

Knowing that he had protection in the club, Indie decided to relax. He did notice that everyone seemed to know who he was, and he garnered respect from both the ladies and gentlemen in

VIP. Groupies flocked to Indie, Mekhi, and Chase as they flirted and flaunted themselves in hopes of snagging a baller.

Indie hadn't had a female companion in months. He hadn't been focused on women because he knew that his heart would need some time to mend after Disaya had crushed it, but as he admired the bodies around him, his manhood began to remind him that he was in need of a good one-night stand.

He stood against the wall in the middle of Chase and Mekhi, as a girl danced provocatively in front of him. Indie wasn't a clown and didn't dance in clubs, but he let the girl do her thing, using him as a prop, while he admired the view and occasionally grabbed a handful of ass and thighs.

Other niggas surrounded the girl and showered her with dollars as if she were a stripper. The way she was shaking her ass and putting it on Indie had his and every other nigga in the club on hard.

Indie had to readjust himself as he slipped away from the crowd and made his way over to the bar. "Let me get a rum and Coke, all top shelf, my man," Indie stated to the guy manning the bar. He turned to focus his attention on the girl he had just left, and as he did, he bumped square into a young woman, knocking her drink all over her all-white freak-'em dress.

"Damn it," she yelled as she quickly grabbed some napkins and tried to soak up the red cranberry from her now ruined dress. "Why don't you watch where the fuck you're going?"

"Whoa, ma, hold up . . . somebody so pretty shouldn't have such a dirty mouth. It makes you ugly," he commented as he looked her up and down, pleased with what he saw.

"There ain't shit in this world that can make me ugly," she shot back with a mean glare.

"I'm sorry about your dress, ma. You should let me buy you another one," Indie stated.

"You don't have to buy me another dress. I'm good. You've done enough. I can't stay up in here like this," she scoffed to herself in irritation.

"Let me take you home," he offered.

The girl shook her head and rolled her eyes at Indie. "Yeah, a'ight," she said. "You buying me a new dress too, nigga."

Indie placed his hand on the small of her back and led her over to where Chase and Khi-P were. "I'm up, fam," he leaned in and whispered to Chase. "You coming?"

"Nah, I'ma chill here and try to take something home myself," Chase replied. "I'll hop a ride with Khi."

"You sure about that? I'm still not a one hundred percent about that nigga," Indie stated.

"I'm sure," Chase answered as he patted his hip where his gun was located. "I'm good."

They slapped hands, and Indie gave Mekhi a head nod.

"Aye, fam, you entering that *DUB* magazine car show next week?" Mekhi asked. "Your wheels ain't fucking with mine or nothing. I'm the king 'round these parts."

Indie laughed slightly. "You ain't seen a whip until a New York nigga done fucked it up," he replied.

"Okay, playboy, I hear you . . . but talk is cheap. You got twenty on it?" Mekhi challenged, all in good fun.

"I got fifty on it, nigga. Have my money ready, baby. I don't take no IOU's," Indie said before he departed with the girl on his arm.

She told Indie her address and kept her attitude all the way to her apartment. When they got there, the girl turned to Indie. "You know you fucked up my night, right?" she asked.

"Nah, you didn't need to be around all those lame niggas anyway," Indie replied as his eyes indulged in her presence.

"Oh yeah, and why's that?" she countered.

"They're a waste of time."

The girl undid her seat belt and leaned into Indie. "Are you?"

"Am I what?" Indie asked.

"A waste of my time," the girl replied.

"I'm the type of nigga that would make you better if I wanted to, but I'm not looking for that right now," Indie answered honestly with a note of sadness in his voice that the girl picked up.

"What? Some other chick done fucked it up for everybody?" the girl asked in irritation.

Indie nodded as his thoughts drifted to Disaya. He had her stored in his mental, even though he hated that she was there . . . he couldn't forget her. "She's a hard act to follow."

The girl smacked her lips. "If she's so damn great, why you here with me?"

"She fucked up," Indie replied.

The girl leaned in close to Indie's ear and whispered, "Then let *me* help you forget about her."

Her tongue caressed his neck, and all of the urges he had suppressed for six months immediately surged through his body. His thick manhood expanded as he felt the girl reach down and stroke him gently.

She opened her door and stepped out, then leaned back into the open window. "You can come up if you want to," she said.

Indie pulled his car into a parking space, keeping his burner on him because he didn't trust anyone, and then exited the car to follow the perfect physique in front of him up to her apartment.

As soon as they entered her place, she was all over him, and Indie didn't fight it as she planted kisses all over his body. His hands roamed her figure and removed the tiny dress that she wore, to reveal a provocative black thong. She wore no bra, and her breasts were perky and round, with big black nipples.

His mouth was drawn to them as he circled her areola with his thick tongue. His dick felt like it would explode. The only sounds that could be heard were the grunting and gasps of their passion.

Indie watched in amazement as the girl seductively dipped to her knees and unbuckled his pants. She planted kisses on his stomach as her fingers worked his zipper, until she uncovered the prize. She took him into her mouth.

It had been so long since he'd been inside something wet that he had to stop himself from nutting too quickly. His hands wrapped up into her hair as he guided himself in and out of her eager mouth. Her head game was ridiculous, and she had him close to an orgasm with her tight jaws and deep throat.

He pulled out of her and she stood. She took his hand and led him to her bedroom. The stage seemed to be already set. Candles flickered gently in the background, and she pushed him down onto the bed. She was about to mount him when he stopped her.

"Hold on, ma, I got to strap up," he said as he leaned down and pulled a condom from his pants pocket.

She took the condom from him, put it in her mouth, and then leaned over him and with expertise slid it onto his dick.

"Damn," he moaned as she came back up and slid down on him. Her walls contracted around his width, and she moved down his shaft, inch by inch. Her tight walls felt like heaven as she began to ride him slowly and deeply. Their sexual chemistry was amazing.

He flipped her over so that he was in a position of control. He opened her thighs and looked down at his thickness as it went in and out of her.

She moaned loudly, as her fingers found their way to her clit. She massaged it gently, causing his manhood to grow another inch from the erotic sight alone.

His rhythm was perfect, and she matched it with thrusts of the hips, causing her bed to rock. Indie leaned in; taking a handful of breasts into his mouth while never breaking his motion. He was digging her back out, and the way she arched it when he went deep let him know he was doing his job.

"Yes! Oh my God, daddy, right there," she called out as Indie death-stroked her, hitting her G-spot and causing her legs to quiver.

Indie pulled out of her and put his head in the space that his dick had just occupied. She squirmed beneath him. He took her pink pearl into his mouth and French-kissed it sensually. She grinded it into him, smothering his face with her juices.

"Damn, ma, you're so wet," he told her. Her pussy was odorless and had the sweetest taste. He devoured it, licking her from her clit to her crack and back again as he stroked his dick.

"I'm about to cum, Daddy," she announced.

Indie continued to bless her clit until she exploded in his face. He lapped it up like it was milk, licking her until she was horny and wet all over again. He knew what he was doing to her. He hadn't had sex in six months, and although the woman beneath him was not Disaya, she would do. She was a great substitute.

He flipped her over and ran his length up and down her opening. He looked at his shaft and couldn't believe the amount of moisture that the girl possessed. She was dripping, and he slid into her, only to discover a perfect fit. Indie thought the girl would run from the size of him, but she tooted her ass up and bucked back on his dick like a pro as he hit it from behind.

"Fuck me, daddy. Take this pussy, daddy! It's yours," she cried out in a mixture of pleasure and pain.

Indie felt his head expand, and he began to grunt as he traced a circle on her walls.

"Ohh shit, ma," he moaned.

Just as he was about to nut the girl eased his dick out of her.

"Uh-uh, what you doing, baby?" he asked.

Before he could protest, she removed the condom and took him into her mouth. She sucked his dick like a cherry lollipop, and in thirty seconds flat his orgasm had built and exploded. She savored every drop of him, sucking him dry, until he collapsed on top of her.

Indie lay there in stunned silence. The girl undoubtedly had the best head game he had ever experienced. "You're the best, ma," he complimented.

"I know," she replied. "Lie down and relax." She rubbed the silk sheets on her bed.

"Can I use your shower?" he asked.

"Yeah, it's across the hall," she purred.

Indie grabbed his clothes and went into the bathroom, where he washed himself thoroughly and got dressed.

By the time he emerged, his sex partner was passed out in the bed, a pillow tucked between her legs. Indie rubbed his goatee and shook his head. *You did a great job, ma, but you didn't make me forget,* Indie thought as he reflected on the amazing sex he had just had.

He reached into his pocket and pulled out a knot of money then dropped a thousand dollars on her nightstand. He knew that the dress didn't cost that much, but for the work she had put in, the girl definitely deserved to be tipped. He located a pen and piece of paper then wrote the girl a quick note. He didn't want her to feel cheap in the morning, so he was polite and hoped that the note would make up for his absence.

Had to run. Thanks for the incredible night. Please accept this money as compensation for your dress. If I see you around be sure to holla at me.
Indie

He took one last look at the beauty before him before he turned and walked out of the door.

"I know this mu'fucka didn't just leave me a fucking note and dip," Leah said angrily to herself. She crumbled up the piece of paper in the palm of her hand and smirked slightly. She wasn't tripping, though, because she knew what his next move would be. She overheard his plans to enter the car show, and she would conveniently be in the right place at the right time so that she could slowly work her way into his life.

Leah had followed Indie to Houston six months ago and had been laying low, watching his every movement and waiting for the perfect time to approach him. She could understand how Disaya had fallen in love with him. He was fine as hell, and his demeanor was sexy, calm, and attractive. It was going to be her pleasure to fill YaYa's spot.

Last night he had fucked her as if his life had depended on it. He was tight-lipped about his previous girlfriend too, which she already knew was Disaya. It was obvious to her that his heart was broken, but she felt no remorse. She had given the nigga six months to get over YaYa; now it was her time to get inside his head and heart.

Indie had almost thrown a wrench in her plan when he told her he had to strap up, but thinking on her toes, she quickly obliged him, but not before biting a hole in the condom before sliding it onto his dick. *After I have his baby, I'll mail the bitch a family picture. I can see her face hitting the floor already,* Leah thought before bursting into a fit of laughter.

It was easy for her to be manipulative and evil. So many people had contributed to ruining her life that she didn't feel bad about causing havoc in the lives of others. Nobody gave a fuck about her, so why should she give a fuck about anybody else. She had let Disaya in, and she had trusted her. *The bitch was selfish. She only thought about herself and this nigga. I should kill his ass, and then she will definitely know that I'm not to be fucked with. Grimy-ass bitch!*

Leah looked in the mirror. She had made a hell of a transformation. After almost mimicking Disaya's appearance, she knew that it would be easy to get Indie's attention. He had loved YaYa; now Leah was determined to make him love her, even if it was only for spite.

Revenge was her motivation, and nothing short of death would stop her from getting it. She wanted Disaya to suffer and she knew that YaYa loved Indie more than she loved herself. By taking Indie and leaving Disaya with nothing, she would hit her where it hurt most.

Within a few minutes of meeting Indie, Leah already had him eating in the palm of her hands. She had fucked him properly like no other woman could and knew that it would only be a matter of time before Indie came looking for more.

Leah took her red lipstick and applied it to her full lips, making a perfect outline before pursing her lips together. Rage filled her as she thought of how Disaya had played her. With the lipstick in her hand, she continued to apply layer after layer, making her circle wider and wider, until red lipstick was painted all over her face. By the time she was done, her heart was racing, and her temperature was high. She punched the image in the mirror.

"Aghh!" she screamed as glass broke all over her dresser.

She had learned to control her temper. It had taken years of counseling to get her head right, but the day she met Disaya, her obsession with her became uncontrollable. *All she had to do was treat me good. She wants to act like she didn't know what's up. I was good to her. We were meant to be together, but the bitch had to get out of pocket. Now look what she's made me become.*

Chapter 23

YaYa's body hurt tremendously. Each movement she made took great effort, and she was weakened in spirit. Her body felt as if it was ready to give up on her. As she looked in the mirror she lifted the hospital gown. A deep-stitched and stapled incision ran the width across her stomach. She felt as if it was all for nothing. She felt lonely and unloved. Where was Indie? Yes, she had lied to him and done him wrong, but there was no denying that she loved him—not even God himself could tell that lie. She would die for him, and when she needed him most he was nowhere to be found. She felt angry at him because their love was supposed to be different. He hadn't even given her a real chance to explain. Instead, he believed what was really a half-truth and deserted her when she yearned to be with him most. He was supposed to protect her, but instead he left her vulnerable to death and destruction.

She let her gown fall around her body, covering up the war wounds that she had received in the crash. Her face was bruised and had tiny imperfections all over from the shattered pieces of glass from the windshield bursting. She had two fractured ribs, and as she limped out of her hospital room, she felt like she would die if she didn't sit down soon.

A nurse noticed her attempting to leave. "Ms. Morgan? Is there something that I can do for you? You really should not be on your feet," the young girl said.

"I need to see her," Disaya replied.

"Okay, just let me get you a wheelchair, and I'll take you to her," the nurse answered dutifully as she hurriedly left and came back to seat Disaya.

The nurse wheeled her to the next floor and into a dimly-lit room. Tears rushed YaYa's eyes when she saw the tiny incubator that was the home of her newborn baby girl.

"She's beautiful," YaYa whispered as she reached her hand through the hole and caressed her baby girl's fingertips. "Hi, Skylar Mona Perkins."

Her daughter reacted to her voice and stirred gently as she gripped Disaya's fingers. Tears fell from YaYa's eyes. She couldn't help it. As she gazed lovingly at the product of her and Indie's love, she felt overwhelmed by her emotions. She never knew that she could love someone as much as she loved her daughter. The agonizing C-section pain was worth the tiny gift that she had been given.

Premature born, Skylar weighed only four pounds, six ounces. The newborn had been traumatized while inside her mother's womb, not once but twice, and she was struggling for her life. The breathing tube that was inserted inside of Skylar's tiny chest cavity helped to sustain her life. No one knew if the baby would make it, but Disaya cherished her anyway and spent every waking hour near her side with her head bowed in prayer.

"Mommy loves you, Skylar. You have to be strong for Mommy. I need you. You mean the world to me, and I will never let anything happen to you ever again," Disaya promised. She sat for hours singing to her daughter, hoping for a miracle. If her daughter died, she knew that it would be no one's fault but her own. *Is this God's way of punishing me for all the wrong I've done?* she asked herself. She hoped that she would be held accountable for her own sins and that her daughter would be spared and allowed to be judged on her own merit. *Skylar doesn't deserve to pay for my mistakes. Please, God, forgive me. Just bring my daughter through this.*

Inside of Disaya ached. She never knew that a pain so great existed. Even when Indie left her, it didn't hurt this bad. This feeling was rotting her faith from the inside out. She felt like she was choking on grief . . . suffocating as she awaited her daughter's fate. She wished that she could change it or fix things somehow, but the situation was out of her control. It wasn't in her hands. She was forced to let go and let God. The only thing she could do was wait. Wait for life to be rejuvenated or taken away. The end decision was not up to her, and the unknown was scarier than the truth.

Indie felt in his gut that something wasn't right. There was just a pit in the bottom of his stomach that seemed hollow. He had no idea what was causing his heart to feel unsettled, but in actuality he was feeling exactly what Disaya was feeling. He just didn't know where his pain was coming from. Something was telling him to call her, but he ignored the feeling . . . his hatred was too great to set his pride to the side. He thought himself noble for continuing to send her money every month. *That's enough. I don't have to talk to her,* Indie thought.

His phone rang, and he reached to answer it. It was Chase.

"What's good, fam? Everything go smooth last night?" Indie asked.

"Yeah, we're good. The nigga Khi is geeked about the product. I don't think we're going to have any problems out of him. He's about his money, and he knows he's about to see more paper with you than he ever has before. It's all love from him. As long as he's getting money, he don't have a problem. What you into today, fam? You spinning through the block?"

"Nah, man, hold it down for me. I got fifty stacks on this mu'-

fuckin' car show with Khi. I got to get a new whip before next week. We gon' get it in, though. Be easy, fam." Indie ended the call.

A milli, a milli, a milli

Indie's MTX subwoofers vibrated Lil' Wayne's song throughout the Reliant Center, where the annual *DUB* car show was being held. He had gotten ridiculous with his car entry and ordered a customized cocaine-colored Maybach Landaulet with platinum rims and twenty-two-inch tires. His name was engraved in the headrests of the seats, and his cocaine-white leather jacket matched the car perfectly as he leaned against it. He looked around casually, as if the car hadn't set him back two hundred thousand dollars, but to him that was nothing, because he had it. Like Lil' Wayne said, *It ain't tricking if you got it.*

Niggas was open as they stared at the luxury vehicle. Those weren't the type of cars that hood fellas purchased in Houston. Every other car was souped-up Chevies or Oldsmobiles, and Indie had to admit that the paint and rims were shining throughout the arena, but he came with his New York swag, and nobody from up top was riding around in twenty-year-old cars. He had been meaning to upgrade his car anyway, and if he was going to buy a Benz, he reasoned it may as well have been the best.

Chase and Mekhi pulled up in Mekhi's candy-wet Cutlass Supreme, and he practically hopped out of the car before he put the showpiece in park.

"My nigga, no you didn't! This ain't you," Khi-P exclaimed, his dick hard from looking at the car.

"I told you to have that paper ready, fam," Indie stated with a slither of arrogance as he slapped hands with his newfound partner.

"Yeah, you got that, because this bitch right here is cold, but shit, you spent more on the car than you winning in the bet," Mekhi acknowledged.

"Sometimes you gotta spend a couple dollars to let a nigga

know his place. It was well worth it, nah mean?" Indie joked with a playful smile.

"Yeah, yeah, let me find out you showing out for these hoes. I saw that bitch with the fat ass that you took home with you the other night," Mekhi stated as he slapped hands with Indie and they laughed together.

Indie, Mekhi, and Chase lounged around and watched as the *DUB* girls made their way around the arena taking pictures with different cars. It was packed, as car lovers from all over the city came to enjoy the event.

The pace of the South was completely different than what Indie was used to. It was anything but sophisticated, but he had to admit, it was growing on him. Everything was always so crunk, from the parties, to the people . . . when Houston came out to have a good time, they came out in droves. Their overpopulated city was like one big-ass Mardi Gras, and Indie was in the midst of the madness, as his car became the center of attention.

Leah licked her lips sensually as she stared across the car show at Indie. Everything about him screamed hood-rich, and she knew Rick Ross must have written his smash anthem for her, because money really did make her cum. She knew that bitches were going to be all over Indie tonight, but she was about to cut all that shit short. She was staking her claim, and the Lela Rose backless dress she was rocking was going to put her on a level all her own.

Her Gucci sling backs click-clacked against the cement floor as she made her way toward her destination.

Recognition filled Indie's eyes when he saw her, and he did the customary head-to-toe scan that all niggas do when they're trying to peep you on the low, but Leah noticed it.

There wasn't much she didn't notice. She was always on her game and if there was going to be a player in any relationship she was in, it would be her. She never got played, because she created the rules.

"I got your note," she said as she stood directly in front of him, her hands finding a comfortable place around his neck, as if she owned him. "I didn't know you were the type to eat and run," she stated as she licked her lips.

Indie smiled. He liked her feistiness. She reminded him of YaYa. The only difference was, the bitch in front of him didn't try to hide her manipulation. She was straightforward, whereas YaYa had him thinking she was someone she wasn't.

"I was hoping you might come back for seconds," she whispered as she let her fingertips trace the imprint of his dick, causing it to jump slightly.

Indie moved her hand and frowned slightly. He wasn't for public hoeing. He wanted a lady in the streets and a freak in the bed. His lady needed to conduct herself like a lady anytime there was anyone watching besides him.

Okay, that's one thing YaYa didn't teach me about your ass. You want me to be the classy bitch in front of your boys. I can do that. Mistake number one . . . it won't happen again.

"You're kind of comfortable, ma. You on me like you're trying to be known. I don't even know your name. Let's start there," Indie suggested.

"I'm Leah," she said with a smile.

"Indie," he replied. "Are you always this bold?"

"Yes. Are you always this cautious with your heart? The other night it felt like you were holding back on me," Leah stated.

"I gave you what you wanted. You wanted to be fucked. You didn't ask me for emotions."

"Well, what if I told you that I'm trying to get to know you?" she asked.

Before he could answer, Indie saw Mekhi approach him. The scene seemed to move in slow motion. Indie's eyes grew wide as he watched Khi-P go into his waistline and retrieve his burner. Indie couldn't react quickly enough. His hands seemed to be glued to his side. *I knew I shouldn't have trusted this nigga,* he thought. He waited for the blast that would end his life.

BOOM!

The bullet flew past his head, and when Indie turned around, he saw a man crumple to the ground, with a hole blown clear through his head and a small .32 caliber handgun dangling limply in his hand.

"Oh my God!" Leah screamed.

"Come on!" Indie grabbed Leah's hand and ran through the crowd with Mekhi and Chase on his heels.

They made it to the exit and ran over to Chase's whip and hopped inside.

"Fuck was that about?" Indie asked.

"The nigga Duke from Tallahassee. He would've rocked your top if Khi-P didn't catch the nigga lurking," Chase stated.

"Good looking out, fam," Indie stated. It was at that moment that any doubts he had in his mind about Khi-P dissipated. Mekhi had proven that he was trustworthy.

He peered at Leah, and oddly she didn't appear to be shaken as the normal female would have been. She was unusually calm and didn't ask any questions. She was thorough, and Indie liked that about her. She knew her place.

"What about your car?" Chase asked.

"I'll pick it up tomorrow once the dust settles," Indie replied. He then gave them the address to Leah's place.

When they arrived he got out of the car, said good-bye to his crew, and accompanied Leah inside, where they picked up where they left off. It was the first night that Indie didn't think of Disaya in his sleep. Instead, his dreams were filled with Leah as he replayed their sexual escapade over again in hisl mind.

Chapter 24

Sniff! Sniff!

Indie was stirred out of his comfortable sleep by the sound of someone sniffing loudly. With his eyes closed, he reached for Leah, but his hand graced nothing but air. He looked up and saw Leah leaning over her vanity.

Sniff!

In her hands she held a rolled-up dollar bill, and she concentrated like a kid in school on the cocaine-covered plate in front of her as she inhaled the substance up her nose.

"I didn't know you fucked with that shit," Indie stated, his baritone causing her to jump slightly.

She snorted one more white line and held her head back as she closed her eyes to savor the feeling. Her euphoric high caused a silly smile to cross her face.

"Who doesn't fuck with this shit? It's the best," she bragged. "It's like candy. Why you think this pussy so addictive?" She held the mirror out toward him. "You've got to try this, daddy. It's the greatest."

"Nah, I'll pass, ma. I'm not fucking with that shit," Indie replied.

"Come on, daddy, it's the greatest shit ever," she coaxed.

He gave her a stern look that told her to drop it, so she did and enjoyed her party by herself. Indie didn't knock what she did, but drugs weren't him, and she didn't know it. But because she did snort cocaine, she had just been downgraded to Indie's just-a-nut list.

"Put that shit up, ma, and come show me what you got," Indie instructed.

Leah, wanting to seem obedient because she knew that it was a quality that Indie found endearing, did as she was told. She stood and untied the short black silk robe she was wearing. She took his morning hard-on into her hands and then went to work on him as if his penis was the microphone and she was the soloist at Sunday morning service.

After three hours of exhausting sex, Indie was ready to depart.

"I'm about to be up, ma, I'm going to get at you a little later," Indie stated as he kissed her forehead.

"Noo," she whined. "Why can't you stay? I was just getting used to you being here."

"A nigga ain't even washed his ass, fucking around with you. I at least got to swing by my place and grab some clothes. Plus I need to pick up my whip from the show. You can ride if you want," he offered.

Leah threw on a pair of jeans and a white Bebe wifebeater, pulled her hair up in a ponytail, then intertwined her arm through Indie's as they walked out of her apartment. She gave him the keys to her car and smiled when she saw his approval of her baby mama Benz. He didn't know it, but she had gotten the whip courtesy of the money she had lifted from his brother's safe.

She rode shotgun as Indie made his way back to the Reliant Center.

Within minutes he was pulling out in the prestigious car, and she followed closely behind him as he led her out of the city and into the back roads of Texas.

Where in the fuck is this nigga taking me? she wondered.

They pulled up to a two-story home, and Leah rolled down her window.

"Get out for a minute," he said. "I might be a minute."

He opened her door, and she stepped outside. She noticed the curtains move slightly, and tensed up because it felt like someone was watching her.

When Indie unlocked the front door, he was greeted by his grandmother.

Leah plastered a fake smile on her face.

"Good morning, Nammy. Sorry I didn't call you. I was out with a friend last night. This is Leah. Leah, this is my grandmother," he introduced.

"Hello, it's nice to meet you," Leah stated.

Indie's grandmother looked Leah up and down as if she stunk. There was something about the girl that she couldn't pinpoint, but she didn't like her or trust her as far as she could throw her. "Hello," she replied plainly, with no extra and no welcoming tone.

Leah could peep a hater from a mile away, and she instantly knew that Indie's grandmother wasn't fond of her. *As long as the old bird stays out of my way*, she thought without ever removing her smile.

"Indie, baby, you and your guest come and sit down for breakfast," she said.

Indie knew better than to decline, so he motioned for Leah to follow his grandmother into the kitchen, where they both took a seat.

Leah watched his grandmother as she gave herself a shot of insulin before seating herself.

"Where've you been, baby? I hardly even see you anymore. You're always in and out."

"Yeah, I know, Nammy. I've been thinking it's about time for me to get out of your hair and get my own place. At first I didn't know if this move was going to be temporary, but I think I'm going to be here for a minute, so I'm gonna grab a spot down-town," Indie announced as he sipped from his glass of fresh-squeezed orange juice.

"That's too bad, baby," his grandmother replied. "An old woman done enjoyed having you around. After your papa died, it felt like something was missing. You being here made it a little less lonely." Her eyes filled with tears that she willed away.

"If you want me to stay, I will, Nammy," Indie said.

"No, no, you go ahead. You don't want an old woman around you all the time no how."

"I'll tell you what. I'll purchase the lot of land next door and get a house built. That way I won't ever be too far away. Plus, with your diabetes, I need to be close so that I can look after you. I'll contact a realtor tomorrow," he stated. "I still have the house in New York, but it can't hurt to have another one here."

Leah cringed when she heard him say he still owned a home in New York. *I know that bitch ain't still living in his shit all comfortable. That's the first thing I'm doing when I get this nigga around my finger. Her ass is getting cut the fuck off. Let the bitch struggle*, Leah fumed silently.

Leah sat under the scrutinizing eye of Indie's grandmother and was more than relieved when it was time to go.

Indie stayed true to his word and began the construction of his home right next door to his grandmother's, but while it was being built, Leah made sure that the nigga never left her side. He spent a lot of his time in the streets, building his empire, and keeping a handle on the blocks of Houston, but Leah couldn't complain. She had assumed the role of wifey without Indie even realizing he had given it to her, and when he came in too late, he always had a bagful of money. She never asked questions, and if she really wanted to know where he was at, it wasn't that hard to find out, since she had already added a tracking feature to his cell phone. She knew where he was at all times, and even though they had never defined their relationship, or "friendship" as Indie called it, he was surprisingly loyal to her.

Leah never had to worry about another bitch stepping to her face, popping off about fucking Indie. If he was messing with other women, he kept them in check. They knew that when they saw him out, they better never acknowledge knowing him, or Leah would get in that ass.

Indie began paying her bills, but that was not enough for Leah, because he was also still paying YaYa's bills each month. She would always find cashier's-check receipts with Disaya's name on it, and even though it infuriated her, she tried not to show it. She simply devised a plan to change it. She knew that Indie was too strong-minded to ever let her get into his business, especially where his past relationship was concerned.

She had to give it to Indie. He was a strong black man, and his plan to get money, then get legit, was one that was guaranteed to work if he continued to move silently through the streets. She had never met a man that was so hard to manipulate. He was a boss, and Leah knew that the only way that she was going to begin to call the shots was if she weakened him.

Drugs. That was the only answer. She knew that if she could get him to hit coke just once, it would cloud his judgment. *This nigga is on some antidrug shit, though, like he's the feds*, she thought.

As she moved around her bathroom, she cleaned up after Indie as her mind raced. *How am I going to get this nigga high?* Her hands ran across his facial products. He was the most high-maintenance man she'd ever met.

As she put his things underneath the sink, her hands ran across his allergy medications. Since moving to Houston, Indie had been having an allergic reaction to the change in humidity and temperature. It was always hard for him to breathe. She smiled as she read the prescription label . . . *Nasonex*. A devious smile crept across her face.

She hurried to her room and opened her top lingerie drawer

and removed a few grams of coke from her stash. She dipped her finger in her candy dish and brought a fingernail full up to her nose and sniffed it. She closed her eyes as the dope penetrated the cells of her brain. *How can the nigga not want to get a rush like this?* she asked herself.

She rushed back into the bathroom and unscrewed the top to Indie's nasal medication then mixed the cocaine inside of the bottle. She shook it up to ensure that there would be no trace of the drug then put the bottle back where she found it. *He puts this up his nose at least three times a day. By the time he realizes he's hooked, it'll be too late. I'm doing him a favor anyway. He needs to loosen up.*

Leah took her candy jar back to her room and pulled out her own mirror. She was about to have some fun, and the games were just beginning.

Leah lay back in her bed and watched as Indie sprayed his allergy medicine up his nose. He sprayed a couple doses up each nostril, so Leah knew that he would be good and high by the time he was done. When he dropped the bottle and closed his eyes, she knew that he was feeling that first-high burn.

"Fuck," he muttered. "I think I sprayed too much of this shit. My shits is on fire."

"Yeah, you probably just took too much, babe," Leah said with casual nonchalance.

Indie held the bridge of his nose and turned his head up, inadvertently intensifying the rush he was feeling. "Damn," he whispered.

After a few minutes the burning feeling in his nose went away, but he felt nauseous. He went to Leah, who had her arms outstretched. "I think I need to lie down for a couple minutes."

"Aww, come on, daddy," she cooed.

He climbed into bed, wrapped his arms around her, and went to sleep.

Leah smiled. It was only a matter of time before she got what she wanted.

As the days moved forward Indie could feel himself changing. He had a euphoric high all the time, but since he had never used any type of drug before, he couldn't place the odd feeling. With the frequency that he used what he thought was allergy medicine, he stayed high most of the day, and the higher he was, the looser his lips became with Leah.

Leah knew that she had him caught in her web of deception when one day she pulled out her candy dish to get herself lifted. Usually he was judgmental and frowned upon her habit, but on this day his head snapped her way in curiosity. It was almost as if his sense of smell picked up on the drug instantly

"Yo, ma, what's that shit like?" he asked. He was confused. He had never had an interest to use drugs, but something inside of him was urging him to hit the cocaine in front of him.

"It's the shit . . . come here and try a little bit. One toot can't hurt. It's not like you're smoking crack, baby. Everybody's doing this shit. Plus, it'll make the sex ten times better," Leah said seductively as she spread her legs and slid her thong to the side to finger her womanhood. She removed her soaked fingertip, dipped it in the cocaine, and licked the mixture of pussy juice and coke.

The image alone was enough to make Indie's dick stand at attention. He rubbed himself as Leah walked over to him, the plump meat on her ass jiggling with each step she took.

She straddled him, and with the mirror in hand she said, "All it takes is a little bit."

She placed the mirror on the bed then leaned over to hit a line. She handed the dollar bill to Indie, who repeated the process.

"You're a man, baby. It's going to take a little bit more to get you right. Hit one more," she urged.

Indie did it without hesitation, loving the feeling that it was giving him.

Seeing Indie so weak aroused Leah. She pushed his head down toward her throbbing clit, and without so much as uttering any instruction, Indie went to town.

The coke had Indie in another world as he wrapped his full lips around her pink pearl and sucked it gently. It was wild, and his dick was reaching record length and girth, just from the smell of Leah.

Leah screamed in ecstasy, her legs spread wide and her hands pressed against the back of Indie's head. "Eat this pussy, Indie. Tell me my shit is the best," she ordered.

"It's the best, ma," Indie stated hungrily as he slurped, licked, and probed her sugar walls with his tongue. "Damn, you got my dick on rock, ma."

The inside of his mouth radiated heat and was sending Leah from one orgasm to the next. He was skilled like no other, especially when he let go of his inhibitions.

"You gon' move me into your new house, daddy?" she asked as she practically forced her pussy into his mouth. She was rolling her body into his face as if she was riding his dick. She couldn't help it. It felt too good to stop.

"I'll give you whatever you want, ma," Indie replied in between licks.

"What about your house in New York?" Leah asked. "Don't you think you should get rid of it? You don't need it anymore, baby. You don't need her. You have all you need in me."

Indie didn't answer, and that irritated Leah, but he had her on cloud nine from the work he was putting in between her legs. He lubricated her ass with his tongue . . . sticking it inside and fucking her with a stiff tongue.

"Ooh shit! Indie!"

Indie came up for air and inserted himself into her femininity. He melted into her folds. He loved fucking Leah, because her skills in the bedroom were out of this world. He felt her contracting different areas of her vagina, until she produced the perfect fit. He slid in and out of her. The head of his length was extra-sensitive, and with each stroke, he felt like he would explode. He tried his hardest to stay in the race.

Leah smiled wickedly. She knew that Indie was holding back an orgasm. The coke had his hormones on high. She was surprised he hadn't shot off when he had first entered her.

"Go ahead, daddy. Let it go. You know you want to," she said. She wound her hips in a full circle, and just like that, Indie moaned loudly as he shot his load all up in her.

He passed out next to Leah, and while he was sleeping she whispered in his ear all night.

"Don't be a fool. You're taking care of a bitch that you're not even with. Fuck her. She killed your brother. Put that bitch out on her ass and sell your house," she urged.

He was so high that he didn't even realize it was Leah's voice in his ear. Instead, he thought it was his subconscious speaking to him. The drugs had accomplished exactly what Leah had wanted them to. They allowed her to penetrate his mind and convince him to abandon Disaya completely.

The fucked-up part about it was that in the morning when he woke up, he would think that it was all his idea to begin with and would forget that Leah was the one with the master plan. To Indie, it was he who had decided to sell his house, and with the psycho-programming Leah was doing at night, Indie was sure that it was the right thing to do.

The next morning when he awoke, he picked up the phone and contacted his realtor. He gave him instructions to have Disaya on the street before the end of the week and to put his house on the market.

Leah sat back with a satisfied smile as she dipped back into her candy jar. Once Indie hung up the phone, she held it out to him.

"You want some more?"

Without even thinking twice, Indie relented and joined Leah's antics. Then they picked up where they had left off the night before.

Chapter 25

Disaya moped around her hospital room, waiting for the doctor to bring her discharge papers. As she looked out of her window, she noticed the dark clouds in the sky. They seemed fitting because they matched her dreary mood. She didn't feel right going home without her daughter. Skylar was still struggling for her life. Disaya wanted to leave the hospital with a smile and her newborn child tucked securely in her embrace, but that wasn't going to happen. Skylar still had a long way to go before she could even breathe on her own, let alone leave the hospital.

She heard her door creak open, and a doctor came into her room.

"Hello, Disaya. I'm here to discharge you," he announced.

She nodded. He explained all of her prescriptions to her. She had hella pain meds because of all of the damage that had been done to her body from the car accident, not to mention the post-surgery cramps from her Caesarean section.

After signing that she understood the dosage instructions, she was free to go.

"What about my daughter?" she asked.

"Skylar is a strong little girl. She's getting better by the day, but she was premature, so we have to make sure she is ready to handle the world before you can take her out of here. You can come and visit her every day whenever you would like," the doctor replied.

Visiting wasn't enough. She didn't want to visit her daughter at the hospital. She wanted to be near Skylar every moment of every day, and she knew that, now that she was no longer a patient in the hospital, she would have limited access to her baby girl.

Disaya left the hospital and caught a cab back home. As the city streets passed by her window, she thought of Mona. Mona had been such a good friend. She was always there for her, and now she was gone. She closed her eyes and sent up a prayer to God, asking Him to forgive Mona for all her sins and embrace her into heaven. She couldn't believe how lonely she felt. She hadn't felt so abandoned since the death of her mother so many years ago. Now all of the issues that she thought she had locked inside of her heart were surfacing again. She realized that she wasn't as independent as she thought she was. All she had ever wanted was someone to love her.

The cabdriver pulled up to her brownstone, and she frowned when she noticed that the door was open.

"What the fuck?" she asked. She gave the cabbie his fare then hopped out with urgency as she raced up the steps.

"Hello?" she called out as she pushed her door open and crept in quietly. She heard voices coming from her living room and was shocked to find three people exploring her house.

"Excuse me? Who the hell are you? And why are you in my house?" she demanded.

A man stepped toward her. "I'm sorry. You must be the tenant that Mr. Perkins informed me of. Are you Ms. Disaya Morgan?"

"Tenant? What the hell are you talking about? This is *my* shit you're in," YaYa protested.

"No, Ms. Morgan, I'm sorry, but this property belongs to Mr. Indie Perkins, and he's decided to sell. He asked me to inform you that you have thirty days to vacate the premises," the realtor stated.

"Thirty days?" Disaya repeated incredulously. "He couldn't call me and tell me himself?" She shook her head as tears came to her eyes. "Just get out!"

The realtor nodded and replied, "I will give you a month. After that, I will come back with the police to have you removed if you're not out."

The realtor and the couple left Disaya alone, and she broke down where she stood, sobbing uncontrollably. It was all just too much for her to take in. She hadn't spoken to Indie in months, yet she always held out hope that he would come home. He didn't even know she had just given birth to their daughter. He didn't know that Mona had died. He didn't know the truth about Nanzi's death, and he wasn't even giving her a chance to tell her side of the story. *He hates me this much?* she asked. She could not help but wonder if he had ever truly loved her. She did not think that there was anything in the world that Indie could do to her to make her abandon him in the same way that he had done her.

Nighttime fell over the house, and she found herself in that same spot on the floor, curled up in a fetal position, still crying her eyes out. Her life couldn't get any worse than this. If she didn't have her daughter to live for, she was certain that she would have taken her own life and joined Mona in hell or heaven; whichever place her soul rested was cool with YaYa, as long as they were together.

You have her to live for YaYa, she told herself. *Now get up. Fuck Indie!* Disaya pulled herself off of the floor. She inhaled, taking a deep breath and released it slowly. She wiped her eyes then stood.

She walked around the house solemnly, deciding what would stay and what she would take, until she reached the door to the basement. She froze as she reached for the doorknob. She had not been down there since the fateful day when Leah had delivered the tape to her house. She opened the door and descended the steps. She was relieved to see that the blood and everything had been cleaned up. Everything was restored to its original condition, and when she closed her eyes, she could see Indie sitting in his favorite chair watching the game on his plasma TV. The memory made her smile.

She walked over to the TV. Her heart thumped as she looked at the VCR. She couldn't stop herself from pressing play, and when she turned on the television she saw the night of Nanzi's murder playing in high definition. She didn't know why she wanted to watch it, but she had to. She saw Leah on the screen posing as her.

Her hatred for Leah soared to new heights. *This bitch went as far as to get the same tattoo put on her ass as me*, YaYa thought in disgust. She shook her head, and then as if a lightbulb had gone off inside her head, she thought, *The tattoo! Oh my God, the tattoo!*

She picked up the remote and rewound the tape to the part where Leah's ass was in full view. Her heart felt as if it would burst from the amount of adrenaline that was pumping through her. She had the proof in her hands. *The bitch got her tattoo on the wrong ass cheek! This is my proof that I didn't shoot Nanzi. Indie will have to believe me.*

Disaya grabbed the tape out of the player and rushed out of the house. She had to find him. He would have to believe her now. She had cold, hard evidence in her hands that she was not the one who had taken his brother's life. She rushed out of the house and back to the hospital. She had to see her daughter. She wanted to reassure her that her daddy was coming home.

Disaya raced into the building and up to the pediatric ward, but as soon as she stepped off of the elevator, her face dropped in horror. She saw teams of nurses and doctors rushing into her daughter's room.

"No!" she yelled as she ran toward the commotion.

She was apprehended by one of the nurses. "You can't go in there right now," the nurse stated. "Let the doctors do their jobs."

"What's happening to her?" Disaya screamed. "What's happening to my baby?" She was hysterical as she tried to fight her way past the nurse that was holding her back. It seemed like every time a ray of hope surfaced in her life, it was diminished by tragedy and strife. "Please just tell me what's going on?"

The nurse took Disaya to the side and hugged her gently. "Listen to me," the nurse stated. "Skylar's lung collapsed. They are rushing her into emergency surgery to repair the damage. You have to pray and be strong for her. She is fighting to get back to you. You have to be strong. Just have faith. Pray for your daughter. I will keep you updated. Anytime I hear anything, you will hear it, okay?"

Disaya nodded weakly as she leaned into the nurse for support. Disaya couldn't do this by herself. She needed Indie. *I shouldn't have to do this by myself. He's her father. No matter what beef he and I have, he should be here for her. I have to find him.*

Disaya waited for three hours before the nurse came out and told her that they had stabilized Skylar. She walked into the recovery area and saw that her daughter was hooked up to all types of contraptions and machines. She leaned down and kissed the top of her head. "Mommy's going to get your daddy, Sky-Sky. I'll be back. I love you, baby. Stay strong for me." She then turned to the nurse. "Please look after her. I'll be back as soon as I can."

The nurse nodded, and Disaya left the hospital. She didn't know where Indie was, but she knew someone who would know . . . his mother. She took a cab all the way to New Jersey, running the tab up to one hundred and twenty dollars, a fare that she could not afford to pay. So instead of being dropped off in front of the Perkinses' house, she had the cabdriver stop around the corner.

"Let me go in here and get your money. My mother will pay you. Give me two minutes," Disaya stated as she got out of the car.

She heard the cabbie protest, but she slammed the door to shut him up. She walked up to the house as if she lived there, but instead of going to the front door, she walked straight up the driveway and into the backyard. Indie's mother's house was directly behind the house where she had been dropped off. She hopped the fence and left the cabbie waiting in the night.

The pouring rain soaked through her clothing and matted down her hair as she walked to the front door. She rang the doorbell over and over again, but was too weak to remain standing.

She was overcome with emotion. She needed Indie. Her daughter needed Indie, and she wasn't leaving until she found him.

Elaine Perkins heard the doorbell ring, just as she was getting ready to retire for the night. She knew that it wasn't her husband because he was out of town at a car dealership conference. "Who in the world?" she asked as she stood up, grabbed her robe, and made her way downstairs. It was close to midnight, and she had no idea who could be at her door at this time of night, ringing her bell like they were crazy.

"Who is it?" she called through the solid wood. She received no answer, but the bell continued to ring. She peeped out of the door hole, and all she saw was darkness.

She opened the door cautiously, and that's when it all hit her. As soon as she saw Disaya's face, she remembered where she had seen her before.

Bam! Bam! Bam!

"Open up this door! Slim, I know you're in there!" they heard someone scream through the door.

"Who the fuck is that?" Dynasty asked. "I know that ain't who I fucking think it is!" Dynasty yelled as she pushed Slim off of her.

Slim quickly threw on his boxers. He opened the door so hard that the doorknob put a hole through the wall. "What the fuck are you doing here?" he asked Lai as he snatched her inside of the room so hard that her arm popped out of the socket.

"What am I doing here? What are you doing here, Slim?" the girl asked him as she shot a hateful glare at Dynasty. Slim could smell the liquor on Lai's breath and knew that she was drunk. It was the only way she would have the balls to boss up against him. The liquid courage she had consumed had her in another element. The girl was determined to come and claim her man from Dynasty.

"Bitch, he's recuperating from that rotten-ass pussy you've been giving him," Dynasty said.

"Sit down. Let me handle this," he said.

"Well, handle it then," Dynasty shot back. She rolled her eyes as she leaned back on the bed and lit a square, intentionally keeping her composure, to show Lai that she was the queen B around here and that the little intrusion hadn't ruffled one feather. She blew the smoke from the cigarette out of her mouth seductively as she looked Lai up and down, shaking her head in disgust. "Obviously if you got to chase him, he don't want you, bitch," she mumbled.

"You were supposed to leave her! You promised me," the girl shouted hysterically as tears came to her eyes. "Why are you doing this to me? I thought you loved me?"

Slim was losing his patience with the young girl before him. He faulted himself for playing with her emotions. He had made her promises that he never intended on keeping. He had crossed the line with her and had gotten into her heart instead of her head. Now he was dealing with the drama of a woman scorned.

Dynasty began to chuckle to herself, which infuriated the girl. "Loved you? Leave me? Maybe if you were rocking some of that couture shit you're teaching my daughter, you could find your own man, bitch, 'cuz mine ain't going nowhere. So you and that bastard-ass baby need to find another sponsor," she stated, her words being absorbed like poisonous venom.

"He doesn't love you!" the girl screamed. "Don't you wonder why he's always in the street? Where do you think he is when he stays out all night? I'm the one cooking his meals and sucking his dick every damn day! He's leaving you!"

Dynasty stood up and walked toward the girl until she was within arm's reach. "I'm not the help, bitch. I don't have to lift a fucking finger. He has bitches like you come and clean our house and cook our meals. The spit you're putting on his dick is only cleaning off the cum I left there, you trick-ass ho. How does it taste?" Dynasty was lethal with her quick tongue and was known for putting chicks on blast and making them feel stupid.

"Like fish, bitch!" Lai shot back.

Without hesitation, Dynasty slapped the shit out of her, but the girl *was not easily intimidated. She snatched Dynasty's necklace clean off her neck, but not before Dynasty hawked up a huge gob of spit and deposited it on the girl's face.*

The smirk of satisfaction drawn across Dynasty's face disappeared instantly when she saw the chrome handle of a small handgun emerge from beneath the raincoat that the girl was wearing.

"No!" Slim screamed, as he lunged for Lai and muscled the gun out of her hands.

Pow! Pow!

Two bullets were all it took to end a life.

The deafening blasts seemed to echo its vibrations into space as the entire room seemed to stand still.

The girl shook uncontrollably as she snapped out of her fit of rage and the realization of her actions hit her. "Oh my God! What did I do?" she asked as her gloved hands shook with terror and regret. She watched in horror as blood leaked from Dynasty's body and soaked into the light carpet beneath her. "Oh God. I'm so sorry. I'm so sorry," she mumbled as she backed out of the hotel room, gun in one hand, necklace in the other. Before she had time to think she bolted from the room, her legs barely strong enough to carry her away.

"Oh my God!" Elaine gasped as she bent down to help Disaya off the wet porch. "Oh my God, sweetheart I am so sorry," she said as she wrapped her arms around the young woman.

Many years had passed since the day she had murdered Disaya's mother, and she had buried the memory so deep inside of her that sometimes she forgot that it had occurred.

As she looked into Disaya's eyes, she immediately recognized Dynasty inside of her. *That is why she looked so familiar.* Elaine had left New York immediately after Dynasty's funeral and had taken both of her sons to Houston to live with her mother. It wasn't until her sons became teenagers did she finally build up enough nerve to return to New York. Back then she was known as Lai, but since then she had not acknowledged that that person existed, and until now she had never thought of it again.

"Oh YaYa, sweetheart, I am so sorry." Elaine and Disaya cried together on that front porch, neither of them asking any questions as to the other's grief, but they both appreciated the support.

Elaine helped Disaya up. She was still flabbergasted as to how her past had come back to haunt her. Indie had fallen in love with the child of the woman his mother had murdered. How ironic could one life be?

"I need to talk to you, Ms. Perkins," Disaya stated. "Please, I have so much to say." She was still sobbing, but Elaine stopped her.

"We will talk, YaYa, but first we have to get you out of these wet clothes. Go and take a shower. I have a nightgown you can put on, and I'll throw your clothes in the washer, so you can wear them tomorrow."

As YaYa retreated to the bathroom, Elaine broke down and cried. She had no idea what Disaya had been through growing up parentless, but she could only imagine. She knew that it was her fault, but she was glad that she was being given a second chance to make things right. She battled with herself whether she should admit to Disaya what she had done and after much debate, she decided not to. It would only add to Disaya's pain, not take away, so she figured it unnecessary. It would also bring a lot of unwanted drama and speculation into her own life, so she decided to keep some skeletons tucked safely inside her closet.

She put YaYa's clothes in the washer, and when Disaya emerged from the bathroom, she seemed to have calmed down a bit.

Elaine had made tea and motioned for YaYa to sit across from her at the kitchen table.

"I know you know that Indie left me," Disaya said. "Did he tell you why?"

Elaine shook her head. "No, he did not. He only said that the two of you had differences and that the baby was not an issue anymore."

Disaya wiped away the tear that trailed her cheek. "Indie left me because he thinks that I killed Nanzi."

The blow hit Elaine like a ton of bricks as new tears threatened her eyes. She truly knew that Disaya's purpose in her life was to dish out karma. *I killed her mother, she killed my son.*

"I didn't kill him, though, Elaine, I swear I didn't. When Indie met me, I was involved in a lot of bullshit. I was running with this organization called Elite. It's like a high-paid escort service. I ended up branching out on my own with a girl who I thought was my friend. We did a lot of sexual stuff together, but I thought it was all in the name of making a dollar. I had no idea she was obsessed with me, until after I fell in love with Indie. She became possessive and crazy over me. I agreed to do one last job with her. That job happened to be Nanzi. She killed him and made it look like I did it. I tried to hide it from Indie, but she sent him a tape that makes me look guilty. That's why he left."

Elaine took a minute to take in Disaya's story. *The apple really didn't fall too far from the tree,* she thought. She knew that YaYa's story was completely possible. In the world of prostitution anything could happen, and there are no fair rules to the game. For some reason she believed Disaya, and even if Disaya was lying, she couldn't be too mad. They had both committed or contributed to the same crime . . . murder.

"You have to believe me," Disaya begged.

"I do," Elaine stated. She reached across the table and gripped Disaya's hand. "I want to tell you that I am sorry for everything. You may not know what I am talking about, but it is something that I have to say. I cannot judge you for what you have been through, and I forgive you for whatever role you played in my son's death."

Disaya smiled. She felt a connection to Elaine that she couldn't describe, but for the first time in years she felt a motherly love that had been missing all her life.

"I have to find Indie, Elaine. I love him so much. He is my reason for everything. He is the one person that showed me I was worth more, and he made me love myself. I know that he doesn't want to see me right now, but it's been almost seven months. I need him, Elaine. Our daughter needs him. She's in the hospital struggling for her life. She needs her father."

"Your daughter? You mean I have a granddaughter? But Indie said—"

Disaya cut her off. "He probably thought that what happened between us caused me to lose the baby, but it didn't. I held on to her, but now she's slipping away, and I can't do this by myself. She needs her family."

"I'm calling him right now," Elaine stated as she arose from the table.

"Okay, but please let me be the one to tell him about Skylar," Disaya requested.

"Skylar? That's my grandbaby's name?" Elaine asked with a fresh pool of joyous tears.

Disaya nodded.

Elaine rushed to the phone. She dialed Indie's number, but his voice mail picked up. She left a message then turned to Disaya. "Come on, sweetheart. You take me to my little angel. I'm going to stay by her side until God brings her out of this, and you are going to go to Houston to bring my son back here."

"Houston?" Disaya said in disbelief. She couldn't believe that Indie had gone so far away.

"Yeah, we'll swing by your house so you can pack a bag. I will watch over Skylar while you are gone."

Disaya and Elaine left for the hospital. Disaya felt like a weight had been lifted off of her shoulders, and she knew that soon she and Indie would be face to face. She would finally get the chance to explain everything to him, and she had the tape to back up her story.

Chapter 26

"Indie, this is your mother. You need to call home. There is something important that you need to know. Call as soon as you get this. I love you, son."

Leah deleted the message. She would decide if and when Indie would call his mother back. She heard the shower water stop running and quickly turned his phone off and put it back where she got it from before he walked into the room.

He emerged. His body glistened as beads of water dripped down his amazing physique. His eyes were dilated, yet his lids were heavy, making him look even sexier when he was high. Getting high together had become a regular routine for them. Once she got Indie started, it was a wrap.

Leah hit a line of cocaine. "You want some?"

He shook his head and declined. "Nah, ma, I've got to hit these streets and play catch-up. You've had me cooped-up in this mu'fucka with you like a newlywed. I also got to check on the house, to make sure everything is going as planned."

Leah felt a wave of nausea hit her like a ton of bricks, and when she opened her mouth to talk, she felt the vomit tickling her throat.

She became hot as she sprinted past Indie and into the bathroom, barely making it before the contents of her stomach came up.

"Aghh!" She spewed vomit into the porcelain bowl and heaved violently, until there was nothing left to bring up.

"Damn, ma, you all right?" Indie asked as he helped her off the floor.

She shook her head. She knew what was wrong. She had set it up from day one. The weight gain, the dizzy spells, and now the morning sickness.

"Indie, I think I'm pregnant," she announced.

Indie's reality rocked as if he had hit life's turbulence. She couldn't be pregnant. He remembered strapping up every time . . . except the times when they had sex when he was high. He wanted to deny that the baby was his, but he wasn't built like that and never would be.

The thought of her being pregnant brought back the deadly memory of him and Disaya. He could hear her scream in pain when he had practically beat his first child out of her. He closed his eyes and put his hands over his face as he shook his head in disbelief. A tear graced his cheek. *Shit isn't supposed to be like this,* he thought, as flashes of YaYa plagued his mind. He remembered her bulging stomach and then looked at Leah and tried to picture her with a pregnant belly. *How could I have been so stupid? I don't even love this bitch.* Yes, he enjoyed spending time with Leah, and she was fun. Half of the reason he dug her was because of her spontaneity and her ruthless, harsh attitude, but with a baby involved, a spontaneous affair became a routine hassle, and he didn't want a woman with a spirit as mean as Leah's raising his seed.

"Hello? Indie? What—you don't want it?" Leah asked.

Not wanting to make Leah feel cheap, Indie lied. "Of course, I want it, ma. You just hit me with a whole lot to think about. How far along are you?"

"Can't be more than a couple months," she replied. "I thought I was getting fat, but at least now I have an excuse."

"Look, I'm up. I've got to clear my head. Don't worry about

anything. I'm here for you. You need to lay off of all that candy, though, now that you're carrying my baby."

Leah smacked her lips and rolled her eyes.

"That's not a request, Leah. It's an order," he said seriously, before kissing the top of her head and leaving.

As soon as he left he picked up his phone and dialed his grandmother's number. Always dependable, she answered on the second ring.

"Good morning, Nammy," Indie greeted. "Do you mind if I stop by for lunch? I have to check on the development of the house and I thought I'd swing by."

"You know you're welcome here anytime. My question is, what's on your mind? You know I know when something is bothering you," she responded.

Indie chuckled because she did indeed know when something was off balance in his life. "Leah's pregnant, Nammy, and I don't know what to do about it," he admitted.

"Leah? That girl you brought over here?"

"Yeah, that's her. She's just not what I want my children's mother to be like, and I don't want to have kids all over the place. I wanted the same woman to bear all of my kids. I wanted to start a family," Indie said.

"Well, I'm not particularly fond of that girl. She's got the devil in her . . . but you chose her. Now you have to take care of your responsibilities."

"I know, Nammy. I just never thought—" He stopped midsentence because he could feel himself becoming emotional as he thought of the child he had lost and of the woman he had once loved. "I'll be by in a couple hours. I have to run some errands first. I love you, Nammy."

"Yep, I love you too, baby. See you soon."

As soon as Disaya stepped off the plane, nervous energy filled her. She was terrified and excited all at the same time. The last time she had seen Indie, he had tried to kill her. She had no clue what to expect from him now. It had been exactly seven months since the last time they had been in each other's presence. She yearned to just see his face again, but she had a feeling that he would rather die than to see hers.

She rented a car and followed the instructions that Elaine had given her to get to Indie's grandmother's house. It took almost an hour for her to find her way, and when she arrived, she had to take a deep breath and calm her nerves before she got out of the car. The heat hit her as soon as her stiletto pump hit the dirt road. She wore her head in a high, genie ponytail, but applied only M•A•C lipglass to her face. There was no makeup in the world that could cover up the scratches that the windshield had caused. She would have to wait for her face to heal before she could even feel normal again.

She walked up to the house, and before she could raise her hand to knock on the door, it opened slightly, and a short, beautiful old woman answered.

"Hi, umm—I'm—" YaYa stuttered nervously as she shifted from stiletto to stiletto. "I'm YaYa. I'm a friend of Indie's from New York," she introduced.

"Hello, YaYa. Indie isn't here right now, but you can come inside and wait for him . . . you've traveled this far, you might as well."

She let Disaya into her home, but she could sense the sadness in the air. It was the same sadness that Indie had brought into her home when he had first arrived. "Are you the reason why Indie left New York?"

Disaya nodded. "I think so. Ms.—I'm sorry, I didn't get your name."

"Just call me Nammy," his grandmother replied.

"Nammy, I made a lot of mistakes . . . and I hurt Indie. But I love him, and there is something that I need to tell him. I can't change my past. All I can do is learn from it and try to make my future better."

Indie's grandmother smiled. Just as quickly as she had judged

Leah, she judged Disaya, only, she liked what she saw in YaYa. Her spirit was good, and she wished that whatever problems her grandson and YaYa had developed could have been worked out.

"I wish you would have come a little bit sooner. Maybe he wouldn't have gotten that hussy he brought over here pregnant. Running from you, he ran himself right into the devil's arms."

"Indie's having a baby?" Disaya asked. She was heartbroken, and she could literally feel her breath shortening, as if she was about to die.

"So she says, but that girl is something else. I wouldn't be surprised if it was all a hoax. Would you like something to eat?"

Disaya shook her head no. "Thank you, umm . . . but I have to go. Thank you so much for your hospitality. It was nice meeting you."

Disaya was up and out of the house before his grandmother could even respond. Disaya ran all the way to her car, and when she was inside of the rental, she burst into tears. *How could he?* she asked. *He's moved on without even calling me to make sure that our baby was gone. He's made a whole new life down here.*

She put her car in reverse, and just as she was about to pull out, a cream-colored Maybach pulled in, blocking her path. She knew who it was before she even saw him step out of the car.

She wiped her eyes and stepped out of the car. When their eyes connected, electricity shot through the gaze.

He walked up on her, shocked to see her, ashamed to see her, furious to see her. They were both speechless. Her once flawless face was marred with deep scratches. His heart broke when he reached to touch her face and she flinched in fear.

She closed her eyes. She had waited so long for this moment, so long to see him. She clenched the tape in her hands as tears fell gracefully from her eyes.

He cleared his throat to make sure no emotion was revealed in his tone. He loved Disaya with everything that he was, but he could not forgive her. He could never forget.

"What are you doing here?" he finally asked, as he grabbed her roughly by the elbow. His anger for her surfaced all over again.

YaYa opened her mouth to speak, but only sobs came out. *He's having another baby,* she thought as she doubled over, sick with grief . . . with jealousy . . . with hate.

"Come on, ma, don't do this to me. We're over. You know what it is," he stated, loosening his grip on her. Seeing her in pain tugged at his heartstrings. He felt sorry for her and for him-self because they had both lost something great when she be-trayed him. Their love was one for the history books, but it had never gotten the chance to grow because of mistrust.

She stood suddenly and smacked his face then beat his chest furiously.

Her punches didn't hurt him, and he let her release them as he wrapped his arms around her waist. He couldn't help it. She was the woman who was supposed to have his child. Not Leah. It al-ways felt so right between them. *Why did she have to go and fuck everything up?*

"I hate you! I fucking *hate you!*" she screamed as she hit him repeatedly.

Indie finally subdued her by grabbing hold of her wrists gently. "Stop, stop! YaYa, stop," he said.

"Do you have any fucking clue what I've been through? Huh? Do you, Indie? I have been *sick* over you for eight months, Indie. Eight fucking months. Eight months! You beat me within an inch of my life, and I still loved you. I still wanted you. I still waited for you to come home. I know I was wrong, but you never gave me a chance to explain. You just left. I gave you time and space to sort things out, but you just moved on. You forgot all about me, Indie. Was it that easy for you to just come here and start a new life? A new family? How could you?"

"How could I not? You killed my brother!" he yelled. "You knew what it was. Bitch got a lot of nerve to show up here think-ing shit is cake. You're lucky I left you breathing the first time."

"Yeah, you know what, Indie. I wish you hadn't. Dying would

have been better than this. Dying would have been better than seeing your best friend's face blown off. Dying would have been better than losing the man you loved more than anything in this world! Dying would have been better than finding out that I don't mean shit to you! It would have been better than finding out you are having a baby!" YaYa wiped her face and stepped away from Indie.

He didn't know why, but he felt badly for YaYa. He missed her, but would never let her know that. It was too late for them to go back. There was no mending what was broken between them.

"Just leave, ma, go back to New Yitty and forget about me. Yeah, I'm having a shorty with a bitch I trust. I don't trust you, YaYa. You're too fucking grimy." It hurt him to say the words, just like it hurt her to hear them.

Disaya thought about Skylar. She was his daughter, but she couldn't tell him about her. She refused to. She didn't want Indie's sympathy love or for her daughter to ever be second place in his life. Indie had a new family now. As much as she hated it, she had to accept it.

Disaya began to walk away, and with each step she took, Indie felt like he couldn't breathe without her.

"Disaya," he called out.

She didn't stop walking. She had to get away from him. He was no longer hers.

"Disaya, I know you hear me," he stated.

"What?" she asked in defeat.

Indie walked up to her and grabbed both of her hands. He took one and placed it over his heart and took the other and placed it on his face, where his tears were free-falling.

"I did love you, ma. Do you see these tears?" he asked.

She nodded, as her own continued to fall, and she heaved in distress.

"Do you feel my heart racing?"

"Yes," she answered.

"You're the only woman that can do that to me, Disaya. You

are my weakness. I did love you, so don't ever lie on me and say that I didn't. *You* broke us, ma. You and only you. I've moved on. I've got a shorty on the way, and I'm not looking back to the past for you. I'm leaving you there. Go back home. Move on, ma. I have."

Indie got into his car and reversed it so that he could let Disaya leave. Watching her drive away was so hard for him to do, but his pride wouldn't let her stay. He had to focus on now and forget about what could have been. He was trying to make a new life that did not include Disaya, and the fact still remained that he was with Leah and she was going to have his seed. He forced himself to avoid her gaze as she pulled out of the driveway. He simply put his car back in drive and put all thought of Disaya in the back of his mind as he watched her speed away.

When Disaya arrived back in New York, she felt drained. She was exhausted, and Elaine could see the anguish written all over her face.

"Where's Indie?" she asked.

"He's not coming," Disaya said. "He's having another baby, Elaine. He didn't even ask about the one I was carrying. He made it perfectly clear that he wants nothing to do with me or anything involving me. I didn't tell him about Skylar. I don't need him. I'll raise her myself."

"That's the pain talking, sweetheart. You're going to need a father for this baby. He has a right to know."

"I have a right too, Elaine. I have a right to move on, just like he did. Please, you have to give me your word that you won't tell Indie about Skylar."

Elaine didn't want to commit to the promise, but she felt indebted to Disaya. "Okay, but I can't keep this secret forever. I'll let you get over losing him first, and then we will talk about when is the right time to tell him. Until then, you and the baby can stay with me and Bill. We will be glad to take you in until you get on your feet. Now let's go check on Skylar."

Elaine could not believe that Indie had another child on the way. She wanted to call him and cuss him out for not telling her right away, but then she would have to explain how she found out. She prayed for YaYa's and Indie's relationship and prayed for the soul of her son Nanzi. She didn't know how this mess would end up, but she felt in her heart that Indie needed to know. He was her son, and he had a right to know. She would work on getting Disaya to tell him, but until then, she would help her as much as she could.

Chapter 27

Three Months Later

"Welcome home!" Bill and Elaine yelled out in excitement as Disaya stepped through the door with Ms. Skylar Mona Perkins in her arms. It had taken three months, but Skylar had made a full recovery, healing from all of her ailments, and had been released from the hospital with a clean bill of health.

Disaya smiled gratefully, and Skylar's eyes sparkled like black jewels as she recognized both of her grandparents.

Elaine and Bill had been great to Disaya and Skylar. Elaine had opened up their home and turned Indie's old room into a room for Disaya and Skylar. They stayed by Disaya's side as Skylar's health dipped and peaked throughout the weeks, reassuring her that everything would be okay.

Disaya was trying to piece her life back together. Most nights she still cried herself to sleep, thinking of Indie. Her heart wouldn't let him go, no matter how many times her mind told her it was over. She knew that she couldn't live under his parents' roof forever, especially since she had let his father eat her pussy. Neither of them ever spoke on it, but it was just awkward.

She began putting a plan together that would get her where she needed to be in life. She had started to take classes at Manhattan Community College. She was tired of hustling. Her Prada Plan had gotten her nothing but heartache, and although she knew her mother hadn't meant any harm, putting that in her head had made her lead a dangerous path in life.

She wanted to use what she had, to get what she wanted, but in the past, she was using the wrong assets. It took her daughter to enlighten her that she had more to offer the world than what she gave herself credit for. She had a Prada Plan, all right, and she was going to use her brains to get her ahead in life. She realized that her physical body would eventually age and wouldn't always be on point, but her mental abilities would last her a lifetime.

That was going to be her new hustle . . . her new plan that would eventually lead her to all that Prada she loved so much. She was seeking intelligence and independence. This time nothing was standing in her way. She had more than herself to think about. She had to think about Skylar, and she wanted to show her a new way to get money. She wanted to break the cycle. Dynasty had reduced her self-worth to make a dollar, Disaya had stepped her game up and reduced her self-worth to make a couple dollars, she would be damned if her daughter continued in their footsteps. Skylar was going to reach for the stars because Disaya was going to set a new example and trailblaze a new way of thinking for her daughter to follow.

"Did we really have to move right next door to your grandmother?" Leah asked as she rubbed her stomach.

"No, *we* didn't. I did. You could have kept your place, but you chose to move in my crib, remember?" Indie stated sarcastically.

Leah picked up the tiny vial of cocaine that she wore around her neck and snuck a line.

Indie approached her and snatched the necklace off her neck. "You're five months' pregnant, Leah. Think about the baby,"

Indie stated in disgust. The more time he spent around Leah, the more he came to despise her. She only thought of herself.

He knew that he would have to make sure he was around once their baby was born. He didn't trust her to care for his seed responsibly and he kicked himself every day for not strapping up.

"Don't act like you don't do it," Leah said.

"I don't. I quit fucking with that shit. I can't believe I let you talk me into it in the first place. You need to get off that shit. I don't want no crackhead for a wifey. Act like a lady," he chastised. "I'm up. I'll be back."

Leah knew that she was getting too comfortable with Indie. She still had to be on her best behavior until she had his baby. She didn't want there to be any chance that he might go back to YaYa. She had learned of his little run-in with her. His grandmother seemed to like Disaya and advocated on her behalf every time Leah was around, which was why Leah hated Indie's grandmother so much. But Leah knew that Disaya didn't have shit on her. *I'm the one with his baby. He'll never go back to her as long as I have his kid*, she thought.

Leah waited until Indie's car pulled out of the driveway before she got up and retrieved her hidden cocaine stash. She put ten grams out in front of her and had her own private party. She didn't give a damn about the health of her baby. She was emotionally detached from the world. *As long as I push this little fucker out, he will be happy. I don't give a damn if he comes out retarded as fuck. I'm gon' get my high.*

Leah continued to snort the cocaine, and when she was high as a kite, she sat back on the couch on cloud nine.

It wasn't until intense cramps hit her did she regret her decision. *Ooh shit, maybe I did overdo it*, she thought. She picked up the mirror and hid any evidence that she had used drugs and decided to lie down to relieve the pain. She slipped into one of Indie's white button-up shirts and tried to rest as she drifted into an uncomfortable sleep.

She was suddenly awakened by an agonizing pain in her

womb. It felt like someone had kicked her in her stomach, and it was so great that it caused her to cry out.

"Oww!" she shrieked. She felt something slip between her legs, and when she lifted the covers, she quickly put them back down. "Oh, my God. Oh, my God," she chanted as she lifted the sheets again and saw a huge mass of blood, mucus, and an undeveloped human body between her legs.

She panicked and reached for the phone then stopped herself. *No, I can't call for help. Indie can't know about this,* she thought. Sweat came across her brow as she grabbed the scissors on her bed stand. She pulled back the sheets and cut the cord that connected her body to the bloody mess between her thighs. She almost threw up, she was so disgusted, and as she looked at the clock, she knew she had more than enough time to cover up her crime before Indie arrived back home.

Her limbs shook uncontrollably as she struggled to stand. She wrapped up the bloody sheets and the baby. She was so delusional that she didn't shed a single tear. She secured the baby under her arm, disregarding the fact that there was blood all over the front of her shirt and dripping down her legs.

Leah walked through the house and out to the garage, where she located a shovel, then headed for the backyard. Sweat poured from her, and she was shaky as she dug a makeshift grave for her unborn child. She was a madwoman. She worked diligently, ignoring all pain, until the sheets and the baby were buried and covered.

When she finally finished, she looked up toward Indie's grandmother's house. Their eyes met, and Leah threw the shovel down then marched toward the nosy old woman's home. *Nammy doesn't like me? Fuck Nammy! I'm not going to let her ruin this for me!* Leah thought as she banged on the front door. She twisted the doorknob and went inside.

"What did you do to that poor child?" Indie's grandmother asked. "You just wait till Indie gets home."

Leah's eyes scanned the room until she found the perfect murder weapon.

"I knew you were trouble the first time I laid eyes on you. He should have just stuck with YaYa."

"YaYa! Fuck YaYa! As a matter of fact, fuck you!" Leah yelled as she grabbed the syringe that his grandmother used to take her insulin. She filled it with air then stuck Indie's Nammy in the neck and injected a large air bubble into her veins. You could see the struggle on the old woman's face as the oxygen bubble traveled straight to her heart and began to block her blood flow.

"I have one more thing to tell you, *Nammy*." Leah laughed, as if watching the old woman die was a joke. "I killed your other grandson, Nanzi."

Nammy's eyes widened just as the oxygen traveled straight to her brain, and within a matter of seconds she fell dead.

Leah wiped down everything she had touched, including the syringe. She then put the syringe in the old woman's hands and left the home undetected. She rushed back to Indie's house and finished cleaning up the blood. She bleached and scrubbed blood from the mattress until her hands were raw.

She saw Indie's headlights pulling into the driveway a few hours later.

"Oh shit, he's here already," she whispered as she ran into the bathroom and locked herself inside.

"Leah, you here, ma?" Indie called out.

She leaned over the bathroom sink and looked at herself in the mirror. Her complexion was green, and she could barely stand from the pain, but she answered, "Yeah, I'm in the bathroom. I'll be out in a minute." She turned toward the linen closet, grabbed a stack of bedsheets, and began to tuck them into her leggings. Once she adjusted them to the right size, she lowered her shirt then turned to the side. It looked as if a baby was still living inside of her. She smiled, then opened the bathroom door.

"Hey, sexy, how was your day?" Indie asked.

"Good," she lied.

"How's my baby?" he asked as he reached to caress her stomach. She dodged his touch.

"Uh-uh, Indie, I've been nauseous all day. Don't come in here touching all on me making it worse," she complained.

"Is that why you didn't cook?" Indie shot her a playful glance as he asked her the question.

"Nigga, you know I don't cook. You better take your ass next door like you do every other night. You want me for my looks, not my cookbook skills," she said.

"Yeah, a'ight . . . I'ma shoot next door for a little bit. Call me if you need anything," he said. He kissed her on the cheek and walked out of the door.

Leah scanned the room in paranoia to make sure she had cleaned everything up. Once she was positive that she left no traces of anything that could arouse Indie's suspicion, she went to peek out the blinds and wait to hear Indie scream for help.

Five, four, three, two, one . . .

"Leah, call nine one one!"

Chapter 28

"Why can't I come to the funeral?" Leah asked stubbornly. "It's something that I have to do myself. I need to be around family right now. You stay here and take care of my baby. I'll be back in a week," he stated. Indie kissed her forehead and headed out the door. His heart was so heavy. He had been close to his grandmother, and her death was so unexpected. He felt like he was to blame. *I should've monitored her medicine more. The medical examiner said she injected herself with nothing but air. I was so wrapped up in what was going on with me that I didn't pay attention,* he thought bitterly.

As he boarded his plane, he felt a sense of relief. He hadn't been home in almost a year, and it would be good to be around the people he loved most. The funeral was in two days, and he planned on staying for an entire week, just to spend time with his people and ensure that they were okay before he headed back. Indie sat in his first-class seat, pulled down his window shade, and let his exhaustion settle in, while the pilot took him back to New York.

* * *

Disaya paced nervously. "Are you sure I should be here when he gets here?" she asked Elaine as she fed Skylar in her arms.

"I'm sure, YaYa. It's about time the truth came out. I have some truth of my own to admit, but we will talk about that a little later. Skylar is three and a half months old, and Indie hasn't even held his daughter. He doesn't even know she exists," Elaine said as she busied herself around the kitchen. "My mother spoke highly of you."

"I only met her that one time, and I was so distraught over Indie. I wish we could have met under better circumstances," Disaya replied.

"There was no need. My mama only needed to meet you once to decide if she liked you or not. She told me that you and Indie were meant for one another. We only get one life, YaYa. Don't waste yours. You love my son. I see your eyes every morning, and I know that they're always puffy from you crying over him at night. At least give him the option to be in his daughter's life," Elaine pleaded.

Disaya went upstairs to put Skylar down for her afternoon nap. She was so afraid of seeing Indie. She wanted to just grab some clothes and disappear for a week, but there was no sense in prolonging the inevitable. Skylar did need her father, and Disaya knew she was wrong for not telling Indie about her in the first place.

"We're here!" she heard Indie's father announce.

She kissed her daughter before placing her in her crib then slowly made her way downstairs.

Indie looked up just as she began to descend the steps and froze in confusion.

"What is she doing here?" he asked his mother.

"She's been staying here, Indie," Elaine admitted.

"She's been what?" Indie asked, his voice raising a few octaves. "Do you have any idea what she's done?"

"I do, son. She told me everything, but let me tell you this."

Elaine turned to Disaya. "Please come down here, YaYa. You should hear this." She held Disaya's hand with her left and Indie's hand with her right.

Disaya shook nervously; just being in Indie's presence was intimidating.

"I've been holding this secret in for a long time, but I feel like I have to tell my story in order for you, my son, to understand how I could forgive Disaya for what she's done. When I was nineteen, I met a man named Buchanan Slim."

Disaya gasped when she heard her father's name.

"Yes, YaYa, I'm talking about the same man that you know to be your father. He was a pimp . . . he was my pimp, and I loved him so much. He and I were inseparable, until he met this other girl. Her name was Dynasty. Your mother, Dynasty," Elaine said to Disaya.

YaYa dropped her hand, but she continued to listen.

"Dynasty got pregnant by one of her regular johns . . . some rich Puerto Rican man, and I thought for sure Slim would get rid of her, but instead he fell in love with her. He assumed responsibility for her baby . . . for you Disaya, and treated me coldly. I had already given him a son . . . Nanzi, but he never looked at me the way he looked at Dynasty. I got jealous one day, and I stormed in on Slim and your mother. I was so angry. I remember the gun being in my hand, and I remember pulling the trigger. I killed your mother, YaYa. Then I told you that I couldn't take you at her funeral."

"Auntie Lai?" Disaya whispered. Elaine was opening up chapters of Disaya's life that she had sealed forever, causing her to break down and face past demons.

"Yes, YaYa, I'm your Auntie Lai. That's why you've always looked so familiar to me. I didn't realize where I knew you from until you showed up on my doorstep three months ago. That's when I saw your mother in you. I have no idea what you went through after that day when I took your parents away, but I am sorry. That secret has haunted me for many years. That is why I am able to forgive you for the role you played in killing Nanzi."

"Was Nanzi my brother? Is Indie?" Disaya asked.

"I truly believe, if Slim would have stayed free, he would have raised you and Nanzi like siblings, even though you were not biologically related to him. Bill is Indie's father," Elaine stated.

Disaya shook her head as she absorbed all of the information. She wanted to hate Elaine, but she didn't. Elaine had done so much for her in the past three months and had welcomed her when everyone else had shunned her.

"I understand if you hate me, YaYa," Elaine said.

"I don't," she replied quickly. "I don't at all."

Elaine hugged Disaya as Indie watched on. It was so hard for him to be in YaYa's presence. To him there was no forgiving her.

Waaa! Waaa!

Indie looked up the stairs where the crying noise came from. Disaya pulled away from Elaine. Elaine wiped Disaya's eyes and kissed her on the cheek. "I love you forever for what you've given me. Go and handle your business."

Disaya walked up the steps, and Indie looked at his mother for further explanation. "So just because you killed her mother in a past life, we have to keep her around in ours? She killed my brother!"

"Go talk to her, Indie. You broke her heart when you told her you had a baby on the way. The two of you need to talk. There is something else you still need to know," Elaine urged.

Indie ascended the steps, shaking his head in disbelief. He walked into his old bedroom and put his hand to his heart when he saw Disaya holding a baby girl. The way she rocked her gently from side to side and held her close to her chest was magnetic. Tears filled his eyes.

"Is she mine?" Indie asked, his voice breaking as he approached Disaya.

YaYa cried as she held on to her daughter. She nodded. "Yes, she's yours, Indie."

Indie took the baby girl from Disaya's arms and held her up in front of him. Everything about her said YaYa and Indie. She looked like the perfect combination of the two, and Indie loved her instantly. He brought his daughter to his chest and inhaled her angelic scent.

"Why didn't you tell me?" he whispered.

"I was going to. That was the reason why I came all the way to Houston, but you said you were having a baby, and I never want Skylar to feel like a second-place child. I decided I'd raise her on my own," she said truthfully.

"She could never be second-rate, YaYa," Indie whispered. He never took his eyes off his daughter. "She's beautiful. So . . . beautiful." He lay down on what used to be his bed and laid his daughter across his chest. Her crying immediately ceased as he patted her back gently. "Why did you have to fuck everything up, ma? This is so perfect, but I'm not my mother. I can't just forgive and forget."

Disaya sat on the bed beside Indie. "I didn't kill Nanzi, Indie, I'm not that coldhearted. I had no idea what was about to go down until it was too late."

YaYa told him the story of how she linked up with Elite. She told it all, leaving out names because she didn't want him to judge anyone but herself. She left out no details, not even the role she had played in the part of Nanzi's murder.

"But you made me want to change, Indie. You were the only reason why I began to love myself." She went to her closet and pulled out the tape that Leah had sent to her house.

"I need you to watch this again, Indie. This tape shows that I'm not the one that pulled the trigger."

"Don't put that in, ma. My heart can't take it."

"Please, Indie. I need you to see this."

She popped the tape in the player and pressed play.

Indie watched it and cringed in anger. As soon as he saw his brother's lifeless face, he began to hate Disaya all over again. Disaya rewound the tape and paused it when it showed Leah's backside.

"This isn't me, Indie. The bitch that set me up got it wrong. She put her tattoo on the wrong side."

Indie peered intensely at the screen and couldn't believe he had never noticed it before. He knew Disaya's body like he knew his ABC's, and sure enough, it was the same tattoo, but in a different location. He looked at YaYa in disbelief, who was now standing and waiting for Indie to speak.

"Say something, Indie . . . say anything."

He stood and laid his daughter down inside her crib then turned to Disaya. "I'm sorry, ma," he whispered in her ear. He swept her hair from her face. He had missed so much in the year that he had been gone from her life. "I'm sorry for putting my hands on you. I'm so sorry for not listening to you."

Disaya broke down in his arms as he held on to her tightly. "Never hide anything from me again. I'm sorry. I should've listened. I hurt you, ma. I'm going to do better, and I'm going to be here for you and my daughter. I understand why you didn't tell me."

It was a relief to be in Indie's arms again, but it wasn't the same. She pulled away from him.

"I don't know if I can do this, Indie. I don't know if we can just go back to the way things were."

"Why, ma? You've got to give me a chance to make it up to you. We have a lot to work out and discuss, but I love you more than I love the air in my lungs, YaYa. Don't do this to me. What am I supposed to do without you?"

"What am I supposed to do with you, Indie? You have another baby on the way. What happened to leaving me in the past? I've been through so much. Our daughter was fighting for her life for two and a half months and you were nowhere in sight. You were out making another one. You were out replacing me. That bitch is probably the reason why you put me out of *our* house. How could you replace me, Indie? I could never replace you. No matter what you did. I don't know if I can look past that," YaYa admitted, all of her emotions coming to the forefront.

His cell phone rang, and he looked at the caller ID. It was Leah. He sent her to voice mail.

"See. That was probably her right there. I can't do that baby mama bullshit. I don't know if it's me and you, or you and her. I just want a new start for me and Sky," she said.

"Fuck all that you talking, YaYa. I love you, and I love my daughter. I wasn't here for you when you needed me most. I understand that you're hurt, but I'm here now, and I'm not asking you to come back to me. I'm telling you that's how it's going to be. Yes, I do have a baby on the way, and I have to take care of my seed. I wouldn't be the nigga you loved if I didn't take care of my shorty, but I need you to stand by me, ma. Be here for me, because you and Skylar are number one. I didn't replace you, YaYa. I just fucked up. You fucked up, and I forgive you, ma. I need you to forgive me and be here for yo' man."

Disaya shook her head unsurely, and Indie pulled her close to him. Disaya couldn't resist his scent. Everything about him was made for her. He kissed her gently. She kissed him back.

"Just try for me, ma. Try to love me like you did before," he said in between their kiss.

"I never stopped loving you, Indie. I just don't want to be hurt again. It took me a long time to get to the point where I could even consider living without you. There was so many times I thought about ending it all, just to stop the pain. Don't do that to me again," Disaya whispered.

"Never, ma, I'm never letting you go," he replied. He picked up Skylar and lay down with her on his chest and Disaya in his arms. "I'm here forever."

Disaya didn't respond as she closed her eyes and thanked God for bringing love back into her life.

Chapter 29

I ndie and Disaya spent the entire week becoming reacquainted. Indie was attached to Skylar like glue, and everywhere the couple went they took their daughter along. Indie was in love with love. He was in love with the idea of being a husband and a father, even though he knew that he and YaYa were a long way from walking down the aisle. He didn't know how he would deal with his situation with Leah back in Houston, but he cherished every single second spent with Disaya. She completed him in a way that only a soul mate could. His other half . . . his confidante . . . his best friend . . . and sometimes worst enemy, YaYa was his woman.

Indie didn't even let Disaya's education get in his way of spending time with her. He dropped her off to and from school every day. He was impressed by how much she had grown. She no longer seemed rough around the edges. She had refined herself and had become a woman of ambition. He loved her more and more each passing minute. She explained to him what her Prada Plan was now, compared to what it used to be, and although Indie thought the concept was cute, he respected it and loved the legitimate hustle in his lady.

YaYa's love for Indie had never wavered, and he was proving to her that she and Skylar would come first if she chose to let him back into her life. She wasn't dumb. She peeped the phone calls that he sent to voice mail, but he never disrespected or lied to her when she asked who was calling him. She was jealous that she would have to share him with another woman who came with another child, but the happiness she felt when she was with him was irreplaceable. She would rather have some of him than none at all.

She helped him through his grandmother's funeral. He didn't take it as hard as he had taken his brother's, yet he still leaned on her for support and gripped her hand tightly throughout the entire eulogy. Every time he smiled at her, she felt loved.

She would wake up in the middle of the night and see him staring at her. When she would ask him what was wrong, he would simply reply, "Everything is right. I just want to look at you. Go back to sleep, ma."

Elaine was ecstatic that Indie and Disaya had worked out their problems. She had never seen Indie so happy or Disaya, either, for that matter, and she welcomed Disaya as if she was her own daughter . . . there was no hyphen for her daughter-in-law. They were a family, and Disaya loved the concept, because she had never had one.

As YaYa and Indie lay in bed silently with their daughter between them on their last night together, an uncomfortable mood took over the room.

"These past seven days have been great, Indie. Thank you for forgiving me," she whispered.

"Stop thanking me, YaYa. You've given me so much more than forgiveness. This little girl lying between us is my world. You are my world, ma. I'ma love you until the day I die."

YaYa smiled, but Indie could see that she was distant. "What's wrong? What are you thinking about?" he asked.

"I wonder, if Skylar wasn't in the picture, if you would love me as much. I can't help but think that you're in love with her and not me. Then what happens when your other child is born? I see your love for Skylar. It makes you love me more. Will your love for your new baby make you love her more? How will you choose between the two of us? And what do I tell my daughter if you don't choose us? I'm afraid, Indie. You're going back to Houston tomorrow. I'm in New York. I feel like we won't make it. There's not enough trust."

"For one, my love for Skylar originated from my love for you. She is an extension and a reflection of you, Disaya. My love for another woman will never measure up to yours. I don't love my child's mother in Houston. It was a mistake, but I can't abandon her, because I'm a man. You never have to worry about being in competition with anyone," Indie said seriously.

Disaya turned her head, but Indie placed his hand beneath her chin and made her face him.

"For two, I never want to hear you say that Sky is *your* daughter ever again. She is *our* daughter, and you will never have to explain my absence to her because I will always be here for you and her. I'll always be with you, but you're right. This New York-Houston shit ain't gon' work. That's why you and the baby are moving to Houston with me."

"Indie, I can't just pick up and leave. I have school. I'm serious about that. I'm not the old YaYa that can just bounce whenever. I have responsibilities now."

"I know. I know. You're on your Ms. Independent Woman kick," he said sarcastically.

Disaya hit him in the arm and rolled her eyes.

"But, seriously, I've already handled all that. You can apply to Houston Community College, and all of your credits can be put on hold until next semester. All you got to do is say yes," Indie finished.

"Okay . . . fuck it, I'll come. But I'm not staying in the house you built for your baby mama. I want my own shit."

Indie laughed and replied, "There go the YaYa I know. I already know how you get down, ma. I called my peoples in Houston, and they've already leased you a luxury townhome. We'll get another house, once I sell the one I just built."

* * *

Indie led Disaya through the airport and took baby Skylar from her arms. "Why couldn't you just move back to New York?"

"We need a new start, and I'm making money here. Once you get your business degree, you can help me go legit," Indie explained as he opened her car door and handed her Skylar. "You need to go shopping and get me all of the things I'm going to need to drive my shorty around with me. A car seat and all that good shit, because I'm gon' keep Sky with me. I've got to show my niggas my favorite girl in the world."

Disaya rolled her eyes in mock disgust then let her behind sink into the butter-soft leather interior of the Maybach. Being back with Indie placed her back on her throne in a life of luxury. The only difference was, she had grown up and realized that if he was poor and living in a cardboard box on the streets, she would still be with him. She was learning what real love was. The old adage that absence makes the heart grow fonder was more than true because being around Indie now was like heaven on earth.

Indie held her hand as he cruised through the hood. He pulled up on Chase, who was manning his most profitable trap house. He rolled down his window and extended his hand.

"Fam, what's good?" Chase asked.

"Shit, just got back in town. How's that money looking? Everything's everything?"

"Money's good, baby. Everything is good. A minor problem from them Tallahassee niggas. They a little salty behind Duke's murder, but it's nothing I can't handle. Just a couple niggas running they mouth. I got that cake for you, though. I'll bring it through to you tonight," Chase promised.

"Did Mekhi get that paperwork taken care of for me on the new townhouse?"

"Yeah, everything's good. The keys are waiting for you in the mailbox."

"Come through tonight around eight. Come to the townhouse. I want to sit down and have dinner with the fam. We've got a new edition, and everybody needs to meet her," Indie stated as he reached over and squeezed Disaya's hand.

Chase nodded and went back into the trap house, as Indie pulled away from the curb.

Indie arrived at the townhouse and helped YaYa out of the car. As soon as she walked inside, a smile spread across her face.

"You like it, ma?" he asked.

"I love it," she assured.

The three-bedroom, three-bathroom, 2500-square-foot town-home was perfect. Everything was new, from the stainless steel appliances to the four-person Jacuzzi in the master bathroom.

"I've got to make a run. I'll be back before it gets too late. Call around and order some food and champagne. My niggas will be through later. They need to be familiar with you, so you will meet them tonight," Indie stated as he made his way back for the door.

"Indie?"

He turned around and saw the worried look in his face.

"Are you going to see her?" Disaya couldn't help but ask.

"Yeah. I at least owe her an explanation, but after tonight, it's you and me. Don't worry about her. I'm with you. I'll always come back to you," he assured.

Disaya blew him a kiss then nodded. "Then go and hurry back to us." She grabbed Skylar's tiny hand. "Wave bye to Daddy, Sky-Sky."

Leah looked at the clock. Indie was supposed to be home at least two hours ago. He had already pissed her the fuck off by not answering any of her calls while he was out of town. Now he was late, and as each minute passed, she grew more and more irritated. She felt like she was losing her mind. Every time she closed her eyes, she thought she heard a baby crying. The shrill cry of what she thought was her dead baby terrified her. Her paranoia was at an all-time high. She couldn't sleep, she couldn't eat, and her womb was sore to the point where it hurt when she walked. She was still bleeding profusely and kept going to and from the window, waiting anxiously for Indie to arrive.

When she heard his keys in the door, she forgot about all the pain that she was in.

"Where the fuck have you been?" she spewed at him.

Indie looked around his home in disbelief. Leah had fucked the interior of his crib up. His seventy-two-inch plasma screen was cracked, there were shattered dishes all over the tiled floor; even his couches were slit and had the cotton popping out of them. It looked like she had gone into a blind rage and ruined everything in sight. He assessed the damage quickly and saw that she had fucked up at least ten thousand dollars' worth of shit.

"Whoa, ma. You need to pump your brakes. Who the fuck is you talking to?" Indie asked.

"Miss me with all that shit, nigga. Who the fuck you been around that got you not answering my calls?"

Indie sighed. He wanted to get mad because she had fucked up his house, but he didn't. He knew that the blow he was about to deliver would set her over the top, so he looked past the fact that she had destroyed a lot of his stuff. He didn't want to make things harder than they already were, so he calmed himself before he spoke to her, to avoid adding unnecessary fuel to the flame of anger growing inside of Leah.

"We need to talk," he said. He noticed that Leah was sweating, and her face looked clammy. "Are you a'ight? You don't look good. The baby been making you sick?"

His concern was genuine, so she played into his hand, "Yeah, I've been a little sick. That's why I was calling so much. Why didn't you answer? What's going on?"

"Okay, look, Leah. When I was in New York, I linked back up with my old girlfriend. I left her about a year ago to come here because of a misunderstanding. Turns out, she has my kid. I got a baby girl. She's three months old."

Leah automatically knew that he was referring to Disaya. She couldn't believe that their baby had survived the beating that Indie had given her. She instantly became enraged because, no matter how hard she tried, she couldn't destroy Disaya. She was supposed to be taking everything from Disaya, not the other way around. It seemed like YaYa always won; especially now that Leah had lost her baby, Indie was sure to go back to Disaya.

"A baby? So where does that leave me? Was I just your rebound bitch? What about our baby?" She asked the question with such conviction that she actually believed she was still carrying one.

"I will always take care of my child, Leah. You don't have to worry about that, but I don't want to lie to you and have you thinking this is going to work. I'm here for you and our child, but I'm going back to my girl."

"What?" she asked. "You cannot leave me!" she screamed.

"I've got to go, ma. Call me when you need me to go to the doctor's appointments, or if you have anything to say about my seed. You can stay here until you have the baby. After that, I'm going to need you to get your own place," he said.

"Indie, please, don't do this!" she screamed.

"I'm sorry, Leah. I've got to go. Call me if you need me."

Leah wanted to run after him, but she couldn't. She was physically unable to do too much. She thought that something was seriously wrong with her, but she couldn't go to the doctor. Then she would have to admit to Indie that she'd lost their baby. *Fuck him and fuck YaYa. They are fucking with the wrong bitch. He's no better than she is. They want to use me and talk sweet in my ear and then leave me. I'm going to make them both pay. I lost my baby, so now I'm going to make them lose theirs.*

"Everyone, I want you to meet my wifey, YaYa. YaYa, this is my niggas Chase and Khi-P. Then this lovely little lady is Chase's baby sister Trina and her little mamas, Miesha and Sydney. These are my cook-up queens. These are the only insiders. Everybody else is an outsider, and we only trust mu'fuckas in our inner circle." Everybody greeted Disaya with love, and the teenage girls were crazy over baby Skylar.

"We'll babysit whenever y'all tryin'-a get your freak on," Trina said with a mischievous smile.

Disaya smiled. "Okay, I'ma hold you to that."

They drank champagne and ate good as they all got to know Disaya. Everybody took to her and embraced her into their family. Disaya loved Indie's crew and knew that if she ever needed anything, all she had to do was dial a number and she would have a squad behind her ready to go to war. Indie gave her a new cell phone with each of their numbers already programmed in, so if she ever needed them they were only a phone call away.

As the evening turned into the early morning, Disaya excused herself to put Skylar down, the girls cleaned the kitchen before departing, and Indie retired to the basement to discuss the beef he had acquired while he was away.

"How long these niggas been lurking?" he asked Mekhi as they took a seat and he poured himself a glass of Rémy VSOP.

"They've been asking around about you . . . you know, trying to get an address, trying to see what type of whip you pushing . . . basically just trying to catch you sleeping. It's been going on ever since Khi wet Duke up at the car show. These niggas is definitely plotting. I can feel it," Chase said.

"I know we need to nip this shit in the bud and dead this beef before it gets out of hand. War is gon' attract attention. We gotta handle this silent and swift," Mekhi suggested.

Indie nodded. "Fine. We'll sit back for a minute, but, Chase, I want you keep your ear to the streets. See what you can find out. Until I say so, we need to stay suited up at all times. Give everybody a vest, even Trina and her girls. If we do go to war, we don't want any casualties on our end."

Indie stood, which signified that he was done talking.

"Your baby girl is beautiful, fam. Congratulations," Mekhi stated as he slapped hands with Indie before departing.

"Thanks, man. We'll get it in tomorrow."

Indie went to his daughter's room and checked on his little angel before retiring to his room. YaYa was already asleep, so he didn't disturb her. He removed his clothes, slid in beside her, and held her in his arms until the calm rhythm of her breathing lulled him to sleep.

Chapter 30

Disaya sat straight up in the middle of the night and looked around the darkened room. She was in a cold sweat, and her heart was beating erratically. She looked at the clock. It read 4:45 AM. She held her breath as she listened silently.

"Indie," she whispered as she shook him out of his sleep.

"What's wrong, baby?" he asked.

"Something's not right," she said, her eyes wide in alert.

"Everything's fine, ma, you just got to get used to the new house," he urged as he kissed her lips. "Go back to sleep."

Disaya sat upright and threw the covers off her body. "She usually wakes up, Indie. Skylar doesn't sleep through the night yet. She wakes up around three every morning." She stood up and raced out of their room. Her panicky mood made Indie follow her into their daughter's room.

The sight of the empty crib brought Disaya to a halt as she stared into the darkness in anguish. "She's gone! Indie, she's gone!" Disaya screamed as she fell into his arms crying. "Where's my daughter, Indie? Where is she? Who would take her, Indie? Who would do this?" Her terrified screams only intensified as the situation sunk in, and the shattered heart of a mother awoke the neighbors and pierced through the still of the night. She had no idea that her worst enemy was lurking around her. She had left New York in hopes of leaving her horrid past behind her, but trouble always seemed to follow. It was the story of her life.

Leah looked down at the tiny child in her arms. She was so gorgeous, she couldn't help but imagine what her own baby might have looked like. The child in her arms was still asleep, but the crying in her ear was as loud as ever.

Waaa! Waaa!

"Shut up!" she yelled. Baby Skylar whimpered, but settled down without so much as a peep.

Leah was confused. *Where is the crying coming from?* As she stood in the backyard of the house that Indie had built, her eyes darted around frantically until she found the source of the ear-piercing sound. It was coming from the grave that she had buried her dead baby in. He was screaming . . . taunting her . . . haunting her.

Leah then looked at the tiny grave she had dug next to her baby's, and a smile crept across her face as she looked down at baby Skylar. Indie and Disaya were going to pay for fucking her over. They were going to pay for all of her pain. "Your mommy and daddy should have never fucked with me. Now their precious little baby has to pay."

Discussion Questions for Fans and Book Clubs

1. Should Disaya have forgiven Elaine for killing her mother?

2. Was Disaya wrong for not telling Indie about Skylar?

3. What could have happened to Leah to make her so cruel and disturbed? Is she crazy, or is there a deeper reason behind her actions?

4. How did you feel when Indie and Disaya saw each other again for the first time? Did he still love her all along? Was he wrong for beating her when she was pregnant?

5. Did Mona deserve to die at the hands of Bay?

6. Did Mona's rape as a child contribute to her promiscuous ways as an adult?

7. What did you think of Buchanan Slim?

8. What do you think will happen to baby Skylar? Will Leah hurt her?

9. Who was your favorite character, and why?

10. If you were in Disaya's shoes, would you have taken Indie back after all that she had been through?

11. Was Indie wrong for sleeping with Leah, even though he didn't know who she really was or what she did? Was he wrong for moving on from Disaya?

12. Are you an aspiring author? If you have a story to tell, then go to www.urbanstreetpublishing.com for more details on landing a publishing deal.

13. Did you enjoy Ashley's solo debut? If so, please e-mail her and let her know. She can be reached at streetlitdiva@aol.com and www.myspace.com/streetlitdiva

The Prada Plan: Part 2 Coming Soon

Urban Streets Publishing is now accepting manuscripts. If you are an aspiring author and would like to submit your work for possible publication, please visit www.urbanstreetspublishing.com.

<u>Urban Street Titles</u>

The Cartel by Ashley and JaQuavis

The Prada Plan by Ashley Antoinette

The Dope Man's Wife by JaQuavis Coleman

Hush by Amaleka McCall

Closed Legs Don't Get Fed by Miamor